Our Father's Generation

by
F. M. Worden

CCB Publishing
British Columbia, Canada

Our Father's Generation

Library and Archives Canada Cataloguing in Publication

Worden, F. M., 1930-
Our father's generation / written by F. M. Worden.
ISBN 978-1-926585-61-1
I. Title.
PS3623.O74O97 2009   813.6   C2009-906000-0

Cover image is in the public domain and is used without malice.

Disclaimer: The book *Our Father's Generation* is purely fictional. Any reference to places or persons living or dead is strictly coincidental. The author intends no harm or injury to anyone.

Extreme care has been taken to ensure that all information presented in this book is accurate and up to date at the time of publishing. Neither the author nor the publisher can be held responsible for any errors or omissions. Additionally, neither is any liability assumed for damages resulting from the use of the information contained herein.

Publisher: CCB Publishing
              British Columbia, Canada
              www.ccbpublishing.com

This is the story of three brothers, Tom – Frank – Albert. Men who grew up on a Southwest cattle ranch during the great 1930's depression and served their country in its greatest hour of need, the Second World War.

* * * * *

This book is dedicated to the men and women of the United States and all its Allies who suffered through the 1930's depression and the Second World War. We honor all the men and women, both military and civilian who sacrificed their lives for our freedom.

May God's light shine on them wherever they are.

God Bless everyone who served.

Contents

Book 1

Brother Tom, The Pilot

Our Father's Generation

Chapter 1

He's the Oldest Son –
Tells His Story First

**Tom's story is dedicated to all the men and women
who flew aircraft in wartime protecting this nation.
He can be a fighter, bomber, transport, fernier,
test pilot or civilian flight instructor.**

I was the first born to my Mom and Dad on a cattle ranch
that my grandfather owned in the Southwest USA. The year
was 1918. My Dad had just come home after the First World
War was over. He had been a rifle instructor at Camp Poke,
Louisiana. That's where he met my mother, a French-American
girl of nineteen and a beautiful woman she was. She was a joy
and wonderful person to know in every way. Dad, so he said,
swept her off her feet and she fell in love with him. They got
married as soon as he was mustered out of the Army. He
brought her home to the ranch. My father had been
grandfather's ranch foreman ever since, I loved them all as
much as a boy can love his parents and Grandparents.

I called Grandfather Popie. He was a big man - six feet tall,
two hundred thirty pounds. He always stood ramrod straight, a
shy but honest and dependable man, and as tough as nails. He
homesteaded this ranch in the late 1800's. He had come from
Germany in his teen years. His Papa had always been a saloon
keeper. Popie always wanted to be a cowboy and raise cattle,
he said he fell in love with the West watching the cowboy

silent movies and reading books about the West, he always had a big laugh saying that.

When he heard homesteading was possible, he made his mind up to come west. He had fallen in love with his childhood sweetheart and married her just before coming west. She was a young German-Jewish girl of sixteen, who could hardly speak any English. Her family had come over to this country when she was just a baby. She had lived in a German community in Illinois all her life; she is a beauty even in her advanced age.

My father was born on the ranch. He had never been more than a few miles away from the ranch until he joined the Army in 1916. I've always called Grandmother, Michelle, and my mother, Mom.

My brother Frank was born a year after me and Al a few years later. Al was the baby of our family, he was just a little spoiled. Mothers, you know, tend to spoil the last born.

I first became fascinated with air-o-planes when I was 10 or 11 years old. I was sitting on my cow horse during a roundup; I could see the airport down in the valley below. I watched one plane take off and circle above me in a lazy fashion in the cloudless blue sky. It was a two-winged plane and as I watched, it made all kinds of spins, loops and turns that looked to be fun to a kid of my age. I made my mind up right then and there to be an airplane pilot; I said to myself, "If a man can fly, so can I."

I knew my Uncle Bob was a flyer during the war. I also knew that he kept an airplane at that airport. Uncle Bob was my Mother's brother. He was a pilot in the war; he married an English girl, my Aunt Helen. He was an architect in the city near our ranch. The man made lots on money and he liked us kids. He and Aunt Helen never had any of their own, he always called me "Tommy Boy."

I was enchanted just seeing airplanes, I started watching them every chance I got. On Saturdays and Sundays I'd take a horseback ride down to the airport to watch the planes come and go, I loved every minute of it, I was hooked.

On one of these rides to the airport a few years later, a man came over to me and asked, "You like airplanes, boy? I see you here all the time. I bet you want to take a ride in one, huh?"

"Yes, sir, I sure do."

He told me to tie my horse and come with him. I followed him around and he took me to see all the airplanes that were parked that day. He asked me the big question, "Would you like to go up?"

"Yeah, I sure would!"

He looked me in the eyes and asked, "You won't be scared, will ya? I don't want ya throwing up all over the plane."

"No, sir, "I said. "I can't wait to see how it feels to be up there."

He told me his name was Jake Summers, he owned the airport and taught people to fly. He told me. "Come on. I'll take ya up in my old Jenny."

I'll never forget that day as long as I live. It was the most wonderful thing I had ever done. Jake looked back at me and saw I was really enjoying flying, he did a loop and I screamed my approval. I had both arms in the air yelling for more. Jake watched me, smiled and turned that old plane loose, I loved every minute of it.

Back on the ground, as we climbed out of the Cockpits, he said smiling, "Boy, you're going to make one hell-of-a pilot, when can we start your lessons?"

"I've got no money."

"Well, boy, what do you own of any value?"

"The only thing I own all myself is a steer I raised."

"Bring him down; I'll trade for some flying time. I'll bet you'll be flying yourself in no time at all."

I thanked Jake and rode home, I was a happy young fifteen year old kid. It took several weeks to convince my folks to let me fly. I told them, "Uncle Bob has flown for years and no one said it was a bad thing to do." Thank God for my Uncle Bob.

Mother took the truck and went to town to see her brother. When she returned, she gave me permission to fly. That was a great day for me.

On the next Saturday, I took my prize steer down to the airport and gave it to Jake. Guess what? My Uncle Bob was there that day. He told me if I could learn to fly, his Jenny was at my disposal any time I could afford to buy the gas. What a great deal that would be for me. He also told me I could work in his office all summer if I wanted to, I did.

It was a good summer although I didn't like the work. I had to work in his office, but I got to fly every weekend. On my sixteenth birthday I soloed, it was the greatest day in my life. I took that old Jenny as high as I figured it was safe. Above the clouds, all by myself, with only the hum of the engine to hear. I was in a world all my own. How peaceful it is to have complete control of an airplane and to be that near heaven. It must be a feeling man has had ever since he began to fly. That day, I did not ever want to come down.

Getting low on gas, I had to. I put her in a bank to the left and down we went. We buzzed the airport forty feet off the ground. I pulled her up and rolled her over on her back, flew past the airport and rolled her over again. I set her down on the ground as easy as a bird landing on a wire.

Uncle Bob, Aunt Helen and my folks with my brothers were there to greet me. All the men at the airport came to congratulate me, too. They all made out as if I had done something a young boy had never done before. I was a big hero for one day. It was a great day for me, I want-a tell ya.

My Uncle Bob was the first to congratulate me. He said, "Tommy boy that was as good as any old timer could do. You're going to make one hell-of an airman." No one could have been happier than me that day. To have Uncle Bob praise me made me proud as a peacock. The folks and my brothers all had good things to say to me. I was never more pleased with myself in my whole life, It was a great day for me. I hate repeating myself, but it was a great day in my life. Little did I know flying would be my whole life and everything I got was from my flying including my beautiful wife Allie?

That winter, I worked my rear off to get myself out of high school. In May, I graduated, now I was on my own. The summer of 1935 I spent in Uncle Bob's office, I was bored to tears, I hated office work. Uncle Bob was one smart guy, he could see I wasn't cut out for his kind of work. He told me, "I have just purchased a four place new airplane. Tommy boy, I want you to be its pilot. I plan to start a charter business with it as soon as you have a few hours flying it."

Wow, was I a happy guy of eighteen. Me, a charter pilot? "When do I start?"

"Just as soon as the plane gets here, it should be delivered anytime now."

Yep, the plane came. On a Sunday afternoon, I took Uncle Bob and Aunt Helen for a two hour ride. Uncle Bob had to take the controls and see what his new plane could do. He looked back at Aunt Helen, told her to hang on and put the plane thru a few paces. That man could fly the pants off a brass monkey. I loved every minute of it. Aunt Helen, before he was finished, looked a little pale and threw up all over the both of us, I think he overdid it a little.

7

This new plane was a Stinson Reliant. The company had only been making this plane for one year, it could carry four passengers and the pilot, it will fly around one hundred and forty miles an hour. Also, it had a range of four hundred miles. I couldn't have been more pleased with the whole operation Uncle Bob had planned.

On the ground, we got Aunt Helen sitting in the car, She needed a drink of water. She really looked pale around the gills. I thought to myself, Uncle Bob was going to catch heck when she came around.

I spent the rest of that afternoon cleaning the spit up out-a the plane. The smell was hard to get out, but I finally did with a lot of elbow grease, soap and water.

The whole crew at the airport had to look the plane over. All the guys were impressed with her looks, it made me feel good to be a part of the operation.

Before Uncle Bob left that day, he gave me some advice about flying in general. "Tommy boy," he said, "Always keep her nose up on the horizon, watch the altimeter and pay attention to the fuel gauge. Never fly when you're tired, it isn't worth having an accident. Take some time to get rested." Several times his advice saved my neck, he also told me to take a hop over to El Paso to get a little cross country experience. I had never been more than twenty or thirty miles from the airport.

I got my brother Frank to go. We flew over the next Saturday and came home Sunday. I followed Highway US 80 all the way, I loved flying this airplane. I even let Frank take the controls a time or two, I thought he might have gotten hooked, he didn't. He told me he preferred to stay on the ground.

The next week I got my first charter. Doc Hanson, his wife and their two little girls booked to go to San Diego for a two week vacation. The Doc sat next to me, his wife and girls in the back. The plane handled alright, I just had a little trouble getting the feel of all the weight. It took a few hours and I set that bird down like it was a baby buggy at the airport in San Diego. The Doc's wife had never flown before. When she got out, she leaned over and gave me a kiss on the cheek. She told me, "Tommy, I'll never be afraid to fly again. You are a great pilot." She made me feel like I was somebody. The Doc told me to pick them up in two weeks.

I asked a man standing on a stepladder working on a plane's engine, near the hanger, "Can I tie down my plane for the night?"

"Sure." He showed me where. I finished tie-n down and returned to where the fellow was working on a plane. I started to ask him questions about the airport. He said he was an airplane mechanic and worked for the owner, a man called {Smiling Jack}.

I was asking questions about the hangar buildings and some of the aircraft, when I saw this gorgeous female dressed in a white shirt, tan boot pants and brown riding boots come thru the big open door. This redheaded beauty stood looking our way. I asked the mechanic who she was. "She's the boss's daughter, Allie. You want-a meet her?" I didn't know what to say. He did for me. He called, "Allie, this boy here wants ta meet ya."

Even at that distance, I could see she was smiling. As she strolled toward us, I could see this beauty was blue eyed with big dimples in her rosy red cheeks. She had wonderful full kissable lips, I fell head over heels in love with this walking goddess.

As she approached us, she said in a musical voice, "I'm Allie." She presented her right hand for me to shake.

I took her hand in my right, pulled her close to me. With my left hand on her upper arm, I said, "Am I ever glad to meet you, you're one good looking young lady."

I thought that mechanic was gonna fall off his ladder. We both heard him say softly, "This kid is smooth." Then he said in a loud voice, "This boy is the charter pilot who just flew in, in the Red Stinson over there." He was pointing at my plane.

She looked at me and said with question in her musical voice, "You're kind-a young to be a charter pilot."

I told her, "I been flying for two years and I'm good at it." I never bragged before in my life, somehow I just had to impress this beautiful girl.

She told me very curtly, "I'm a pilot, too, and I've been flying a couple of years." She grabbed me by the arm and said, "Come on, I want you to meet my daddy." I told her I was hungry and had to find a place to sleep. She pulled me right along and said, "I'll see to your needs." How lucky could a guy be to meet this girl?

We entered the hangar and walked over to an office inside the building. There standing in the door way talking with a couple of men was a handsome man who looked to be forty years old. He had graying temples, reddish brown hair, a firm ruddy face and a big friendly smile. He stood six feet tall maybe two hundred pounds.

Allie broke right into their conversation and said, "Daddy, I want you to meet...." She stopped and asked, "What did you say your name was?"

"Tom."

"Daddy, I want you to meet Tom, he's a charter pilot."

I put out my hand to him. He took it and said, "I'm Smiling Jack. How ya do-n?"

I looked at him, then at Allie and said, "I'm do-n great."

He got my drift right away. He said, "Easy boy, this is one fine girl."

"Yes, sir. I can sure see that."

All this time, Allie was giving me a big beautiful smile. My heart was gone. She told her Daddy, "He's hungry and needs a place to sleep tonight."

"Take him to the diner. It's on me. He can have the cot in the office for tonight."

"Thank you, sir."

He said, "Call me Jack, Tom, everybody calls me Jack."

Allie grabbed me by the arm and said, "Come on, Tom, my cars outside." She led me outside to a 1934 Ford Roadster; it was yellow with black fenders, what a beauty. She slipped into the driver's seat. I ran around, opened the door and climbed in beside her. Off we went in a cloud of dust. How could I be so lucky to meet this beautiful girl? And a pilot, too!

With the top down, the wind made her hair swirl around her face, reminding me of pictures of the females I had seen in history books of the Roman Empire. Her looks were outstanding. I couldn't take my eyes off her, she is one beautiful woman.

In about a mile, we turned into a diner's parking lot. The diner was an old train car. Inside, everyone gave Allie a big hello. She must have known all the people who were eating there. She had all the men's attention in that diner, I'll tell ya. She told me that she, her daddy and all his work men ate here all the time.

We sat at a two-place table by the front window. Facing this beauty, I was captured completely. I hung on her every word. She had the sexiest voice I had ever heard. I was gone, I had fall-n in love with this girl. In high school, I never had time for girls and really didn't care for them at all. Most were a pain, if you get my drift.

A shapely young blonde came to take our order. This girl had a big friendly smile and I could see she had an interest in me. How could I be so lucky? I could see Allie didn't take kindly of this blonde's attention. Allie told her to take our order, "Quit make-n eyes at my boyfriend." That made my day. The little gal took our orders and took off in a huff, I watched her go and I was smiling at her as she went. She stopped and smiled back at me and I gave her a wave.

Allie made a noise, cleared her throat and said, "I'm still here."

"Yes, you are," I said.

She put out both her hands to me across the table and I put mine in hers. She pulled me to her a little and said, "Tom, I hope you and I become an item around here." Wow! She liked me. She told me as soon as she became a pilot the boys quit asking for dates. "I intimidate them doing something that they don't."

I told her I could see how that could be. "All boys like to be manly, if you know what I mean?"

She nodded her head yes. I pulled her as close as I could and proceeded to kiss her lightly on her red lips. Boy-O-boy, she kissed back and we got a big hand from the people in the diner.

I got a big juicy hamburger to eat and a Nehi orange soda to drink. She had some kind of seafood. When we left, I didn't see the little blonde girl again.

In the car, she asked if I would like to go see a movie. I, of course, said, "Yes." I wanted to prolong my time with her as long as possible. We went to a movie house and saw the Marx Brothers in {A Day at the Races.} At least I think I saw the movie. We sat in the last row and I want-a tell ya I couldn't take my eyes off her. How many times I kissed and hugged her

I couldn't tell ya, but it was very much, she was very receptive to my advances.

She drove me back to the airport and showed me where the cot was in the office. Then she left. I want-a tell ya, I didn't get much sleep that night; Allie was on my mind all night. I finally fell asleep around four a.m.

At 6 a.m., she shook me awake, sat on the edge of the cot and said, "Tom, will you marry me?"

Holy Cow! I blurted out, "I sure will."

About that time, her daddy came in and she told him she wanted to marry me. He didn't take that very well. He told both of us, "NO!" Then he said, "If you two are still in a marrying mood a year from now, you got my blessing." That seemed fair to me.

As I flew back home that day, I vowed to never say a word about Allie to anyone at home. I was the guy who never dated girls; I was truly in love with Allie. Frank and Al would make all kinds of fun about me being in love.

I considered myself the luckiest guy in the world. I could fly and I had just met my dream girl.

Chapter 2

My Girl Allie

At home the very next week, I had a charter to El Paso, Texas for a businessman and his companion, a lady friend. They stayed overnight and I flew them back home. There was a lot going on in the back seat, I couldn't see but I heard a lot of laughing and strange noises. The guy tipped me well and told me to keep mum, if ya know what I mean.

The next weeks really dragged while I was waiting for my return trip to San Diego. The day finely came. I had purchased a new flying outfit, boots, pant boots, the spitting image of a pilot of the times. I was a happy young guy singing to myself all the way to San Diego, I sang ever love song I could remember.

At San Diego, I circled the airport several times, just to let Allie know I was arriving. I set the bird down as gently as a mother caressing her baby.

Before I could taxi to a tie down spot, Allie was running along beside my ship, waving with both hands. She was in my arms before the prop stopped spinning. We sat in the plane talking, hugging and kissing for most of an hour that day. I got to tell ya, I felt I was the luckiest guy in the whole world to have this beauty in love with me.

After greeting all the people at the airport, Jack wasn't there; Allie and I went to get a bite to eat at the Diner, the little blond gal took our order. She said, "I think Allie is in love with you, she talks about ya all the time."

"I hope so." That made me happy.

The little gal said, "If you have any doubts, look me up."

She gave me a big smile and walked away.

Allie didn't take kindly to the girl's advances. "She's got some nerve trying to steal my boyfriend. Right here in front of me."

I said, "Haw, she's just teasing and making conversation."

Allie was mad. "She better watch out and so should you."

I laughed and told her. "No one can ever take your place."

She put out both her hands to me, I gave her mine. She pulled me over the top of the table to give me a big wonderful wet kiss on my lips.

That evening we took in a movie show at the Bee-U Theater. The movie was King Kong. Allie acted scared and held onto me all thru the show, I knew she was kidding. A gal who can fly like she can is not going to let a silly movie freak her out.

Later in the car she told me she wanted to hold on to me as she said she was in love. She said she wanted to make sure I was for real.

Back at the airport office Smiling Jack was there. We talked late into the night. Jack told about barnstorming around the country and how he had worked for Hollywood pictures. One of his best friends, Ormer Locklear, had been killed doing a stunt for a picture. He talked about Ormer and what the man had done for thrills in his barnstorming days. Jack said that Ormer was the first to walk on the wings; he transferred from plane to plane, hung off the wings and landing gear without a parachute. Jack told us there will never be another like him. I could see Jack admired the man and missed him. Jack seemed sad to talk about Ormer. Jack said barnstorming still was a good way to make money. People like to be thrilled.

He said, "Taking passengers up is a good money maker." He was looking forward to the next summer to get going on a tour.

I slept in the office that night and dreamed of Allie and barnstorming. I was awake on and off all night, I was wondering if I could do the things with an airplane Jack had talked about.

At sunup Allie was setting on the cot when I woke up. I got a great good morning kiss. We had breakfast at the diner and a long talk about our future together. She had it all planned out. "We'll buy a big airplane and charter together and make lots of money. This depression will soon be over and everyone will want to fly, it'll be great to fly with you."

I told her she is my whole future, flying or not. "I love you and I want to be with you all the time." How great it was that she wanted me.

This wonderful time had to come to an end and it did, too soon to suit me. Allie had left in her car to run an errand for Jack.

The doctor and his family showed up around nine a.m. We were loaded and ready to taxi to the runway when Allie showed up. She came running over and banged on my side window. I opened the window and stuck my head out, she gave me a goodbye kiss on the lips and yelled, "Phone me when you get home, I have to know you're safe." I waved and shook my head yes.

I taxied to the runway and gunned the Stinson into the air, she lifted off like a bird on the wing. We headed east toward home.

The doctor sat beside me and asked about Allie. The engine makes a lot of noise so we had to talk pretty loud, I know his wife heard our conversation. I told him I was going to marry the girl, but I didn't want people at home to know just yet. He said he would keep my secret. He told me my girl was a beauty. Of course, I agreed.

When we landed at home, Uncle Bob was there and told me

he had charters lined up as far as the eye could see. My Uncle was one good hustler, no wonder he was a rich man.

All that winter I stayed in the air most of the time, I must have gone to or crossed over thirty states.

On one trip, I flew a party of hunters to Colorado for big game, another party to Texas to hunt birds. All the men were nice to me except two state reps. I flew them to the state capital. We hit some rough wind and got bounced a bit. The two men said I was a bad pilot and would not recommend me to anyone. What can you expect of a couple democrats?

In December I flew two well-dressed men to Chicago. We arrived just as a big snow storm hit, I want-a tell ya, I was lucky to find the O'Hare airport. Somehow I had a guiding angel that day, the whole country was socked in and I got a break in the clouds just in time to get landed. I could see both guys were sweating heavy, I acted like it was nothing, but I'll tell ya, I said a few prayers that time before I got on the ground.

The airport was snowed in, I couldn't get off and the airport authority wouldn't give me clearance anyway.

One of my passengers, the little guy, invited me to stay at his home in the suburbs. His house was the biggest place I had ever seen. He had a wife, two young girls and a house full of servants. All the people there treated me super, I had a really nice bedroom and the food was great, I spent the better part of two weeks there.

The storm let up and the airport called and said I could get off, I was sent out in a taxi. On the way, a police car pulled us over and I was held in a police station the rest of the day and all night.

It seems I was the guest of a gangster. The little guy I was staying with was Al Capone's Jewish bookkeeper, Sam Coleman, the other man was Al's bodyguard, Eddie Gurney.

The cop who questioned me said Eddie was a killer. They kept me for two days until a lawyer showed up and told the police to charge me or let me go, they let me go.

I went back to the airport, the storm was in again. Several other pilots were grounded, too. I met one who was Charles Lindbergh {Lucky Lindy} the guy who flew to France over the ocean. It was great to see him and listen to the men talk flying, these men were the real flyers of the day, most were flying the US mail.

The storm over, I took off early morning and landed in Oklahoma City for fuel and an overnight stay. All the time I was in the city I had cops watching me; I guess they thought I was some dangerous criminal.

Back at home, I told Uncle Bob about my stay and that the two guys were gangsters. He said he knew they weren't businessmen as they were both packing guns. He got a big laugh out-a the whole thing.

Looking back at that time, I was very lucky to have made it thru the whole thing with no trouble.

Christmas Day, I called Allie and we talked for more than three hours. The airport office looked me up when the bill came in, for two dollars and fifty cents I'd talk to Allie every day if I could.

The first of the year I flew a honeymoon couple to Mexico City. That's a trip I will never forget, the Mexicans tried to confiscate the Stinson. I was held in jail for a week as the American counsel worked it out, I was a happy guy to get away from there. I pushed the Stinson as fast as she would go to get home.

At home I had a charter waiting to go to Florida. The Stinson needed some work so I got to stay another day. My passenger was a good-looking woman, Wow! I mean good looking. She was about twenty-five and a living doll, trouble was she knew she was beautiful.

Uncle Bob told me she was a beauty queen and that I might get to fly her all over the country. "How ya like that Tommy boy? This girl is going to tour the country, as a representative of some beauty products. I can set it up if you want to do it."

I told him I would rather not spend time with this girl. I should have told him about Allie but I didn't.

We took off on a Sunday morning. After three overnight stops, when mostly the weather held us up, we landed in Miami, Florida. She went into the airport office and did some telephone calling.

Soon we had people everywhere, newspaper reporters and loads of people who just came to look. This fellow came to me and told me he was her manager and wanted me to fly him and her to New York City. I asked when I could have the money for the trip. He said he would get the money when we got to New York, I had to call Uncle Bob for advice. He told me to stay put until I got the money, I relayed that to the man and he got mad and started cuss-n me. I told him money first, and then I could fly them to New York. He said he could have the money in a few days. I told him I'd call my owner and see what he had to say. Uncle Bob told me to get to New Orleans as there was a passenger waiting.

I took off early the next morning and just for fun I flew out over the Gulf of Mexico. This was the first time I had flown over a large body of water. Now I knew how Lucky Lindy felt flying over water as far as you could see in all directions. If you go down in the Gulf, it would be all over, not a good feeling.

I came over New Orleans an hour before sunset. It took awhile to find the airport. I landed just as darkness set in, found a tie down and tied the Stinson down, then went to the office to see if they knew where my passenger was. A woman in the office told me my passenger was at a hotel in town, I was to call and let him know I was here. I did, and then I took a taxi to a hotel myself. After eating in the hotel café, I hit the bed for a long night's rest.

Next morning I got my passenger and to my delight he wanted to go to Los Angles. What luck, I could slip down to San Diego and pay Allie a visit. I made one stop for fuel and onto LA. I dropped my passenger off in LA, by the time I got to San Diego it was dark. I buzzed the field and someone turned the landing strip lights on, I sat down very easily. Tied down and ran to the office, I called Allie and in a few minutes the Ford roadster was pulling into the hanger. Allie gave lots of hugs and kisses. I had a most pleasant evening and all the next day with her. We had a nice talk with Jack and I got up the nerve to ask about Allie's mother, I hit a sore spot on Jack as he got up and left without saying a word.

Allie told me the story about her mother. She ran off with a guy while Allie was still a baby. Allie said that Jack was devastated when she left. Allie said he had never got over her mother. "He still loves her and he would take her back if she wanted to come back."

I asked if she ever tried to see her Mom.

"I've only seen her two times in my life, she came one Christmas when I was five and another time when I was ten. Tommy, you'll never have to worry about me running out, I saw how it affected Jack."

I thanked her for telling me the story. "I'll never ask again about your mom."

"Its okay, Tommy, I don't really care one way or the other about her, I have the best father a girl can have, he is swell to me." She was smiling as she spoke. "Now I have a man I can love." She sure knows how to make a guy feel good, now I know why I became a pilot.

I flew home the next day. Oh how I hated to leave Allie. I had really become attached to her, me the guy who never cared much for girls before. Love is a funny human emotion, it had hit me hard.

The spring of 1937 came with a fury of news about wars in the world. The Japanese had attacked China, the Italians had invaded Ethiopia in '36 and the Germans were building an air force bigger than any country had in the whole world.

On one of my trips home, I asked Dad and Popie about the world situation. Popie said he didn't think there would be a war that the U.S. would get in. Pop was more concerned. He said, "Yeah, there will be a war; men just have to fight each other."

I asked if he thought I should join the Army.

"No, if they want ya, they'll come for ya."

I talked to Uncle Bob and he said there will always be talk of war. "Don't worry, the U.S. won't get into it." He made me feel a lot better.

The first of May, I flew the Doctor and his family to San Diego for a vacation. I hadn't finished tying down before Allie was in my arms again. After hugs and kisses she helped me tie the Stinson down.

We spent a most pleasant evening with Jack. Supper at the diner, then we talked with Jack at their home until he retired for the night. He said I could sleep on the living room couch. He made Allie mad telling her to go to bed in her room.

She said it in a sharp voice, "I will when I get ready." I could see she had a temper when she got angry, Jack let it pass.

She got Guy Lombardo on the radio and wanted to dance, of course I didn't know how. Anyway I made a good try and I got to hold her in my arms while listening and dancing to the sweetest music this side of heaven. My life couldn't have been better, loving this wonderful woman. We danced until the radio played the Star Spangled Banner, afterwards we took a long walk and didn't go to bed until three in the morning.

Allie woke me up at eight a.m. and had fixed a great breakfast. This girl could cook, too. After breakfast we took a ride in the car, she drove us over to Coronado Island. We sat in the car and watched a Navy PBY take off and shoot landings.

I asked her about the war situation. She said, "Na. I don't believe America will ever get in a war again." She told me the US Congress had just passed a draft by only one vote. She didn't want to talk of war anymore, she drove around showing me the sights of San Diego. We ended up at Mission Beach watching the people swim into the surf. We hadn't had lunch so we had an early supper of seafood.

Back at the airport Jack invited us into his office. "Sit," he said, "I need to talk with you kids."

Allie spoke first, "Daddy, Tommy and I want-a get married."

Jack raised his voice and said, "Absolutely not, you're both too young; you'll have to wait a while longer, that's all I'm going to say."

Allie started crying and yelling, "You promised we could in a year if we were still in love, Daddy we're still in love." She kept telling him he had made a promise. "Daddy you never broke a promise before." Now she was crying hard.

"I'm sorry, baby, you can, but not now." He got up went out, got in his car and left.

She went out, got in her car and was crying almost uncontrollable. What could I say? I got in the car and told her it wasn't the end. "We'll just have to wait."

"No," she said and started sniffing, I gave her my hanky. "We're going to get married tonight, okay, Tommy?"

"Whoa," I said, "How can we?"

"We'll go to Tijuana; they have marriage chapels over there, open all night."

I told her, "I can't go against Jack, I need his approval."

"Do you love me Tommy? Do you want me?"

What could I say? "You know I want you, my whole body aches for you, I need you, Allie."

"Let's go now, right now." I couldn't turn her down.

Yeah, we went to Mexico and got married, it was legal and all, I made sure of that. We spent the most wonderful night in my life. We got a room at the Coronado Hotel, the moonlight streamed into our room making Allie look like the goddess she is, I never spent a night like that again as we consummated our marriage. I was so much in love I didn't care if Jack approved or not.

Next morning, on the way to the diner to have breakfast, I told Allie I was going to confront Jack and tell him we had gotten married.

"NO!" she said. "We'll let him think he got his way. I'll tell him when I think its right. He'll be mad, but he'll get over it when he sees how happy we are."

"Allie, I hate to deceive him, I like your dad."

"He likes you, too, Tommy. He's told me that several times, he said I couldn't make a better choice than you." Boy, oh boy, did that ever make me feel better.

We had ordered and were being served our breakfast by the little blonde when Jack came in. He came over and stood looking at us, he looked a little mean, he had a snarl on his face.

The little blonde gal said, "Allie, you got a glow on this morning, I've never seen ya look better."

Jack looked me right in the eye and said in a loud voice, "You did it, didn't ya?"

I gave him a blank look, "What?"

"Ya slept with her, didn't ya?"

I thought for a minute he was going to punch me, he had

his right fist made. He turned on his heels and at the door he turned back, smiled at me and gave me a half-hearted salute as he went on out. Right then I knew it would be alright.

I stood and pulled Allie to me and told her, "Now, babe, you're all mine."

I gave her the best kiss on her ruby red lips I had ever given. I said, "I love you, Allie." Did we get a big hand from the people there? You bet we did, even the little blonde gal was clapping. I was the happiest young guy in the whole dang world that morning, that time is etched in my brain forever.

Chapter 3

Air Shows 1937-39

The morning after the night Allie and I got married in Tijuana, Mexico, we had breakfast then ambled on over to the airport to face Jack, Allie's daddy.

At his office, he invited the two of us to come in. "Come on in and sit down, I have to talk to you two." He had already placed two chairs in a way that we had to face him. With legs crossed, hands folded on his stomach he began talking. "I have some serious talk for you two kids." We both sat wanting to hear his every word.

"Kids, I'm in a whole lot of trouble." We both looked at each other with questions in our faces. He continued, "This depression has put me in deep debt, I have this place mortgaged to the hilt, I need your help."

Allie and I looked to each other in wonderment. He went on, "Barnstorming isn't paying like it used to, people are tired of wing walkers and hangers. The crowds won't come out to see that anymore. We can still get a few spectators, but nothing like the old days. We can still make a few dollars giving rides, but that's not gonna cut it anymore. We will never be able to pay the bills; I've come up with this idea. I've just purchased two Alexander Eagle Rock biplanes; they're the best stunt planes you can buy. One is up in LA, the other is at the factory in Colorado being refurbished."

Allie and I were still looking at each other in wonderment at what Jack was getting at.

"I need you two kids to be the pilots."

I was looking at him like, you're kidding me.

"Tommy, you're an excellent pilot, Allie is already a stunt pilot. Tommy, you can be the best if you try."

I looked at Allie, she had a big smile on her face. She said, "Now we can get married Tommy."

"Wait one darn minute." Jack wasn't going to be pushed into anything. "Later, after we get this thing going. I'm going to bill ya as the two youngest stunt pilots in the world, I'm telling ya, you two will be as famous as Earhart and Lindbergh. How ya like them apples?"

Allie was smiling all over. I could see she wanted to do this. I had reservations.

"Jack, I can't just walk away from my Uncle Bob. He needs me."

Jack was ready for that. "I've talked to your Uncle; he thinks it's a great deal for you."

What could I say? Looked like Jack had covered all the angles.

"Okay," I said, "I'm ready if Allie is."

She didn't have to answer. I could see by her face she was ready.

Jack commenced telling what he had in mind for us. "The two biplanes are being painted to match. You two will do synchronized flying." He showed us with his hands. "You'll take off together. That's after an introduction in front of the bleachers and the crowd. I want you two to stand in the cockpit and wave, then fire-up, taxi to the runway and take off together side by side. Up you'll go, do a loop and a bank to the right, then bank to the left, then climb, one break right the other left, do separate loops and then one will pass under the other, all the time trailing smoke. That will be a sensational stunt, the crowd will love it."

I could see Jack was really fired up about the whole thing. He told us we would have to practice and practice to get it perfect. "We'll only have a month to get it done, what do ya say guys?"

Allie was all ready to do it. "Tommy," she said, "I bet we can't miss, will you do it?"

How could I say no?

The next day I flew the Stinson home. Uncle Bob told me he would fly me up to Colorado to get the Eagle Rock. "That way you'll get the feel of the plane on the way back." He also told me he had a pilot coming to take over the charter flying. He said he had put some money in the air show to back Jack. "Do a good job, Tommy boy, I'm counting on ya." He sure made me feel good about the whole thing.

Uncle Bob and I flew up and got the plane. On the way back I got the feel of her all right. She was a beauty to handle, I had never flown a ship so maneuverable. What a joy it was to fly this plane.

We came home on a Saturday. Sunday I announced I was gonna do a few stunts in the plane. Somehow I attracted a crowd. Louise, Mother, Popie, Pop, my brothers, Helen and Uncle Bob were there and about half our town.

I really had rung the ship out doing loops and rolls. For a final, I came across the runway on her back upside down about forty feet off the ground. Mother had a few words to tell me about my flying. I don't think she was thrilled at all, just mad I would do that. She said the whole thing was silly to fly that way. "You could be killed. Do you know that?"

I told her not to worry, It was safe as riding a horse. She just shook her head at me. Everyone else told me it was great the way I handled the plane.

That evening we all had dinner at Uncle Bob's and I stayed the night with Frank in his room. Frank worked the summer in Uncle Bob's office. We had a nice brother to brother talk, he went on and on about his girlfriend Gloria. He kept asking how

I liked her. I never told him I was married, but I told him I had a girl in California who would make Gloria look like a skinny boy. That shut him up about Gloria.

The next day was Monday, I took off early and arrived at Jack's Airport early in the afternoon. I could see the other Eagle Rock tied down outside the hangar. Of course, I had to buzz the hangar, took her up and did a roll or two then higher up, I put her in a flat spin. What a ship she was to handle. I sat her down easy and taxied to the hangar. Allie, Jack and the whole bunch were there to meet me, Jack didn't say anything then, but when we were alone he gave me holy-hell for doing stunts without his OK. He told me in no uncertain terms not to do that again. I said I would respect his wishes.

The next morning Allie and I began our synchronized flying. Jack would lay it out on the ground and we would go up and do it. I'm telling ya, Smiling Jack can chew butts and in a way to make ya like it, he chewed on the two of us every time we got back on the ground. He kept saying, "Little mistakes can kill ya."

I was trying my best to please him. We flew eight hours a day, seven days a week. By the time we finished I could do the routine in my sleep. When we told Jack that he said, "That's just what I wanted you two to say." Allie and I were ready.

Most nights, Allie and I would take off and spend the night together. Jack never said a word, but I knew he was suspecting something was going on between us, he never said anything.

We spent several weeks getting the planes ship shape. We were taking four Jennys, a Ford Tri-motor plus the Eagle Rocks on the tour. The Tri-motor carried our mechanics and equipment.

We had two parachutists from France join our company. They do what is called skydiving, that is, they don't open the chute until about one thousand feet from the ground. It was a new technique developed in Europe. Jack said it was as close as man could fly without an airplane, I was anxious to see that myself.

I did a few days later, the two went up in the tri-motor and leaped into space like nothing I had never seen before. They flew down and landed on the runway, I was impressed.

Our first show was in Salt Lake City, Utah. I must admit I was a bit nervous the first time I had to fly before a crowd. Allie could see my anxiety, she got me aside and said, "Tommy, I can see you're the same way you were the first time we made love, I told you then all would be okay and, Tommy, I want-a tell ya, you were great then, you'll be great now."

Boy, oh boy, did she make me feel better, what a gal I have. We did do a good job, Jack made a few changes, but he said on the whole it was a good show.

The next three stops were on the northern cities along the west coast. The only problem we had was the wind coming off the ocean. Everybody adjusted to it and we did have big crowds. We got super write ups in the local papers, Allie and I got big hands everywhere we went even to cafes and all. She really took the attention in stride, me, I kind of liked the way people made over Allie and me.

After the west coast we headed inland to Denver, Colorado. Allie talked me into spending the night together in the back of the tri-motor. We were in blankets and getting it on, when a light lit up the place. It was Jack and he was mad as hell, he had me by an arm and with a fist doubled up he was about to pop me in the face. Allie started screaming, "NO! NO, Daddy! We're married, we're married!"

I was damn glad she stopped him or I may not be here now. Her words took the air right out of him, he kind of fell back and sat down. For a minute I thought he was gonna cry.

"God dammit," he said, "I can't trust you two at all." He

covered his face and said, "You can get us in a hell-of-a mess. What if you get knocked up Allie? How you gonna fly then?"

"How long is the season gonna last?" she asked.

"We'll be through the last of September."

"That's great, daddy," she said, "I won't even be showing by then."

I looked to Jack, he looked to me and we both looked to a smiling Allie.

"Showing?" I asked.

"Yeah," she said. "You got me a month ago, you're going to be a daddy."

I had no idea she was pregnant. "How long have you known?"

"About two weeks, I went to a doctor last week, he said I been had a couple weeks."

I didn't know what to say. I jumped up, pulled on my pants and hustled out the door of the plane. On the ground I was feeling sick. Me, a father? I could hardly believe it. Then it hit me; me, a daddy! I started dancing and singing at the top of my voice. I looked to Allie and Jack standing in the door of the plane, both laughing and singing, too.

I heard Jack tell Allie, "Baby, you're gonna be a special Mom."

She told him, "You'll be a wonderful Grandpa."

Allie and I got dressed and Jack took us to the best hotel in Denver. I was so happy our marriage was out in the open. Jack said he was overjoyed for the two of us, he even called me "Son."

After breakfast, I called home and got Grandma Michelle. All the folks were out working. In her broken English she told me how happy she was I was married and had a child on the way. "Your Mommy will be so happy, we all knowed you's different. Tommy, we all love you and your new wife. Your brother Frank is on the way to Europe to study architecture. Your Uncle Bob is sending him, come home as soon as you can, we want to meet your Mrs." I told her I would and to tell the folks I'll come soon.

After Denver we went to the mid-west and toured all the big cities. Allie and I were being billed as the youngest stunt flying married couple in the world; the people came out in droves. Allie loved every minute of the attention she was getting. We made radio appearances and were interviewed by newspapers everywhere we went. Jack was so happy he was almost beside himself, the money was pouring in.

We did a show a few miles from the Great Lakes Naval Training Station. A squadron of Grumman F3F1's flew in and landed just before our show got under way. These were the Navy on line fighters at the time, a biplane with closed cockpit, I got to look one over. The Navy guys were friendly and informative, I even talked the commander into letting me fly one. What a nice guy he is, I took her up and she seemed awfully slow to me. Back on the ground I was informed I had forgotten to raise the landing gear that was the first time I had flown a retractable gear. All the Navy pilots got a big kick out-of-that.

Our whole company was invited to dinner on the Navy. All the guys paid a lot of attention to Allie and why not, she was the best looking woman in the world.

After our swing through the mid-west we went south into Texas. At one of our shows the Army Air Corps made a fly in visit. They were flying a squadron of Boeing P26C's. This Fighter is known as a pea-shooter, it's an open cockpit, fixed gear, and dumb looking airplane.

Yeah, the commanding officer let me have a go with one. On the ground I complained the craft was a bear to handle. He agreed and told me all the pea-shooters were going to be sent to China to fight the Japanese. I told him, "I hope the Chinese can fly better than I." Again we had an invite to dinner on the Army, yes, Allie was the center of attention. She told me it was a good thing we were married as the Army boys were good looking and she said there where one or two she could go for.

I told her, "Lady, you been had, I got ya." We both had a good laugh.

While we were in Texas, Jack purchased a Boeing Stearman biplane. I didn't have any idea why he would buy a plane like this. He took the ship up and did he ever give her the works, the man could fly an airplane.

The next day he had a post with a harness attached and two steel shoes fixed to the top wing. "Now," he said, "All I need is a volunteer to take a little ride standing on the wing." He was looking at me.

"Oh no, not me!" I said. "Not in this world."

Allie popped up and said, "I'll do it, Daddy."

"No, you won't. Not carrying my baby. I won't let you." I meant it, too.

Jack said, "No babe, Tommy will do it, I know he will."

What could I say but "I'll do it."

Allie was not only pretty to look at; she was as brave a person I have ever come across. Did I do it? Yes I did and you know what? When I got into it, I really, really enjoyed standing on top of the wing.

The first time I went up, Jack was the pilot and the next time Allie flew the plane. We kind of did the same as our other act, we both stood in the cock-pit and waved to the crowd then took off. Allie trailed a white scarf from her neck and as we came across the runway I would climb from the front cock-pit and get myself to the standing position on the top wing. Strapped in the fun began, me standing hand and arms out to my side, we came back across the runway then straight up. At three thousand feet we did a big slow inside loop, some fun!

I began to enjoy the stunt, Allie was tickled to death that we were a big hit with the people. We were on a national radio show a couple of times and we were getting all kinds of mail, that is, when it caught up with us. Allie loved to read the mail and she would talk about it all the time, me, I could care less. Allie wanted to be famous; she said a woman flyer would help make aviation better for all the people, I think she was right.

We flew the same routines for the next two years. Yes, Allie had a beautiful little girl baby, she became the delight of everyone connected with the show. She was the apple of Grandfather Jack's eye, he carried her everywhere he went, and he even helped us give her the name Elsa. It was his mother's name; he was so pleased that we used the name.

The flying seasons passed so quickly I couldn't believe we could be thru so soon. The whole troupe returned to San Diego every year to get ready for the next. We had a show in all the 48 states each season. Jack declared each season a great success. That made Allie and me happy.

We were having lunch at the diner when a Navy pilot Jack knew came in and joined us. He told us he had signed a contract to fly for the Flying Tigers in China. A General Chennault was asking military pilots to resign to go and fight the Japanese in China. I could see Jack was interested in this man's talk, Jack was a real old war horse. Big money was being paid to military pilots.

I started asking questions, but Allie cut me short and said, "Don't you get any ideas, you're not going anywhere without me and Elsa."

After the Navy Officer left, I asked Jack if he thought there would be a war that the US would get in. "You can bet on it," he said. "Have you been reading the papers?"

I told him, "I only listen to the radio, I don't seem to have time to read."

Jack said, "It looks to me like the Germans are on the march again, they have the biggest air force in the world, most modern, too. They sent planes to fight in the Spanish civil war."

"My brother Frank is a student in Germany, I hope he is okay." I was real worried about Frank.

I must have had real concern on my face as Allie said, "He better get out of the country, I read the Germans are drafting the young men. Wouldn't it be something if your brother got forced into their military?"

I could only say, "God, I hope not. That would kill my Mon and Dad."

We finished our meal and headed back to the airport. A news flash came over the car radio. "Germany has just invaded Poland and England has said it would declare war on Germany if they didn't pull their troops out today."

Jack said firmly, "The war is here now."

That was the first time I had ever seen or heard Allie cry, I could say nothing to console her. I knew in my heart, the USA was going to war sooner or later. Jack told the two of us that our government had not prepared us for war. He was mad as a hatter and said, "President Roosevelt and his cronies let us down, the writing has been on the wall for some time, our big shots don't even think about war, the way the draft went proved that."

The next thing we heard was England and France both declared war on Germany and Germany was in the process of invading France. England had sent troops to France to fight the Germans.

Our world was at war alright, where the heck was Brother Frank?

Chapter 4

The Battle of Britain: RAF

It was the saddest day in my entire life, up to that time, to see my Allie crying. She knew as I did what we were in for. As we sat in our car listening to the car radio, I could only hope this coming war would be over soon. Little did I know then what was in store for me and my family?

Allie, the baby and I flew to the ranch for Thanksgiving; all the news was of the fighting in France. The Germans had overrun Belgium and the Netherlands. France and England were having a rough time keeping the German Army from taking France.

My Dad and Popie were beside themselves that Germany would go to war again. All of them were worried sick about Brother Frank. No one had a word from him in weeks. I tried to console them by telling them that he could take care of himself. That didn't seem to help a bit. Mother and Michelle would tear up at the mention of Frank's name. I kept telling them, "He will be okay."

My Dad took me aside and wanted to know what my plans were about the military. I told him I had no plans, he advised I should think about joining a service before I got drafted.

"I'll look into it when I get home."

Back home I went to see the Navy recruiter; he said I could join, go to boot camp then take my chances about flying. "Maybe you can go to flight training, but right now we don't need pilots." I tried the Marines, same story. "We need good strong guys like you, but we need Infantry."

Not me, no Infantry for me. I got the same song and dance

from the Army, I could go to basic training, then I could try for pilots training. I kind of said to hell with it, I was too young to be drafted at this time. Allie wasn't really happy about the whole thing, she just didn't want me to join at all. I told her I would have to go sooner or later. She said she knew that but wanted to prolong it as long as possible.

The month slipped by, Christmas and New Year's came and went. We had spent the time with Jack, I was at the airport helping one of Jack's mechanics clean up an engine when three guys who had been pilots in the air shows flew in and landed, I walked over where they were talking together.

"Hi guys, what's up? What brings you boys to this bird nest on a day like this?" It was cloudy and getting ready to rain.

Big Jim said, "We're waiting to meet a plane to take us to Canada; we have decided to join the Canadian Air force. How about you, Tommy, you want-a go too?"

"What's the deal?" I asked.

"Any licensed U.S. flyer can join if you can pass the physical."

I had found my calling. I called Allie on the phone to tell her, I wanted to join the Canadian Air Force. To my surprise, she said, "Go for it." That's how I joined the Canadian Air Force.

In Canada I spent three months training, it was called "a quick up." I spent most of the time learning about how to be a military person. After finishing the course, I was made a Flight Sergeant. We received new blue uniforms, with flight wings over the left breast pocket, and a Canada patch on the left arm at the shoulder, I was pronounced a fit combat Fighter Pilot.

Allie and Elsa had spent two months with me while I was in this training. That made life a lot better for me.

Orders came down that fifteen pilots were to be in England ASAP. I was made the CO of the detail; we were to fly two

Lockheed Hudson twin engine aircraft to England.

Allie booked a flight to San Diego; I saw the baby and Allie off at the airport, it was a sad day to see Allie crying so hard, as she entered the plane; I threw a kiss and mouthed, "I'll be back."

We left the next morning, we landed at Nova Scotia to refuel and flew across the Atlantic to an airdrome in central west England. There I was posted to a Patrol Squadron at the tip of northern Scotland. I was to patrol the North Sea looking for submarines and other German sea going vessels, I complained. "I came here to be a fighter pilot, not a sub chaser."

The C.O. told me, "We need experienced pilots to instruct the others, you are our best."

What could I say but, "Okay."

My duties started as soon as I unpacked, the Hudson was the ideal aircraft to use, it carried ten, one hundred and ten pound bombs. We patrolled sunup to sundown. My first go was fourteen hours, and then we would get eight hours on, eight hours off. A month of this and my butt was dragging. We hadn't spotted one sub, I was beginning to think the Huns {as the Brits called the Germans} had no subs in the North Sea.

If I hadn't been getting letters from Allie and Mother, I would have gone berserk. Funny how news from home will make a guy feel so good. Allie said she was working at the Lockheed Aircraft Company in Santa Monica, California, I kind of figured she was building airplanes. Little did I know she was a test pilot for the aircraft Lockheed P38? It was several years before I learned about it, what a gal I married. She was in more danger than I.

All the news was of the fighting in France. The Brits had sent a force {with fighter planes - Hurricanes - no Spitfires} to stop the Nazi advance. Seems they were having no luck stopping the Germans.

Two of our pilots were called to Fighter Command, they were older chaps. I felt cheated for weeks, I said so too. I was to feel better soon.

It was on an early morning patrol, we had been out for an hour, when the observer called on the intercom, "Sub dead ahead."

Sure enough, I could just make out a Sub on the surface coming our way, what luck! I banked the Hudson hard right and at full throttle we climbed into a dense cloud bank. At 15,000, I leveled off and turned north, every once in a while we could get a peek at the Sub through a break in the clouds. She was steaming right along on the same course. Apparently, their lookout had not seen or heard our aircraft.

I gave it five minutes, dove down and a few feet off the water headed for our target. At five hundred yards, I climbed above the Sub. "Bombs away!" She never knew what hit her, the hundred-ten pounders hit square on the deck, what a shot! As we climbed away, I banked left to get a better view. The Sub jumped out of the water and broke in half, in two minutes, the Sub was gone. I had total remorse; I knew a hundred men had just died. War had come to me in a striking realization.

After the patrol, a celebration was had in the village pub. Now there were fourteen crews patrolling the North Sea from our airdrome. Our Commanding Officer, Jeff J. Jones, a tall Scott, came to me that night and told me I had been posted to Fighter Command, I almost broke down as I wanted that so bad.

"Tommy," he said "You will make one great Fighter Pilot." He had been one in the first war. "I wish you the best in the world, England needs you now." Boy, oh boy, did he make me feel good; I had a lot of respect for this man.

The news was of the retreat of French and British forces.

They were trapped on the beaches of a French coastal town - Dunkirk.

Two days later, I was on a train bound for Fighter Command. I was to report to Air Vice-Marshal Park at Uxbridge, Group 11 Headquarters in south east England. I arrived at Park HQ at seven a.m. He welcomed me with open arms. "We need fighter pilots. You will be a member of Squadron 29 at Tangmere Airdrome, it's the hottest group we have." He was a no nonsense guy.

"We need pilots," he said again, "Not heroes. Follow the orders of your squadron leader."

I said I would without fail.

The news about Dunkirk, France was that the Brits had taken most of the soldiers back to England, 250,000 in a flotilla of civilian small boats. That was an impossible feat, to say the least.

I was given a ride to the Tangmere Airdrome. In the dispersal hut; I met my Squadron Leader, a chap named Flight Officer Major Sailor Martin. A stern looking individual, he looked to be about thirty-five years old, Six feet tall about one hundred eighty pounds. He was a friendly fellow and introduced me to a good number of my brother pilots, most were young as I. I met my wing man, Lee Johns, an Aussie, tall, blonde, dark blue-eyed, handsome, weighting in at about a hundred and sixty pounds. a really good looking young guy. He told me he had been with the squadron all of three days. "I have four hours of combat time, No kills but some misses."

"I'll get one soon," he told me with much confidence.

Major Martin asked if I had ever flown a fighter aircraft.

"I have a few minutes in a Navy f4f Grumman Wildcat and an old Pea-shooter, a Navy Officer let me fly them at an air show we were giving at a Navy field; nothing to brag about."

Major Martin the Squadron CO and I walked outside and

over to a Hurricane fighter plane parked in the dispersal area. Four ground crew men were busy working on it.

The Sq. CO said, "This is your aircraft, it has just been refurbished at the factory. These men are fueling and putting a few finishing touches on it. The ship was shot down and the pilot killed, may you have better luck with her."

I must have looked a little apprehensive. He told me. "She's as good as new."

He introduced me to my ground crew chief, Corporal Jason Smith. "She's all ready to fly, sir."

The Corporal looked really young, maybe nineteen at the most. He was a rather tall, lanky chap with a smooth face and a friendly smile. I could see we were going to get along fine. He gripped my hand and said. "We'll get a lot of Huns, won't we Sir?"

"You bet we will."

"Your airplane is in good hands, I'll take good care of her and you, Please call me Smithy, everyone does."

"I sure will."

Squadron Commander, Flight Officer Major Martin said, "I want you to take your Hurricane up. You need to get the feel of her before you go into combat."

Smithy told me, "She's full of petrol and ready to go, no ammo though"

"Go south out to sea, give her a good jolly go, you have an hour. Watch for enemy aircraft, the Huns are lurking about."

I climbed into the cockpit. This aircraft had more instruments than any plane I had flown. He stood on the wing giving me instructions I needed to fly my Hurricane. "When you turn upside down, the engine will spit a few seconds. She has a carburetor, it takes a second for the fuel to catch up. Remember that, the enemy has fuel injection, so you are most vulnerable at that time." When he got down, Smithy helped with my seat and parachute harnesses, I was ready to fly my Hurricane.

As I was flagged out and taxied to the take-off area, I tried to run over in my mind the instructions Officer Martin had given me. There was no runway here, just a grass field,the ground was somewhat soft. At the end of the field, I turned into the wind, set the brakes and revved the engine, I released the brakes and she leapt forward in response. Away we went, back on the stick, in a split second we were airborne.

"What power this baby has."

I circled the field two times, climbing all the time, I needed to get my bearings. At three thousand feet, I banked right and headed south. Climbing all the time, I was out over water in a few minutes. I put on the oxygen mask at twelve thousand feet, and flattened out, all the time watching for enemy aircraft. None, I never saw any all the time I was out when I figured I was out about twenty miles, I put her through some aerobatics.

WOW, what an aircraft this was! If I had done some of the same stuff in the old biplanes in the air shows, I wouldn't be here, this plane could take it. Loops, rolls, spins, she climbed like crazy. I had never flown a plane like this before, I was having a ball, what fun! When I checked my instruments, I only had a few minutes fuel left. The gauge was clicking on "E." I was at fifteen thousand feet, I rolled her over and went into a steep dive.

WHOA! The Hurricane began to shudder and kept in the dive, I was pulling back on the stick with all my strength, I was sweating like a run-a-way horse. She pulled out at one thousand feet, Whew! Hooray, I was about to relieve myself— pee in my pants.

Back at the airfield, I sat her down as gentle as a baby buggy. Smithy helped me out of the cockpit. "How ya like her?" he asked.

"This is a real aircraft."

He grinned and shook his head yes.

A lorry pulled up next to the Hurricane, a young female in a blue uniform got out and started to unload cartons of 303 ammo. I asked Smithy about her.

"She's a WAAF, we have lots of girls like her, and they do everything for us. Drive lorries, tractors, you may see them with a shovel filling bomb craters after a raid, mostly they work on the tracking tables."

"Tracking tables?" I asked.

"Yeah, they track the enemy as soon as they take off in France; track our fighters as they intercept them. You will have to go see, it's something to see, we can't do without them, they're wonderful." He introduced me to the WAAF, her name was Sarah. I learned more every day, about Fighter Command.

I walked past the dispersal area, there sat eight pilots waiting for the call to scramble. They were lounging in lawn chairs, one got up and introduced himself. "My name is Patty," he said as he shook my hand. He told me the seven other chaps' names. "How do we call you? We give nick names to everybody."

"My name is Tom. I'm called Tommy at home."

"Tommy is an English Bloke, we need one better."

One of the pilots chimed in. "Let's call him Yank."

"That's okay by me. "

"Yank you are," Patty said. "The CO wants to see you."

"See you chaps later." I walked over and entered the dispersal hut, there were three pilots and Officer Martin sitting around a table.

"Come on in," Officer Martin said. "How was your flight?"

"Great, that's the most powerful aircraft I've ever flown."

"Did you have any trouble at all?" he asked.

"She was a little hard to take out of a steep dive."

"Ha, ha," Martin said laughing. "You forgot to trim. Many first timers pull the same thing, you won't forget again."

I assured him I wouldn't.

"Two critical moves you must make when you dive in a Hurricane trim her and don't forget to switch on the firing button when you go into combat. Also, you only have nineteen seconds of ammo. Try to use two second bursts, watch your tracers, they will tell you where your hitting. We recommend starting firing at two hundred and fifty yards from the target. We use the Hurricane for the bombers; let the Spits take on the German fighters. Our tactics as of now are to dive from above, out of the sun if possible. Try to pass thru the enemy formation, firing as you pass by. Climb as soon as you can and get in position to make another pass. I know it sounds simple, it's not. Most of all, you will have to train yourself. We all do, we don't have the time to train to shoot. Most of the pilots never shoot their guns until they go into combat."

"I understand, I'll try not to spend ammo."

Major Martin then introduced the three pilots, all three where NCO's. "These men are your bunk mates. Flight Sergeant Adolf Lyseek, he's Polish" He was a rather short husky individual, with a ruddy face, balding head and a strong hand shake, my hand will never be the same. He spoke good English when he welcomed me to the squadron. Officer Martin told me Sgt. Lyseek's story. He had come over to Great Britain a year ago with five other pilots from Poland. Sgt. Lyseek interrupted the Major.

"Yes, we came to England as we saw the Germans marching; my country's aircraft were obsolete, we could not fight the Germans with them."

Officer Martin continued, "He was with us in France, his wife and two young sons were killed in the bombing of Warsaw."

"I'm sorry to hear that." I felt sadness for him.

Sgt Lyseek said, "She would not come to England with me, I should have made her. She did not want to leave her parents." He bowed his head as he spoke.

I really felt sorry for him to lose his family that way.

"This fine fellow is from South Africa, Flight Sergeant Lee Rolland." Sgt Rolland came and shook my hand.

"Glad to have you aboard, Old Chap, Please call me Lee, I like the name." He laughed saying his name.

Lee was another good looking young guy. Looked to be six feet tall, brown neatly combed hair, brown eyes, weighed about one-seventy or -eighty pounds. Looked like the kind you would want to be your friend.

The last NCO was standing next to Lee. He looked young, maybe seventeen or eighteen.

"My name is J.W. Allison, call me JW." He was very handsome, reminded me of the American movie star Tyrone Power, I could see he was full of himself. You have to be that way to be a fighter pilot. He shook my hand. "Glad to meet you."

Officer Martin said, "Your gear and kit are in your hut, these men will show you where. The NCO mess is open all the time, If you have any questions, feel free to come and ask. You will not fly until tomorrow morning, we rise at four a.m., be ready to scramble by five a.m."

The three Sergeants led me to our hut. The hut was primitive to say the least; it had four cots, a wall locker for each, a clothes hanger, four chairs and a small writing desk. A small lamp hung over each cot.

I had letters from Allie and Mother lying on my cot. I waited a while to open them.

We four sat and talked awhile, I wanted to get to know these men. I asked Lyseek about his time in France. He wanted to talk, he told of the fighting in France, he was hit by ground fire and had to bail out, he landed in a field near a road that was being used by hundreds of refugees. He told of the German aircraft bombing and strafing the road. There were people and animals killed all along the road, it was pure slaughter. "I was lucky not to have been killed. It took two days to get back to my airfield, I shall never forget that time." He showed a lot of anger in himself. Who could blame him?

The pilots left and went out to the dispersal area as they might have had to fly at any time.

I was alone and got to read my letters. Allie said all was good at home, the baby was growing like a weed. She enclosed two pictures, I would not have recognized our little girl. Mother said Popie had been sick with the flu and Uncle Bob was getting bad with cancer. They were worried about Frank, they had no word from him in weeks. Boy, oh boy, I hoped he was all right. The last they heard he was somewhere in Europe trying to get to Italy.

I spent the last hour before mess writing letters. After mess, we all returned to our hut. As I was finishing my letters, my wing man, Flight Officer Tim, came by and asked if anyone wanted to go to a pub. J.W. was ready so I decided to go along. Tim said we would be back by ten p.m.

Tim has an English Ford four-door sedan. JW and Tim got in the front seat; I sat in the rear seat behind the driver Tim. We were pulling out of the airfield gate when four WAAF's in blue uniforms waved down our auto. One of the girls called, "You chap's going to a pub?"

Tim, through the open driver's window answered, "Yeah. You girls want-a go with us?"

One of the ladies yelled back, "Yes, we do."

Tim invited them to hop in. Three of them got in the back seat with me. The other one opened the door next to me and popped right in onto my lap. She remarked, "You're the Yank all the girls are talking about, right?"

"Yeah, I am." She was the WAAF with the ammo I met at my plane.

"Hope I'm not too heavy?"

"No, you're just fine."

The WAAF who stopped us said, "I'm Maggie." The one next to her said, "I'm Edith." The other one said, "I'm Ginger." The one on my lap said she was "Sarah."

I told them, "I'm Tom, the Yank."

"Are you a single man, Tom?" Sarah asked.

"No. I'm not, but I like pretty girls just the same."

"Look out Sarah," Ginger quirked, "He'll have you in bed shortly."

"No way," I said.

Maggie looked in the dim light to be in her late twenties, rather husky and sharp featured lass.

We arrived at the Red Barn shortly and our entire group entered a typical English pub. There were three men and two ladies at the bar. Sarah, Edith, Tim and I sat at a table, Sarah sat next to me. Maggie, Ginger and JW went straight to the bar. Maggie ordered a jinn, she took off and laid her cap on the bar exposing her short cropped man's hair cut. I thought, "That woman is the bossy kind."

Edith was a very quiet sort; she was pretty, five-two and nicely built. Ginger was the party type, a beautiful blonde with blue eyes and a well-built body that even the blue uniform could not hide, she was a real butterfly. Sarah was pretty with her dark brown hair and flashing brown eyes, full lips and gorgeous smile. A most pleasing voice, I liked her immediately. She reminded me of a woman in the American movies, darn if I could remember her name. I could see Sarah wanted to talk. The waiter came; I asked Sarah what she would have to drink. "I'll have a pint," she replied. I ordered the same. And I put money on the table, she said in no uncertain terms, she was paying. She was so forceful I put my money away.

I asked her how she became a WAAF. "I wanted to be a nurse, but my father talked me out of it. You see he was a Doctor, a Surgeon, in the first war in France. He was gassed by the Germans in a field hospital. All the time he was with us, he was kind of sickly. He told me he didn't want me around sick people, so I trained to be a WAAF, my father died when I was fifteen. I have a little Brother, who will be ten this year. I was born in a small hamlet north of London, I want to hear about you. How come you came over here to fight?"

"I know America will have to soon be where I am." I asked, "Where are your Mother and Brother now?"

"They moved in with my Mother's Brother as soon as the war started. They live on a farm in the center of the country. I hope they won't get bombed there."

We made small talk for over an hour, I really like her.

Maggie announced, "We have to go, we must be back in our quarters by ten fifteen."

Tim got to his feet and said loud and clear, "Drink up, we're leaving."

We all returned in Tim's auto. We sat in the same arrangement as before with Sarah on my lap, Sarah put her left arm around my neck and whispered, "I like you Tom,"

"I like you, too, Sarah." She rubbed her cheek against mine.

Ginger heard it and said, "O-o-o-o-o what's going on here?"

I said, "Nothing, Ginger. We two are just being friends."

"I bet, if I were her, I would like it." Ginger was laughing.

Tim turned, "I better get to know you Ginger." We all

laughed.

We dropped the girls off at their quarters. Sarah waved and called, "I'll see you again Tom."

As we pulled away I remembered, "Teresa Wright," I said out loud. "Teresa Wright. You chaps help me to remember that name." They both said they would.

At our hut, Tim let JW and I off. Inside, the black-out curtains were pulled, Lee and Lyseek were both in bed. Lyseek was snoring the roof off. I got out my pj's, robe and slippers and a set of ear plugs. I undressed, put on the pj's and robe, grabbed my kit and went to the wash room. I brushed my teeth, washed up and hurried back to the hut.

Lyseek was still snoring, with ear plugs, I went to bed. I turned my lamp off, dark as sin in the hut. I lay in bed thinking I had a good day. When I fly, it is always a good day. When I had shut my eyes, I could see war planes in my mind, black ME 109's, lots of them. All of a sudden I was tired, I felt a little guilty about Sarah, what would Allie think if she knew? Oh well, tomorrow I fly my first combat scramble. I adjusted my head on the pillow to get more comfortable and soon fell asleep.

Chapter 5

1st Combat – September 1940

I was awakened by a bright light, I pulled out my ear plugs and sat up in bed. The sound of aircraft taking off filled the room. Sgt. Lyseek was up and dressing, when he finished dressing, he opened our hut door. The smell of fresh mown grass sifted through the screen door. Birds could be heard chirping from the trees, A new fresh fall morning. The morning sunlight had not begun. Lyseek called, "It's four a.m., everyone up."

Lee slowly put his feet on the floor, he stretched and yawned, "God. What a terrible time to get up." JW was the last to rise, he took a cigarette and lit it. I watched as the smoke he blew drifted up and disappeared.

I took off my pj's and hung them and my robe in my locker. Dressed, I slipped on my flight boots. Carrying my Mae West, Lee and I went together to the NCO mess for breakfast. Two eggs, bacon, hash-brown potatoes, sliced tomatoes, toast, tea and coffee.

All the pilots who were to fly this morning gathered at the dispersal area. Our Squadron commander came to talk to us. "We will fly the {vic} formation. Tom, any questions?"

"No sir. I know the {vic}."

"You will be number eight, Lee number nine."

I was ready.

The telly rang, "SCRAMBLE!"

What a rush. By the time I reached my machine, Smithy had the engine started, I was in the cockpit in a flash. Smithy helped me buckle up, first, the parachute harness, then the seat straps.

I taxied out with the other planes. We were all in the air in minutes; up we went and formed into the Vic formation. Oxygen masks on, we leveled out at twenty thousand heading east, only slight cloud cover.

In a few minutes, we could see below a guppy of forty or fifty J 87's Stuka, dive bombers. They were ready to attack the radar towers on the Dover coast, no escort fighters could be seen.

Our Squadron Leader called on the R/T, "Tally-Ho." He peeled off and dove down at the Stukas. The Squadron followed one by one. Me, I was in the eighth place, I lined up a Hun and gave him a two second blast. Shit 0h dear, too far out, the tracers showed I was missing badly. In closer I hit home, he started to smoke, I must have hit the engine, he rolled over and dove into the ground, HA! My first kill.

As I started to climb, I saw three Stukas heading east. They had dropped their load and started scampering home. "Not so fast old boys," I said. "Sitting ducks, just my meat." I proceeded to chase them. After a few minutes, I was on the tail of the rear Hun. A two-second blast found the mark, pieces of aircraft began to fly at me, one hit my wind screen, no damage. The three man crew bailed out. We were out over the Channel; the Huns were going to get wet.

I was closing on the next one so fast I had to throttle back and hit the flaps to slow my speed a little. It worked fine. Now the rear gunner was firing at me. The blink-blink of his machine gun sent red fire tracers at me, he was missing badly. I squeezed the firing button, dead on, sparks of my tracers showed I was hitting damn good. He began to show black patches of smoke, I must have hit his engine. The Stuka began to shake and flop around, it did a slow roll and dove straight toward the water, and No one had gotten out. I looked to the last one, he was quite a ways ahead. I opened the throttle, I was closing fast. Damn, black smoke flak bursts began to fill my space, Ack-Ack. To my surprise, looking down I was over land, I had flown into France. I banked hard right and did 180, I wanted away as fast as I could. I said out-loud, "I'll get you Huns some other time." I just wanted to put distance between me and the Anti-aircraft guns; luck was with the Hun this day.

Out over the Channel, I was feeling darn good, and then it happened. My wind-screen began being covered with green slim. Crap, my engine coolant was leaking, Ack-Ack had scored a hit, in a few minutes my engine would freeze , the coolant was gone, I knew I didn't have very long as the engine would seize. I was now at three thousand feet altitude and I hadn't seen any enemy aircraft, luck was with me. I had a heading of dead east toward England; my engine began to miss badly.

The white cliffs were coming closer, I was going down fast. I tried to gain more altitude. "Come up baby, come up." I kept yelling, "Come up, come up." No go, I had to get higher or I would crash into the cliffs. I pulled back on the stick with all I had, still no go, I had to ditch. The plane was going down fast, fear grabs at you. What if the plane summersaults? Scary, one dead pilot. My best shot was to drag the tail in the water and try to make a soft landing. Still pulling on the stick, I thought, "Flaps, flaps," no good.

Still hauling back on the stick, I could feel the tail dragging in the water. All of a sudden the plane stood on her nose, turned to the right, then settled back down. It was all over and I was in one piece. I pushed back the canopy, unhooked the harness and got out on the left wing. The wing was slowly sinking into the water, I crawled over to the right wing.

Looking around, I could see I was in about four feet of water, I could wade to the beach. Looking north, I saw a small boat coming my way, maybe Germans? I pulled my pistol ready to make a fight. As the boat got closer, I could see a woman in the bow waving. As the boat drew up to the wing, the woman yelled, "Jump!" I did right into her arms.

The boat backed out and turned around, we headed north. She said, "Come into the cabin, I want you to meet my husband and father."

I followed her to the cabin. I soon discovered these people look for downed pilots in the Channel all the time, these are great people. A cup of hot tea and a biscuit, the lady introduced her husband and father. The husband was a rather stout fellow with coal black hair and a friendly smile; he darn near shook my arm off. The father was smoking a stinky pipe, a cap cocked on his head, he gave me a big bear hug and said, "We saw you go after the Huns, we saw you coming back trailing smoke, we headed for the spot where we hoped you would come down, we will take you in."

"You people do a great job." I had to ask questions. "Do you pick up many downed pilots?"

The father answered, "Everyday."

"Enemy pilots?"

"Everyday."

"Do they give you trouble?"

"Not often; they are happy to be saved. We do run into German boats once in a while, we never have any trouble from them, we both respect what we do."

In a short hour, we entered a small inlet, leading to a pre-war fishing village. The boat people dropped me and headed back to the Channel. I got a wonderful reception from the villagers. All the food and drink I could take and I got a lot of attention from the children of the village, all kinds of questions. When I told them I was an American, I really got a lot of cheers and they sang, {He's a Jolly Good Fellow.} I got on the telly and informed the airdrome where I was, I was told to sit tight; a car would come for me.

Just as darkness fell a car arrived, the driver, to my surprise and delight, was none other than the female WAAF, my friend Sarah. I thanked the village people, got in the car and Sarah and I started for the airdrome.

Sarah said very little until I thanked her for coming to pick me up. She got very talkative, "Did you know your R/T was open and sending during your flight."

"No, I hope I didn't embarrass anyone with my language, I had no idea you guys were listening."

"No, the operation room got a real kick hearing you, all of us were praying for you. There's a pub just ahead, would you like to stop and have a pint?"

"Yeah, I would like that."

We stopped and had a pint and some fish and chips. The pub was warm and the people friendly. We fighter pilots leave the top button on our tunics undone. People all know when they see that we are fighter pilots. I got a lot of slaps on the back and lots of cheers. It was all a lot of fun for me.

We heard many stories about the dogfights that raged in the sky above them. One older man told us, very proudly, that he had captured three Nazi Airmen when their bomber crash landed in his field. With a shotgun he held the airmen until the home guard came for them. Another said he had pulled a pilot from his burning crashed Spitfire. We heard several similar stories. Lots of cheers after each story.

We both hated to leave such a friendly group. Sarah and I arrived at the airdrome commanding officer's office around ten p.m.

As I started to leave the car, Sarah grabbed me by the right arm and said, "Tom, I'm becoming very fond of you." She was such a sweet girl, she pulled me to her and pecked me on my cheek, I hardly knew what to tell her. All I said was, "Good night, you sweet thing." I hurried into the office, I knew I had a good balling out coming, I was not disappointed. Officer Martin gave me a real tongue lashing for disobeying orders. "Don't chase the enemy across the Channel again." Then he said in a demanding voice, "Go get some rest."

As I left, he said with a big smile, "Jolly good bloody show, old chap, you will get a new Hurricane in the morning." I gave him a quick salute and headed for my hut. A hot shower and some sleep was all I needed.

At six a.m. on September 15, 1940, I entered the NCO's mess and got a rousing welcome from my brother pilots. I got a lot of "good shows" and slaps on the back. The roar of aircraft engines filled the morning air, three new Hurricanes arrived. After my breakfast, I hurried out to my park to find Smithy giving my new aircraft a real going over. The ground crew refueled and armed her ready to fly.

I climbed into the cockpit to look her over, she smelled new. An envelope was pinned on the dash, I opened and read the letter inside. The ladies who had worked on the aircraft wrote they would pray every day for my safe time in this machine, six ladies signed the letter. We have great people we have backing us up.

I heard over the loud speaker, "SCRAMBLE!"

Smithy helped to fasten my parachute and seat straps, and then he pulled the wheel chocks. I turned the engine switch on and pushed the starter button. The twelve hundred and eighty horse engine burst with a roar into life. Following my squadron leader, we taxied to the downwind end of the grass airfield, I lined up for takeoff. I followed number seven in my takeoff run. Throttle forward, airborne, we lined up in formation. We headed northeast, climbing all the time. A near cloudless sky greeted us, at ten thousand we leveled out.

The raiders shown on the operations screen appeared below. Six Heinkell-15 float planes were flying at four thousand. I guessed they were going to plant mines in one of the inlets just off the Channel, sitting ducks for us.

"Tally Ho, away we go." I switched on my firing button, trimmed her and followed the squadron in a dive on the target. I never got off a shot; the first six squadron fighters took out all six floatplanes. We returned to the airfield and landed in about half an hour, a job well done. Most of the remaining morning my squadron sat on alert at the dispersal area

At ten-thirty a.m., we were scrambled again. Airborne, we climbed to twenty thousand feet on an easterly heading. In a few minutes, I saw what looked to be a hundred Nazi bombers with at least twenty ME 109 escorts crossing the English coast at ten thousand feet below us. The sky had turned to high, thin scattered clouds, with a strong north wind.

My Squadron Commander did not hesitate, "Tally ho," he called over the R/T. We peeled off one at a time, I picked a Dornier 17 on the outside rear of the formation. A two second burst, followed by another, and the left engine of the bomber started to flame, a good hit. Down through this formation I went and pulled up below the flight, I put the Hurricane into a sharp climb. This new machine could really climb. Looking north, I saw three Squadrons of Spitfires joining the melee. They were intent on breaking up the escorts, they did a good job. The sky was full of shooting, diving, flaming and smoking fighter aircraft.

I made two more passes before I ran low on fuel and out of ammo. I made it back to my home airfield. Smithy and his crew had me airborne again in ten minutes. He told me the RAF said this was the biggest Luftwaffe raid England had ever had in one day. Back in the air, I could believe that, London was catching all kinds of hell. Smoke from the fires in and around London could be seen fifty miles away. Once on the north of London, I saw a Big Wing of Spitfires coming to join in the fight, looked to me like ten squadrons.

My contribution to the fight was same as before. Climb above the bombers, dive through and try to get hits as I passed an enemy plane. On a pass from the north I had just leveled off ready to make my climb when "holy shit" an ME 110 passed right over the top of me and flew straight away. All I had to do was push the firing button when he filled my wind screen, pieces of the aircraft began to fly passed me, some hit my aircraft, I was lucky no damage was done. The 110 burst into flame and exploded within one hundred yards of me, the crew never had a chance to bail out.

On my next pass, I was north of London again, low on fuel and ammo. I looked for a field to resupply, I found Hornchurch and landed. A ground crew was on my plane before the prop stopped. A WAAF climbed on the left wing and handed me a cup of tea and some crumpets. I sat in the cockpit and finished eating just as the crew finished.

Airborne again, it was the same—climbing, diving, shooting and repeating the same over and over. Around four p.m., I had had it, the bomber Gruppe formations had vanished. I headed to my home airfield and landed, Smithy directed me to my parking spot, I was completely drained of all my energy. I sat in the cockpit as Smithy and the ground crew refueled and rearmed my aircraft, Smithy climbed on the wing and told me, "Looks like the Huns have stopped for the day."

All I could say was, "Thank God."

I climbed out and walked {on shaky legs, I might add} to the debriefing hut. The debriefing officer spent twenty minutes on a question and answer session, he released me to get food and some sleep.

I awoke to loud knocking on my door. Half asleep, I

answered to find Sarah standing there.

"May I come in?" She asked

What could I say but, "Sure, come on in." I went and sat on the bed, she sat down beside me.

"Quite a day you had, we heard much of your time on the R/T, I was praying for you all the time." She pulled me to her by putting both her arms around me. She kissed me tenderly on my cheek. "I love you, Tommy."

All the emotion I had in me overflowed, I pulled her to me and kissed her hard on her beautiful lips. "I love you too, Sarah." At that time, I loved her as much as Allie., but I came to my senses. "I can't love you, Sarah. I have a wife and child, I love my wife dearly."

"I know you love me, Tommy. We are here now, let's make the most of our time together, tomorrow may never come for us."

Chapter 6

Sarah and the USA

Sarah and I went to the NCO mess and had breakfast. While eating, Commander Martin came in and informed me I had been promoted to a Flight Officer. He also gave me orders that instructed me to be a new Squadron Leader, he told me I had to be an officer to be a squadron leader, he also said I only had one experienced combat pilot in my squadron.

At the dispersal area, the CO introduced me to my new command. They were young, real young, most of the young men were 18 and 19 years old. I questioned these pilots, most of them had very little flying time, some had as little as ten hours in an aircraft. "How in the world can I make fighters of these young men? It's murder to send these kids against the Luftwaffe." I gave the CO a hard look, he spun on his heels and remarked as he walked away, "You have your work cut out for you."

Sarah was standing a few feet away and she heard all of the conversation. I looked to her. She only shook her head "no." I dropped my head and said out loud, "Dear God, I need your help."

Sarah joined my payer, saying softly, "God bless and be with you."

I thanked her by saying, "You're a real jewel, Sarah."

She walked a few feet away, turned and put her right hand fingers to her lips and threw me a kiss, I threw one back, she walked away.

I started teaching the boys what I expected from them. "We don't engage fighters unless we have to, Hurricanes are used to go after the bombers. We dive on the formations from above; we try to break them up, dive through and get your shots in quickly, climb back for another run." All the boys shook their heads "yes." I could see they knew what I meant.

On our first sortie, I lost two fighter boys, one flew into a bomber, I don't think he meant to, he came out of a dive and rammed a Heinkel before he could turn away. Needless to say all the bomber crew and my boy were lost. The other pilot clipped wings with a bomber, my boy went down with his aircraft. The others pilots got on the job training.

In the months that followed, I worked my butt off trying to protect my boys and teach air- combat. Somehow I got thru to them, I saved a lot of our kids. With a lot of praying and God's help, I might add.

I received letters from home quite often. Allie wrote beautiful letters and always sent pictures of our little girl and snapshots of her and the baby. Oh, how I longed to hold them and see them, I got letters from Mom and Dad. My brother Frank had checked in and was safe, that made me feel better.

I got to see Sarah a lot; she seemed to be around when I had free time. I really got to enjoy her company, we talked and walked every chance we got, I looked forward to seeing her. What a nice woman. Who wouldn't like her? She was filling a real void in my life.

My squadron had returned from a scramble. After a debriefing, the CO came and told me to take three days off. "Take this girl of yours, go somewhere away from the war for awhile," he demanded.

I had just got to the door of my hut when Sarah pulled up in an MG Roadster. I had to change my clothing and get my kit. We were on a road south in a few minutes, the air was cold as December was fast approaching.

She told me, "We're going to a village my father always

sent Mother, my little brother and I to spend the summer months. He would come and join us on the weekends. I love it there, I want you to love it, too."

We arrived around seven p.m. in the south coast village of Hastings. We registered in the Hotel Royal, room # 205 front. The room looked down on the street below and the small beach that was below the sea wall. We had dinner in the hotel dining room, the people there were cordial and friendly. The cook managed to fix a splendid meal. Sarah had removed her cap and let her long dark brown hair down, she was as pretty a woman as I had ever seen, her big laughing brown eyes set in an angular face, she had a smile and laugh that could light any man's heart, I was a goner. Feeling guilty was not enough, can a man love two women at the same time? I know it's so.

There were two other couples as guests at the hotel and twenty or so people living there. Someone put a dance record on a player {Once in Awhile by Tommy Dorsey and Frank Sinatra.} We all had a go at dancing, a most enjoyable time for Sarah and me. By eleven p.m., we retired to our room. The next hours were spent sleeping and making love to each other, she was a most wonderful loving person, how bad I am? I was feeling guilty, I told Sarah.

"Tommy," she said, "Let's take this time as we can, we may not be here tomorrow." She was right, that helped my feelings.

The next day, we walked around the village and talked to the friendly village people. We hiked in the hills north of the town and stumbled into a well hidden antiaircraft battery. From the crew we learned a lot about the defense of the south coast of the UK. There had been many troops there, but since the invasion by the Nazis looked to be called off, the men were back in training for the invasion of their own of France. There were patrols by land, sea and air, also spotters all along the coast. I asked if they had shot down any enemy aircraft. The crew chief told us, "A bomber crashed and burned a meter north of us, we were damn sure we got him." When he told us that, all the crew let out a big cheer, we visited with the boys several more times.

The day we were to leave, we had to drive at night as enemy fighters were strafing the roads all day. It was safer to travel the roads at night. On our last walk, we entered a small jewelry shop a few doors east of the hotel, Sarah wanted to shop, I wanted to buy her something. She asked the shop keeper, "Do you have a ring with an Aquarius birth stone? I want-a keepsake to remember our days spent together here in Hastings."

He showed us a ring with a purple amethyst stone, she had to have it. I paid the man.

"I want to buy you something, Tommy." I shook my head no. He showed us his last German wrist watch, she purchased it and wanted my old watch, I gave in.

Back at Tangmere Airfield, my days were consumed with my Squadron, flying and air combat. My charges were learning quickly, our squadron became one of the top. The Huns were not letting up, we had plenty to shoot at. Most of their bomber boys were less trained than ours, we had many sitting ducks.

I hadn't seen Sarah in weeks, so I went looking for her. At her quarters, I ran into her friend Maggie. "Have you seen Sarah?" I asked.

"Didn't you know? She transferred to North Weald."

"When did she do that?"

"Soon after she came back from your trip, don't go looking for her, I don't think she wants to see you anymore."

I was dumbfounded at this news, I didn't know what to say, I just walked away in shock.

At the airfield, I had a note to see the CO. "Tom,

Headquarters wants a Photographic Reconnaissance Pilot, you want the job?"

"You bet," I answered. I was ready for something else. I checked in at Heston Airfield a day later. I was to fly an unarmed Spitfire and take pictures of different sections of the coast of France from Antwerp to Cherbourg. The headquarters wanted to know about all about the defense the Nazis were building along the coast. My Spitfire was as fast a plane that was in existence, it would outrun anything the Nazis had. Thank God, I had to use the speed all the time. I got to see some of the pictures I took; it made me do a better job knowing what to look for.

I had been on the reconnaissance job for several weeks. I decided to go find Sarah. On the first day off, I borrowed an auto and drove to North Weald, I checked with the WAAF office. They told me that Sarah had been transferred to Hornchurch. So I was out of luck finding her this day.

It was quite awhile before I got some time off. I borrowed an auto again and drove to Hornchurch., Just by accident, I found Maggie.

"Maggie, have you seen Sarah?" I asked.

"Haven't you heard? Sarah and two other girls were killed in a raid last May, they were in a bunker that took a direct hit."

I was devastated; Maggie could see I was in bad shape. I sat down on the ground and covered my face with my hands, Maggie sat down next to me and said, "I'm sorry, Tom, to be the one to tell you." I couldn't help it, the tears flowed.

Maggie sat there with me for I don't know how long, I was so sick I wanted to die. Maggie finally got up and said, "I have a letter for you from Sarah in my quarters, I'll go get it." She got up and left. Soon she returned and handed me an envelope addressed to {Tom, the only man I will ever love.}

I put the letter in a breast pocket, thanked Maggie and

somehow drove back to Heston. Really, I can't remember the drive back. I sat in the car until one of the ground men asked if I was ok. I went to my quarters, laid down and went to sleep; I had never felt as bad in my life. It took days before I could make myself open and read the letter.

It was so personal and loving. I cannot repeat what she wrote. From then on, I carried the letter, a snapshot of Sarah and pictures of Allie and our little girl in my left breast shirt pocket. Any time I felt sorry for myself, I would read the letter.

I flew the Spitfire day in and day out taking pictures. The Luftwaffe came up with a new and faster Focke-Wuif 190. This aircraft was faster than even the Spitfire, we had to take new tactics to counter this threat. I got caught by two 190's over Normandy late one evening, flying low, just off Channel waters, I made an exit for home, and the radar on our coast saved me. The two enemy fighters met a flight of Spitfires. They managed to get both Huns; lucky me. Several times I had to climb into cloud cover to escape the Focke-Wuifs, only their best flew them.

The time did anything but drag. Time passed so fast that a new year loomed shortly, I had a long flight on a Sunday. I had fallen into bed and had a long nap, a fellow pilot shook me awake. "TOM!" he yelled, "Wake up, your country is at WAR!" It took a few minutes for me to come alive. "Come to the mess, it's all over the BBC."

It was Sunday, December 7, 1941--- Pearl Harbor. My county had declared war on Japan. Germany had declared war on the USA, all things changed rapidly in the UK. New airfields sprung up overnight, big tent camps grew almost overnight.

I had a few days off and went to London for a short visit with my fellow American RAF fighter boys. There were ten of us serving with the RAF. In London there were American service personal everywhere, looked to me like the US was taking over the UK. We American RAF pilots didn't know how we would fit in the scheme of things. Guess we would just have to wait and see, we saw soon enough. All American RAF pilots were offered to fly for the US 9th Air Force. We would come in as 1st LTs and we could have our own Squadron. We all agreed to join our own country's Air Force.

In late 1942, I joined a forming P-47 fighter group, the 358th, stationed at Sunninghill Park Berks, England. Not as we were promised, not all American ex-RAF pilots, we were told the squadrons needed experienced pilots to help train the new boys, I guess it was best.

I got my first real up close look at the P-47 Thunderbolt fighter aircraft. The thing was big, I mean a monster compared to the Spitfire. The Spitfire could park under the wing of a P-47. The pilots named it the JUG, It did look like a milk jug, it weighed seven tons and was a huge plane even compared to the British Hurricane. My British friends made a lot of fun of the Thunderbolt. They said the Luftwaffe would eat us alive, Boy, oh boy, were they wrong! The first time I flew it, I knew they were badly fooled. The thing was not a climber, but oh how it would dive. If any plane got in competition with it in a dive, it lost.

American aircraft came in and filled the airfields as fast as they were completed. Hundreds of bombers - B-17s, B-24s, B-25s, B-26s, and many C-47s - appeared in the English sky. There was no shortage of American fighters either - P-38s, P-39s and even a few of the newer P-40s.

On one of my first flights to France as an American, I was flying a Spitfire. I saw for the first time a P-47 Thunderbolt Squadron in flight over France. They flew so close I was afraid of a midair collision. I thought to myself the Luftwaffe was going to have a field day with these new fighter pilots and I was not far from wrong. Most of the dogfights ended with an American shot down. The bombers had no better luck, half of the crews never came back from their missions.

Daylight raids needed escorts. The brass got a little wiser but not enough. They sent P-47s, but they would turn back short on fuel before the bombers got to their targets. The Huns would wait for the fighters to turn back then have a field day. God, I felt sorry for the crews who were shot down, some never had a chance. My squadron did escort duty for six months, we never got to see enemy fighters let alone have combat with them.

In late 1943, some smart brass hats got the message. The need for escorts all the way to the target and back had to be. The P-51s were equipped with drop tanks and what a difference it made to our daylight bomb runs, it cut losses in half and then some.

My Squadron got a new mission. By the way, I was promoted to squadron leader, and made a Captain. We were to go for ground attack targets. The hunter had become the hunted. The P-47 was an ideal plane for that kind of mission, the P-47 was a flying gun platform. Eight fifty-caliber machine guns, twelve rockets, it could even carry a one-ton bomb. My boys and I were tearing up the roads in France. In daylight, not much got by us, railways were another big target.

I got a letter from home from my Dad. He knew my little brother Al was here in England in the Infantry. He wanted me to try to look him up; I got nowhere. All US personnel locations were top secret, I wrote Dad back I would keep trying.

Chapter 7

The Ground War

My squadron's basic mission was to hunt and destroy any military target we could find in occupied France. We were ordered to go no farther than half our fuel would take us. Destroy everything we could find and hightail it for home before we ran out of fuel.

Enemy airfields were a major target. We destroyed a lot of the Luftwaffe on the ground. Trains were another good target along with truck convoys. The hunting was really good day after day. We heard thru the French underground that the P-47 was the Huns most hated aircraft. All the pilots got a big kick from that. We knew then we were doing our job.

I was in the officer's club having a late night drink with my boys when I got orders to go to a secret meeting. I was furnished transportation and an escort of two MP's. At the assigned meeting place, I was ushered into a room full of top brass, both British and America. In a few minutes, I was educated to why I was sent for.

The Gestapo in Paris, France, had captured several top leaders of the French underground and was holding them in the Gestapo headquarters building in downtown Paris. The underground had sent word a top interrogator was coming from Berlin to take charge. The brass was afraid the entire underground would be compromised as the Gestapo were experts at torture. The only solution was to destroy the building. I was told my squadron was picked to do the job, I didn't get a chance to think it over, it was orders. I was told by a General that high level bombers were likely to kill many

French people and would probably destroy many buildings. He said, "We don't want to mess up downtown Paris." I could see his reasoning.

Here's the deal, my squadron would attack from the west and from the east. Half the squadron would hit the building at first light from the west. The other half would be in position to strike from the east as soon as the first attack finished, I would lead the first strike. We would have cover from both British Spitfires and American P-51s. We must go low under the German radar, go tree top until Paris is sighted, then pull up to make the attack.

A complete mock up of Paris was made for me and my guys to study. My attack would be critical, as the others would follow my lead and hit the same building. Our whole mission would depend on the French underground to give us the word to go. Members of the underground would be in position to help anyone who could escape from the building.

We got word the mission would go the following morning, I want-a tell ya, I didn't get much sleep that night. We took off at four-thirty and flew at less than a thousand feet all the way across the Channel. I thought several times I was going to get my feet wet. At the French coast, we pulled to fifteen hundred. Soon, my second group parted ways. When Paris came in view, I had some doubts as nothing seemed to fit, I was sweating blood. Our timing was right on, I knew the target was just north of the Eiffel Tower and a few blocks east. There she was in the early morning light, What a relief! The Tower lights were still on.

I gunned my jug and climbed five hundred feet, left bank then right bank. The Gestapo building loomed ahead, a big red Swastika hung above the entrance. I put my sight on the flag and fired the rockets and machine guns. As I pulled up, I released the five hundred pound bomb, a direct hit.

Looking back, I could see my guys were making hits, too. Above I could see our cover aircraft; I banked left hard and made a heading for home. On landing, we were met by lots of happy brass, they weren't the only ones. The French reported the raid was a complete success. My whole squadron received the AIR MEDAL. Many prisoners escaped and we got the Gestapo big shot. The only sad part was that many good French people had to die that morning, I'll never forget or get over that.

We returned to our hunt and destroy missions. The main objectives were the Luftwaffe airfields, we were hunting, bombing and strafing any military equipment or conveys we could find.

One sunny afternoon, we were working about fifty miles from the German border and in southern France. I spotted some trucks pulling out on a road from a wooded area. I called and told the boys what I saw, circled around, dropped down and strafed the trucks, I banked hard right, a bad mistake. The next thing I heard was a loud explosion, I was hit by ground fire; my engine was pouring black smoke. I tried to gain altitude, no good, I turned south. I saw my guys fly by, I had to get out.

Opening the canopy, I fell out on the wing and rolled off. I knew I was too low and I hit the ground hard, luck was with me. I missed the trees and fell into an open area. God I was hurting, I couldn't stand and the chute was dragging me. I hit the release and the harness came off, the chute blew away toward the trees.

The next thing I knew there were black boots standing around me, Germans. One of the soldiers poked me with his rifle and demanded in German, "Get up!" I tried but couldn't. Two of them pulled me up. Ah, my left hip, leg and ankle were killing me with pain, I could hardly stand. One German started taking my things, my pistol, my wallet, the picture of Allie and

Elsa, he was a sergeant. He was grinning at me all the time. I tried to fall, but they stopped me and started pulling me into the trees.

Oh, I had so much pain, I cried out to stop. They just kept pushing, I don't know when it happened, but the Germans held up their hands. We were surrounded by French partisans at least thirty, women and men. I got my stuff back, the German wasn't grinning any more.

Two men carried me until a young boy came with a short pole, then the two men carried me on it between them. Gun shots filled the evening stillness, I assumed the Germans were shot. Soon, I was put in the back of a truck, it had German markings. In the back of the truck, the pain became so bad I passed out.

When I came to, I was lying on straw in some kind of shed. An older man was leaning over me. He asked if I could hear him, He spoke in French, I murmured, yes. He told me I had a broken hip, leg and ankle. A young woman was there also, she gave me a bottle of red wine. I drank almost all of it on the first offering. He said I would be moved the next morning into Vichy, France. He told me many Allied airmen were being smuggled by the French underground through Spain to Portugal and picked up by British warships. Somehow, I made it through the night with help from the wine. The young woman stayed with me all night.

I was taken to a Nun's Convent and put in a small room. A man and lady went to work on me, he gave me a shot that put me out. When I woke up, I had a cast on my left side from foot to shoulder.

I stayed in this room for what seemed like months. There was one small window, I could see the sky and some tree branches. I did have a lot of company, now and then, Allied airmen would stop by and visit on their way to freedom.

Different people fed me all the time and changed my diaper.

Just out of the blue, the man who put my cast on came in and told me it was time to cut it off. It took three weeks for me to walk well and get my strength back. When it came time to leave, I felt sad to leave these wonderful people, I told them so.

Two men had the task of getting me to Lisbon, Portugal. We traveled by auto, train and sometimes horse cart; all the time I had good company. How can I ever repay them? I was taken out to sea in a small boat to a waiting British warship. We were taken to a port on the west side of England.

After my ordeal of being shot down and the long recovery, I felt fit for duty and reported in to the 9th Air Force. Instead of duty, I received orders to go home. I was told the war was about to wind down. A transport ship would be available for my transportation home in two days, I took the time to see my guys and some of the RAF people I had served with.

On the scheduled day, I reported to the waiting ship, I had just climbed the gang way up to the ship. I hesitated to look at the people on the dock. Leaning on the rail, I suddenly saw a familiar figure. The lady looked up and then tried to hide her face. I knew instantly who it was, I rushed back down to the dock, ran and caught the lady by her arm, I spun her around. "SARAH!" I yelled.

I couldn't believe my eyes. "It is you, Sarah. Why?" I gasped.

She fell into my arms and gave me a gentle kiss on the lips. She explained. "Tom, I knew it would not work, go home to your wife and forget about me."

"Sarah, I do love you, I hope you can understand, I can love two women at the same time. Give me your address, I want to write."

She gave me an envelope with her address on it. I had to

leave as they were calling from the ship that it was time to go, I barely made it back on the deck. I stood there watching Sarah as the ship pulled away from the dock. I watched as long as I could see her standing on the dock. She gave a little wave and then disappeared in the fog. God forgive me, I did love that woman.

Out to sea, I wrote her a long letter, I paid a Steward to mail it in New York.

The ship's Captain announced we could send cables to our love ones.

When we docked, I had on my pinks and greens and carried my flight bag. Twenty-five hundred people wanted off the ship, it seemed, at the same time. As I moved along the rail, I spotted Allie; she had a little girl by the hand, my little daughter Elsa.

Allie didn't see me until I was almost off the gangway. When she did, that wife of mine went wild, hugging, kissing, crying and laughing all at the same time. When I got her settled down, I picked up my little girl and with Allie on my arm we walked down the dock into a new world and new life.

Chapter 8

Allie, Tom's Wife, Finishes the Story

I was deliriously happy to have Tom home at last after four long years. I met him with our daughter when his boat docked at the harbor in New York City. I had never been so happy in my entire life to have him home again, Oh, how I had longed for this day. He was so handsome in his uniform, all the ribbons on his chest and he was a Major. We stayed in a hotel in New York City for a week, just lazing around and sightseeing. Tom wanted to go home to the ranch to see his folks. I had to tell him my Daddy Jack had died and both his Grandparents were gone. Uncle Bob was awfully sick, but he was still getting around. He didn't say much about his grandparents, just that he was sorry to hear they were gone. I guessed his Mother had written about them.

We stayed three days at the ranch. Tom took long horseback rides, he always wanted to go alone; he would be gone for hours. His Mom told me that he did that a lot when he was a boy. He never said much when he returned.

Tom was mustered out of the service in Santa Monica, California. I had purchased a house in Santa Monica when I worked for Lockheed Aircraft Company. My house was only a few blocks from the plant. At the house, Tom was not sleeping well, he took midnight walks, he sat on the back porch a lot and he played the phonograph record {Once in Awhile by Tommy Dorsey and Frank Sinatra}. He played the music over and over again. I became concerned and went to see an Army shrink at Brentwood Vets Hospital. He said not to worry; it would take awhile for him to adjust to a normal life again. A lot of help he was.

One afternoon, I was shopping and ran into Howard Wilson, my old boss at Lockheed. He had a crush on me and he admitted it.

"How's that lucky guy of yours?" he asked

I started to cry. He grabbed me in a bear hug. "What's the matter, Allie?"

Howard was such a great guy I had to tell him I was sick over the way Tom was acting. He knew right away what had to be done. "Flying, that's what Tom is, a flyer. We need test pilots. Do you think he would work for us?"

"I don't know," I answered.

"I'll stop around tomorrow and ask him."

Tom jumped at the chance. In a few days, he was at an airfield in the California desert flying the new jet planes. He became a different man, happy, he was so happy.

We sold the house in Santa Monica and moved into a mobile home near the Base. I had another girl; we named her Emily after Tom's Grandmother. We purchased a house in a new project near the Base. We spent most holidays at the ranch with the families, Tom's parents, Frank, Al and their families. Life was darn good to us. The years just flew by, we both grayed a little. Our girls were getting to be young ladies.

One morning, I was in the kitchen cleaning up. The girls were off to school and Tom had an early morning flight. I heard the sirens at the base. Out on the back porch I could see thick black smoke from the Base, I knew it was coming from one of the runways. I jumped in the station wagon and drove to the Base. The MP on the gate told me by his look that something was wrong. I drove to the headquarters, Howard pulled up in a jeep. He came right over, reached through the window, took me by the arm and said, "Allie, its Tom."

"Is he hurt?"

"No, Allie, he's dead."

I passed out, when I woke up, I was in the Base hospital. Howard had sent for our girls. We cried and cried, I asked if he had been burned. Howard said, "No, we got him out in time."

Howard told us, "Tom was doing the thing he loved, flying. No man can do better than that."

A service was held at the family cemetery on the ranch. Hundreds of people came; some from England and all over the country. An Air Force Chaplain gave the service, an Honor Guard fired a 12 gun salute, it was a beautiful Military Service.

Tom and I would visit the little cemetery most of the time when we would go to the ranch. Tom always said, "This is my final resting place; here I can watch the planes take-off and land, put me here, Allie."

After the service, Tom's brother Al, he is the manger of the ranch, invited me and the girls to come live on the ranch. "There's a nice adobe house, needs some repair, but you and the girls are welcome to it. If you want, I'll have the repairs done right away."

The girls wanted to move as soon as possible, horses and girls, you know. I told Al we wanted it. He said he would call as soon as it was finished. I put the house at home for sale, it sold in a week. I sold Tom's car and we started to get things ready to move as soon as Al would call.

I was in the garage picking through tools and stuff to give away. Under the work bench, I found a small metal locked tool box. I cut the lock off and inside I found a pack of letters from some woman in England. They were addressed to Tom at a mail box in town. Opening a letter, I was astounded to learn this woman was writing what I saw as love letters. I took the letters in the house and began to read the oldest one first. Reading between the lines, I could surmise Tom and she had had an affair while he was in England. I was devastated to think Tom had deceived me. I cried all night and well into the next day.

Howard stopped by to see how I was doing; he saw right-a way I had a problem. I told him about Tom having a lady friend while he was in England.

"Allie, most flyers will find someone. They go to bars and Allie; there are girls there ready for a relationship. A guy in combat where life is cheap has needs; those girls will fill that need. Don't be sad Tom is—was--only human. The ladies are giving you a go-a-way party Saturday night, talk with them."

Saturday evening, I joined twenty women friends at the party. It was really nice. I talked with my friend Georgia, she's a little loud, is really good looking and kind-a life of the party. I got her aside and talked about Tom and his having a lover in England. She gathered all the ladies around and told them my Tom had a lover overseas. She asked, "How many of your husbands had lovers overseas?" All raised their hands. Some told me they were sending money to children of their husband's.

Georgia said, "Allie, Tom loved you and he probably loved the women over there. Accept it and go on." I decided to do just that, although it was hard.

We moved to the ranch. Al had completely rebuilt the adobe house, a real nice job he did. A Spanish type, three bedrooms, three baths and a gorgeous patio with flowers and all. That Al was a real fixer.

We had supper that first night with Mom, Dad, Frank's family and Al's family. After the meal, Al told me I was a partner in the ranch, I got Tom's part. He said as manager he would be reporting to me once a year. I felt I had a real family.

Frank wanted to talk. We walked up to the little cemetery on the hill and sat on a bench. t "Allie," he took my hand. "Allie, Mom told me about the letters you found. You know,

Allie, Tom never had a girl in high school. Girls never interested him; flying was all he cared about. When he came home after meeting you, he told me he was in love. I knew you must be special. Allie, I always had a girlfriend; God, Allie I had a lot of them, I loved them all. Only trouble was, every time I thought this was the one, I lost her. Until Laura came along, I thought I was jinxed. Over there, Tom needed someone to hold, he loved you more than his own life. This woman must be something for Tom to care about her. Allie, write her, tell her about Tom, I'm sure it will make you feel better."

I did that very night, I wrote a letter, no, I wrote a book about me and Tom. I carried the letter in my purse for days. Then, one day the girls and I were in town shopping, I stopped by the post office and mailed it.

A week later, I got the most beautiful, tear stained letter I had ever received with a picture of her and Tom sitting on the wing of an airplane both in their blue RAF uniforms. She was lovely. I invited her to come for a visit, she did. The girls and I were in the waiting room when she came through the door, I knew immediately it was her. A lot of hugging, kissing and crying went on there. People must have thought we were crazy.

That first time, she stayed a week with us. No wonder Tom fell in love with her. Our whole family did. We visit back and forth all the time now. Every day she is here she goes up to the little cemetery and stays an hour, she was truly in love with Tom.

We visit each other at least twice a year, I go to the UK and she comes here. The last time I was leaving London, we hugged and I said to her, "Sarah, I feel you are the sister I always wanted." She said she felt the same.

If you ever go to England, go to the south coast village of Hasting. A few doors from the Hotel Royal is a small jewelry shop. Go in and you will be met by an aging lady, and if you look close you will see on her left hand ring finger an amethyst purple stone ring. If you ask, she will tell you her name is SARAH.

Our Father's Generation

Book 2

Brother Frank, The Architect

Our Father's Generation

Chapter 1

Frank Tells His Story

Munich, Germany, April 1, 1938. Here I stand rigid as a stone statue with at least two hundred guys my age, on the railway station platform in Munich, Germany, waiting for a train to arrive to take us to some unknown destination. I was rousted from a sound sleep at the home of my friends where I have resided for the last six months while attending the University of Munich, by a knock on my bedroom door. Two burly black uniformed SS men entered my room and demanded I get dressed pronto; I had no choice. I dressed as fast as I could and was herded passed my wide-eyed German family to a waiting truck with a dozen young men like myself and made to get aboard. All the young men on board acted happy at this development they were in.

It was pitch black this morning as we drove thru the streets of Munich to this railway station, where I had arrived a few short months ago. Half asleep, I was awakened by a voice coming over a loud speaker telling us we were the latest members of the German Wehrmacht, the finest military organization in the world. We would be joining the German army infantry as private ranked riflemen, to serve our beloved fatherland.

The morning was filled with "Sieg Heils" and everyone there gave the German arm and hand salute. I was poked in the back and motioned to reply with a raised arm, hand and Sieg Heil of my own. I had no choice. The black uniformed SS man looked mean and I could see he meant business.

In the distance I heard the train arriving. Soon the engine

came huffing past, spewing white steam as it screeched to a stop, throwing sparks from steel to steel as the engineer applied the brakes. We were ordered to get aboard, I found a seat by a window. We sat there for what seemed like an hour, and then the train pulled slowly away from the station. As the morning light came from the east, I watched the scenery pass with tears filling my eyes and for some unknown reason my mind wondered back to my last day of high school in my home town in the good old Southwest USA.

The road leading to the school bus stop was as dusty as I had ever seen it. We hadn't had any rain in so long I had forgotten how good rain felt. The best thing today had brought was my last day in high school. Oh, how long I had waited for this day. No more Mr. Simmons, the teacher I disliked, he didn't like me either. No more walks to the bus stop. Next Friday, I would graduate and Monday I would go to work steady for my Uncle Bob, an architect. I'd spent the last two summer school vacations in his office as a gofer, I made four dollars a week. Not bad in 1934 for a kid my age, we're in a depression, you know.

As I reached the top of the hill and looked back at our house in the valley below, I spent some time thinking of my family. I continued onto the bus stop and sat on the bench there as I had done so many times before. Four long years, I could hardly wait to get out of school. About my family, let me tell you about my Mother, the light of all our lives, she met my dad in 1916. She was studying to be a teacher, a French teacher, she had come from France as a small girl, her family lived in Louisiana. My dad had joined the Army and was stationed at Camp Polk. They met at a carnival on a hot July night and a hot romance developed. They got married three weeks later.

My older brother Tom was born nine months later. I came into the world twelve months after Tom. Dad stayed at Polk for the rest of the war as a rifle instructor. He felt cheated not to get to France. My baby brother Albert was born six years later on my Grandpa's cattle ranch where we all lived. My mother's older brother Bob went to France as an airplane pilot stayed and married an English nurse after the armistice. Her name is Helen, a lady I dearly loved. Bob studied architecture in Paris and Germany. He came home to the city near us and started an architecture office in partnership with Clem Hanson, a man he met in Europe. Their business was very successful to say the least; you might say he's rich, he has a fine home, two big cars and an airplane, but they have never had any children, he took us kids as his own.

Tom worked for Bob the summer of his sixteenth year and he was so crazy about airplanes Uncle Bob helped to teach him to fly, much against mother's wishes; I might add. Today he's working as a barnstorming pilot, not too bad for a kid of nineteen. Me, I like the office better. Albert loves the ranch and horses. I went to work for Uncle Bob steady that summer and lived with Helen and Uncle Bob at their home. I would make eight dollars a week and pay Helen two dollars a week for my board.

Yeah, I graduated Friday, not at the top of the class, I might add. If you don't want to hear my story, you might as well drop out now.

When I went to work that Monday it was a red letter day. I met Gloria, a twenty year old beauty; WOW, what a beauty! She had started to work in Bob's office the week before. Let me tell you about this girl, she would take any guy's breath away as she did mine. She was five-nine, one hundred and ten pounds; a blonde haired, voluptuous beauty with an hour glass body.

Oh, I want to tell you the first time she spoke to me I was so tongue tied I could hardly speak. My God, this woman was beautiful, honey dripped from her lips, but I got over it and we became good friends...you might say more than good. I'll tell ya more about her later.

My first encounter with beautiful girls was on the ranch. You see my Dad hired a Mexican cowboy with a family. We had a house on the ranch where help could live. Juan, the cowboy, moved in with his family. Juan, my Dad said, was the best hand he had ever seen. He was a good guy in every way. Juan had a good looking, hard working wife and three daughters. Two were young and Maria was my brother Tom's age. Of course, Maria went to school with us. She was the best looking girl I had ever seen. All the boys at school went mad over her. She, I think, was sweet on Tom, but he never paid any attention to girls.

Anyway, here's what happened to me. Some years ago Grandpa and Dad built a dam across a spring stream that was fed from the mountains. They hollowed a little low place and made a small pond, it was about an acre big. Grandpa wanted to grow catfish but never did. Through the years, the pond became a really nice spot, Mom planted willow trees around the pond and cattails in the pond. The pond was about five foot deep in the middle and three foot deep along the sides. My brothers and I learned to swim in that pond.

In the summer time, if you needed to cool off, a dip in the pond was a good idea. Everyone loved the pond; Juan and his family used it as much as we did. One Saturday, all the people had gone to town to shop. It was my junior year of High School vacation. I had to stay home to feed the horses at feeding time. It was a hot day so I decided to go for a dip, the pond was about half a mile from the houses.

Down I went, stripped off and jumped in. Paddling around, I stood up in the north end. There looking at me through the cattails was a naked Maria. Holy cow, was that a surprise. She said in a sultry voice; "FRANK, come here." As you can surmise, nature took its course. I became rather found of all females and was no longer a virgin.

While I was in Europe, Mom wrote that Maria married a man at the bank where she worked. That time with Maria helped me get over being shy around the fairer sex.

More about my family. Grandpa came from Germany and met Grandma in Illinois, she is from the old school of German girls. She was so clean she squeaked and you must talk slow to her as she still spoke mostly in German. It helped us kids to learn a little of the German language, we also got some French from mother.

Let me continue, Grandpa came west and homesteaded the ranch we all lived on. It was a real cattle ranch with about twelve hundred head of mother cows, a real cow-calf operation. Five bulls and thirty or so horses. Five full time cowboys helped my Dad, he was the foreman. During branding and roundup time, we had another five or six come in to help. Enough said about the ranch.

Let me get back to Gloria, I like to talk about her. What red blooded American boy wouldn't? I had to take some drawings and specifications to a customer in a small town sixty miles north of our city, since I didn't have a driver's license Uncle Bob had Gloria drive me in the company Model A. On the way back, she taught me about the birds and bees. She was a great teacher, I want-a tell ya, I won't tell about the particulars, but it was a great day in my life, she was awesome to say the least.

I knew something of the birds and bees living on a cattle ranch, but as far as humans went, I knew very little, except what Maria taught me. The folks never told us boys about that. Well anyway, we got along fine that summer. I got my driver's license so she didn't come with me any more on out of town trips. Oh crap, that was bad for me. We still got together on the weekends, I would borrow the office Model A and we'd take a ride out in the country and sometimes had ourselves a picnic. Those were the days, my friend; I hoped they would never end.

Around about September I looked for and purchased a Harley-Davidson motorcycle. The thing was almost as old as I was, but she ran like a top and besides Gloria like to ride with me. We spent many a pleasant Sunday afternoon on that bike.

Uncle Bob got me to working on the drawing board. I'd do specifications, building material estimates and a few drawings of buildings I made up in my head, you know, office buildings, private houses and so on. Heck, it was fun and I really liked to do it. Uncle Bob told everyone I was a natural architect. He'd laugh and say, "Boy, you may be the next Frank Lloyd Wright." I liked hearing that.

Well, any way, the next spring Tom came to town with a new biplane. On Sunday afternoon, Tom invited the folks down to the airport to see a few stunts with this airplane. Somehow the whole dang town turned out at the airport for the show, all our folks came. I want-a tell-ya, Tom did things in that airplane I didn't think were possible, he turned that plane inside out. Why, all the people were gasping for breath just watching. Mom almost fainted when he came upside down across the runway. His head wasn't more than forty feet off the ground.

That Gloria kept saying, "That's your brother? I want-a meet him." I thought the jig was up with her and me.

The family had supper at Aunt Helen's and Uncle Bob's that evening. Of course, I introduced Gloria to Tom, he didn't bat an eye. I thought to myself he must have gone blind in that airplane. That girl couldn't keep her hands off him, it was so obvious my Mom took her aside and told her something I couldn't hear. Anyway, Gloria stopped pawing him.

Tom stayed in my room that night and I asked him about

Gloria, you know, what he thought of her. He surprised me when he said, "My girl in San Diego would make her look like a shinny boy." Holy cow, she must be something I said to myself. "Her Dad owns the airport we fly out of. Man, she is the best looking woman I've ever seen. I'm gonna ask her to marry me." When Tom said that, I knew he was no competition. Well, things got bad for me with Gloria anyway.

This good looking guy came to work in the office; he had just graduated from architect school. Gloria went bonkers for him and likewise him for her. Their romance was the talk of the office and town. Holy cow, she quit talking to me altogether. The next thing I knew, they ran off and got married, that was the end for me and Gloria.

That winter, Uncle Bob came down sick, I went to visit him in the hospital. Aunt Helen told me he had cancer, a bad kind. Heck, he smoked liked a smoke stack all the time, he was a chain smoker. When he worked, he smoked and drank coffee all day and all night, he worked a lot.

At the hospital on one of my visits, he wanted to have a heart to heart talk with me. Helen was there when he said to me, "Frank, what are you planning to do with your life?" He really puzzled me.

"What do you mean Uncle Bob?" I asked.

"What kind of work do you want to do the rest of your life?"

"I really haven't thought about it," I told him.

"Frank, you're a natural architect. If you don't study that, you're just gonna waste your time and mine. Now, I'm gonna make you a proposition, are you ready to hear?"

"Sure," I was ready.

"I want you to go to Europe and study like I did. Helen and I will furnish the money, will you go?"

I couldn't help it; the tears began to flow down my face.

"You are the best uncle a guy could have; you bet I'll go." Then I asked, "What's wrong with studying in this country? You just hired the fellow Gloria married, he studied in this country."

"Hell," he said, "That guy won't make a pimple on an architect's ass. He's just a draft man, that's all he'll ever be. You can do that now, I want you to be a real architect. Helen and I have made an account you can draw from any time you want. There's money in it to last a few years. Money will be sent to you every month as long as you stay in school. Will you go?" How could I say no?

That next Sunday I rode the motorcycle home and had Mom's usual pot roast for dinner. After dinner, we all went out on the front porch. Grandpa sat in his rocker, Mom and Grandma in the porch swing and Dad walked back and forth. I sat on the railing and told the folks the proposition Uncle Bob had offered me. Dad was the first to speak. "Looks to me like there's gonna be trouble over there. Have you read the papers about the goings on in Europe? Some reports say there are war clouds forming in Germany. Frank, you sure don't want-a be caught in one of their wars. I'd give it a lot of thought before you make up your mind."

Grandpa said, "Na, the German people know all about war, they ain't gonna let no one lead them into war again, it's all talk."

My Dad got hot under the collar. "What are you talking about, Dad? Haven't you been reading the papers? Hell, the people there think this guy Hitler is the second coming of Jesus Christ. Frank, I'd think along time about going over there. What do you think, honey?" he asked my Mom.

"I don't think Bob would send him over there if there was any danger. I think it would be good for him to go and get a good education. He'll never get a chance like this again, he should go."

Grandma added her two cents, "Fred," my Dad's name was Fred, "We German people are good. They won't let anybody start another war over there. I say go, Frank, and learn all you can."

Dad was hot again. "Damn, you people sure don't see things the way I do. I'll bet my last dollar there's going to be another war, even the radio is talking war."

I really hadn't given a war any thought at all. All I wanted was a good education and Uncle Bob had given me a way to get one. I told my Dad, "I would like to go, even if war comes, it won't bother me, I'll just stay out of the way."

"Frank, you're old enough to make up your own mind. If you must go, go, but I'll be worried until you get back home."

It was all set with the folks. I was going to Europe to study architecture. Hot dog, I may be a big shot some day, like my Uncle Bob.

My next visit to Uncle Bob in the hospital, he told me he had sent money to the schools in France and Germany. "An endowment I set up years ago, I have written letters informing them you're on the way. There are some people I know over there who will help you if needed. What you must do is make a portfolio of drawings of buildings you would like to build. They will ask to see some of your work. Go to the office and design a modern structure and a church, they like churches. Tell Clem to help, he's damn good at evaluating good work."

I did. I made all kinds of drawings until Clem said enough. He even told me he liked my work.

Uncle Bob came home from the hospital, I spent several days talking with him. He said he was feeling better and would be okay, I was sure glad to hear that. He told me to go to the White Horse department store and fit myself with a whole new wardrobe. I did...two new suits with vests and two pair of pants, an overcoat, two pairs of shoes and new underwear, I also got a suitcase and a small trunk, I was ready to go to Europe.

The day came; I got on a train headed for New York City and a boat to Europe. All the folks, Aunt Helen, Uncle Bob and people from the office all came to see me off. As I sat by a window and waved to the folks, a strange feeling came over me as the train pulled slowly away and they all disappeared in the distance. I was homesick already, I had never been more than one hundred miles from home in my entire life.

Chapter 2

Rita and the Ship

On the train, I sat next to a window so I could wave good-bye to the folks, there were plenty of seats available. Soon, a railroad man came to me, he had a badge that read {Conductor} on his cap. He asked for my ticket. "New York City," he said, "Young man, that's a long trip, you can get food in the dining car, have you ridden a train before?"

"No sir. My first time."

"Have you any questions I can answer for you?" He was a nice man to ask.

"Do I change cars on this trip?"

"No, we will change engines two times. Just stay in this car, it will take you right into Grand Central Station in New York City."

For a dumb Southwest hick, I was pleased to know I would not have to worry about changing trains. As I looked around, I found that my car was fairly empty. At the next stop, that changed. Two large families got on, there were eight kids ranging from about four to fourteen. The whole scene changed and got very loud. Oh well, I couldn't do anything about that, but I couldn't get any sleep.

Around noon, a young boy came thru and sold me a box lunch and a drink. A sandwich, an apple and an orange Nehi soda pop. The afternoon dragged on. About five p.m., my hunger returned, I went looking for the conductor and found him two cars back. He told me I could get dinner in the dining car father on back, I found it and an empty table. A white coated young Black man brought me a menu. It had my full attention until a sexy female voice asked, "May I sit at your table?"

I looked up to see the most gorgeous woman I had ever laid eyes on. I stood up and said, "I would be pleased to have your company." Gloria had cured my tongue tied posture with beautiful ladies. This lady slid into the chair like a swan, I was completely captivated by her looks. The man brought her a menu, I had lost all interest in food, I just sat watching her.

She asked, "Have you ordered?"

"No, not yet."

The waiter came and we both ordered. This was a most pleasant meal, this trip was looking up for me. She asked where I was bound for. When I told her New York City, she said she was going there, too. What a break for me, we sat talking over coffee.

She started telling me about herself. "I've been a dancer with my father since I was eight. We've danced all over the U.S. in night clubs. Now, I have left him and am going back to New York, to be in actress school in the city, I hope to dance in Broadway shows and maybe the movies."

"Lady, if good looks get it done, you're a shoe-in." She laughed the best laugh I had ever heard. I told her I was on my way to Europe to study architecture.

"Your looks are good enough to be an actor; you should come with me and study to be one." That really made my day.

I asked if she was traveling in a chair car; she was. I asked if I could sit with her? She was very pleasant and said she would be pleased to have me as a companion. She was in the car ahead of mine. We went and got what she called her overnight case, came back and sat in the seats I had. We made small talk way into the night, I found she was born in Brooklyn.

The Conductor came by and gave us pillows for the night,

they cost ten cents each. She didn't need hers as she used my shoulder and chest for hers, O, how good she smelled. I can still smell her perfume, it was the best.

Somewhere around midnight, our Conductor came by and told us he was getting off and a new one would be getting on; he wished me a lot of luck. He looked at the lady asleep on my chest. "Son, I see you are all ready having good luck." he smiled and left.

We must have been changing engines as we sat still for some time, and then moved on. The lady was curled up in her chair and stayed sound asleep. It was well passed day light when she woke up. She took her case and went to the ladies room and returned looking like a true living Goddess, Holly cow! She was beautiful.

The new Conductor came by and asked if we were man and wife. Boy- O- Boy, did that make me feel good. She told him, "Maybe someday, but not now." That made me feel even better to think I might have a chance with a lady like her.

He asked our names, I had never thought to ask hers. She told him, "Rita Casino, I'm changing it to Rita Hayworth, that's my Mother's maiden name, that will be my stage name."

I remarked, "It's a beautiful name."

We went to the dining car for breakfast. The whole day flew by, too fast to suit me. That night I had her sleep on my shoulder again, but this time I had my right arm around her all night. How lucky could a guy be to have her beautiful face so close to mine and to smell her perfume? It almost drove me crazy. The next day, we did the same as the day before, it flew by. The night was the same, her asleep on my shoulder. I want-a tell ya, it was pure torture being that close to her and not being able to make love to her.

The next day, in the early afternoon, we entered Grand Central Station. What a place, she knew her way around like the native she was. Off the train, I followed her to the baggage room, I told you she knew her way around. The man in the baggage room said it would be awhile before our trunks would come. We sat on a bench talking for most of an hour, it was the most pleasant hour I had ever spent.

When the trunks arrived, a deep feeling of sorrow came over me. She called a man in a red cap to come and take our trunks to the cab stand. He set them on a cart and we followed him out to where a line of yellow taxi cabs sat. The driver, with my help, put the trunks on a rack on the back of the cab and strapped them down.

Inside the cab, the driver asked where we were going. She gave him an address uptown and I said, "Pier 19." He told us he would take her uptown and then me to the Hudson River. As we rode, I sat feasting my eyes on her, I bet I looked like some love sick kid. At her destination, I helped the driver carry her trunk inside, she was checking in at the desk. The driver said he would wait in the cab. She turned to me and floated over, put both arms around my neck and gave me the best kiss on the lips I had ever had. She backed off and said, "How do you like that, Frank?"

Without a word, I reached and with both hands pulled her to me, put both arms around her and kissed her as hard as I could on her beautiful lips. She backed off again and said, "Why don't you stay in New York? We could get to like each other."

"I can't, Rita, I made a promise to my uncle. If I stayed, I'd be a basket case around you. I have to go." As I reached the door, I turned back and thru her a kiss, she thru one back and waved good bye.

As I entered the cab, I said to myself. "I could fall in love with that woman." The driver brought me back to the present. "You ever were in the city before?" He could tell I hadn't by the way I had been gawking around looking at the tall buildings. "My name is Dave, that girl we dropped off is the best thing I ever saw, bar none, you her boyfriend?"

"No, sir" I told him. "I sure wish I was."

"I'll tell you friend, if she don't become a star on the stage or in the movies, I'll miss my bet." Dave was taken with her, too Then he said, "I'll drive ya down Fifth Avenue, when I tell ya roll down the window on your right, you'll see the tallest building in the world, the Empire State Building." I did as he said, why, I couldn't even see the top from where I sat.

At Pier 19, he stopped the cab in front of an office with a sign that read {Grace Ship Lines.} Dave helped me set my trunk off and said, "If you ever get to the city again, look me up I'll be here." What a nice man, everyone I'd met so far treated me nice, I hoped it would continue.

In the office, a man behind a counter asked my name. I told him and he took an envelope from a cubby hole and handed it to me. Inside, I found a ticket telling me I had a passage on a boat going to Cherbourg, France. I asked the man, "Where do I get the boat that's going to France?"

"Turn around, son you'll be looking at it, and it ain't a boat, it's a ship. I'll get someone to take your trunk aboard." I thanked him, went out, picked up my suitcase and walked up the gang plank.

At the top, I met a man on board the ship, he asked for my ticket. Looking at it, he told me I was in cabin 10. "Go down these steps," he pointed to a door. "Number 10 cabin is the third door on the right." Then he said, "Breakfast is from seven to nine, lunch eleven to one and dinner six to eight. Your life preserver is in your cabin, you have any questions?"

"Yes, sir," I said, "Do I get a cabin to myself?"

"No, you'll have a Bunkie."

"A beautiful girl?" I laughingly asked him.

"O sure, just what a young guy like you needs," he said with a smile "We try to fix you up with a guy your own age. If you are hungry, go to the kitchen, the cooks will feed you."

"Sir," I said, "I have no idea where the kitchen is."

"In the hallway your cabin is in, the Dining room is up the stairs if you keep going straight on, you will find the kitchen there, is that your trunk on the dock?"

"Yes, sir, that green one down there." He told me a man would go get it and bring it to my cabin. I thanked him and hurried to cabin 10. Inside, I saw two bunks on each wall, a desk and a closet, a door led to the bathroom. There were no port holes in the cabin.

I went to the Kitchen; there were ten cooks in white clothes sitting around a table. They fixed me a great meal and I had a lot of conversation with them. They told me the people would come aboard tomorrow and we would sail the next morning. I walked the deck of the ship around and around. The lights of the city were spectacular, a sight I could not in my wildest imagination ever expect to see again.

That night, I wrote mother and Uncle Bob, took a shower and turned in. The next morning, I was up early, washed and hung my other suit in the closet. I went up to breakfast. After the meal, I went to watch the people coming aboard. There were all kinds and lots of young girls. Hot dog, this trip was going to be ok, I said to myself.

That afternoon, I got to meet my Bunkie, an old fart who started in bitch-en before he even told me his name. He was a German and lived in Berlin, he said he was a professor of languages.

I returned to the deck to watch the people. I walked around the ship and met a guy who said he was a sailor on this ship, we had a nice conversation. He knew I had never been on a ship before, how he knew I never discovered, anyway, he seemed to be a nice person. He told me we would sail the next morning about nine a.m. "Be on the port side when we pull out and you will see the Statue of Liberty, I always get a little choked up when I see her. Mister, this is the land of the free and the home of the brave, I always think of that when I see her."

I thanked him for talking with me and went to the stern of the ship and sat in a deck chair to watch the lights of the city come on as the darkness fell. A great stroke of luck fell on me there, I hadn't sat there for more than a few minutes when this comely young girl came and asked if she could sit in the chair next to me. I stood and told her I would be pleased to have her company. She was no Rita but wasn't bad and I couldn't be too choosy, what did I have to lose? Turned out I came to like the young woman. Her name was Jane Hardy and she was the daughter of Judge Hardy. Did you ever see the movie with Mickey Rooney where he played Andrew Hardy, the son of a Judge Hardy? This girl was not the daughter of that judge.

We sat and talked until eleven o'clock. This girl was really easy to be with, I found out she had just had her seventeenth birthday. I walked her to her cabin, no she and her folks were in a state room cabin. She introduced me to the folks and right away I could tell her mother didn't care for me. Her mom was quite a bit younger than the old judge, I felt he liked me right way. Did I care one way or the other? "No!"

I went to my cabin to go to bed; Holy Cow, that old fart was snoring so loud I had to plug up my ears. That night I couldn't get much sleep. The next morning, I went out on deck on the port side.

All the people on board seemed to be there, there was a crowd of people on the dock yelling and waving like crazy. This girl Jane came and took my arm and told some of those crazies were from her family. We both starting laughing so hard, I couldn't control myself, I grabbed her and hugged her so hard she asked me to stop, then she did the same to me. In all this confusion, I planted a kiss on her lips, boy, did she kiss back. Come to find out her steady boyfriend was on the dock waving, she just did it to make him jealous.

If he had been on this ship, he would have reason to get jealous. We did a lot of hug-n and kiss-n before the trip was over, I never tried anything like Gloria and I did. This girl was too ready to suit me, I wasn't about to get locked into a relationship I could not control.

Any way, as the ship pulled out, I could see the Statue of Liberty and I really got choked up myself, she is a beauty. Soon we were in open water and on the way to France. Jane and I spent the whole day together and went to the dance in the ballroom that evening, a most enjoyable time. Thank God, the professor changed cabins; I had one all to myself.

The whole ship could see me and Jane we're getting pretty thick. A few days later, a kindly old gentleman stopped me in the hallway. We were about ten days out from New York. He asked if I knew about Jane's father. All I knew he was some kind of judge.

He said they were from Newark, New Jersey. She had told me that. He said during prohibition, he was a bootlegger and was in with gangsters. That was enough for me. I became very cool with Jane. She knew something was wrong and started fooling around with a bunch of college students on vacation. That suited me just fine.

I found another girl the next day. She was French and said her name was Mamie. Hot Dog, I got me a French teacher. She said she was nineteen, she looked twenty-five. Anyway, we hit it right off. All she wanted to do was hug and kiss; I found she was good at that. We docked at Cherbourg, France, late in the evening. There was a big dance in the ballroom that night. The

Captain gave us a speech about how he had enjoyed all our company.

The next morning, I caught the train with Mamie to Paris; Guess what? Mamie's husband met her at the station, I had been messing in someone else's garden. Live and learn.

Chapter 3

Paris – Lilly

At the station, I got my trunk and suitcase out to the taxi stand and was lucky to get a driver who liked Americans. He said he was here during the war and liked the doughboys. That really made me feels good. I asked if he knew a boarding house near the La Villette School of Architecture. He said that was in the Latin Quarter on the left bank of the Seine River and he happened to have a lady friend who had a boarding house in walking distance of the school.

What good luck to find this taxi driver. The boarding house was a very old house with three stories. A woman in her fifties owned and ran the house. She said it would cost me thirty dollars a month in American money; she made me feel right at home. I would get breakfast and supper with my board. She said four men and three ladies lived there, and I would have a room on the third floor. That suited me just fine. I unpacked and wrote the folks and Uncle Bob letters.

As the darkness filled my room, I could see from my window why Paris was called the city of lights. The Eiffel Tower stands out in a beautiful golden glow. I was so tired I washed up and went to bed without supper. The next morning, my land lady scolded me badly for not eating the evening meal. She fixed an excellent French breakfast. Yes, sir, the French do make French toast.

After breakfast, I took a walk to see the school I was going to attend. It took about ten minutes of walking to enter the grounds of the campus. It sat in a park-like setting with only three buildings, old beautiful buildings. I found out later they were built in the seventeenth century. On the way back, I took a little detour up a narrow street with shops and cafes. It was near noon, so I decided to stop and have lunch in one of the cafes. I sat at a table alone. This young girl came and took my order. She really got a kick out of my French, laughing as she took my order. I saw her go tell another waitress about me. She was still laughing hard. This other girl came right over and asked, "Are you an American?"

"Yes, I sure am; how can you tell?"

She plopped down in a chair next to me and said, "Your French gives you away." Then she said with a big smile, "I'm half American; my daddy was a soldier in the war." Right then I knew I had an in with this beautiful girl.

I leaned over to her and said, "You're the most beautiful half American girl I ever saw." I gave her my biggest smile.

She said, "You are a funny boy," and she laughed so nice I had to laugh with her. As I ate my lunch of cheese, bread and milk, I asked if Americans came to her café often. She said she had never seen one here before. I told her I was going to school to be an architect. I asked if she would take a walk with me when she got off work.

"I'd be pleased to," she said smiling. "I want to ask you about America."

It took over an hour before she got off. I walked up and down the street for that hour and window shopped the small stores along this narrow street. She found me a few doors down from the Café. We walked around the streets talking for the rest of the afternoon. What a delight she was. She told me her mother worked in the Le Jules Verne restaurant in the Eiffel Tower.

She asked where I came from in America. When I told her the Southwest, right away she asked if I ever saw a cowboy. I told her my folks lived on a cattle ranch and I had been a cowboy. I thought she might have wet her pants; she got so excited about cowboys. What a sweet girl she was. She asked me to go home and meet her mother. "I know she would like to meet you, she always says good things about Americans."

While we walked toward her house, she took my hand and said, "I haven't met many Americans, just the tourists that come to Paris. Most of them are in such a hurry, I never get to talk with them." In a few minutes, she guided me up the steps to her home. It was a block from my boarding house.

Wow, what a beauty her mother was. She looked to be twenty-five, but this girl said her mother was thirty-eight. I couldn't believe this lovely lady was in her thirties. She was a raving beauty, the most beautiful eyes I ever saw and the rest was pretty darn good, too. She spoke perfect English. She introduced herself as Marie La Vou and her daughter's name was Lilly. "I like Americans, they gave me my Lilly." She was smiling all the time and hugging Lilly.

We sat and talked late into the evening. I got a lot of questions about America. Marie had fixed supper for us. I made a date with Lilly for the next day. I had a week and a half before school started. As I walked home, I felt I was the luckiest boy in all of Paris to have met the most beautiful ladies in all of France.

At the boarding house, I had a letter from my Mother. She said that my brother Tom went to work for Smiling Jack as a stunt pilot, flying in an air show. Tommy was to be one of the pilots in the show. Her letter said everybody else was good. I'll bet Tommy was one happy guy.

The next morning, I had just finished breakfast when Lilly came to my boarding house. She had taken the day off to take me sightseeing. Holy Cow, how lucky can a guy get?

"Is there anything you'd like to see?" she asked.

"I would like to see where Lucky Lindy landed in his

airplane."

"That's out at Le Bourget Airport," she said. "Its a few miles north of the city, we can take the Trolley out there." We had to walk quite a ways to catch the Trolley. We had to stand all the way to the airport. She stood close and she smelled so good I had to contain myself, if you know what I mean.

We arrived at the airport at noon and had lunch in the airport lounge. When the people there learned 1 was an American, they all had a story about the night Lindbergh landed. It took several hours to get away from those people. We walked around the field. Lilly told me she was there that night with her mother. "I was 10 years old, I remember the night well." She showed me the exact spot where the plane set down. "The people would have taken his plane apart if the Gendarmes hadn't stopped them." She was so good at explaining what happened the whole time Lindbergh was there. We had a fun afternoon.

We took the trolley back to the city. It was the same, standing room only. Again, she stood so close; I had to steady her by keeping my arms around her. Her forehead bumped my chin all the way back. She still smelled so good I could hardly stand it, but I did. When we arrived at her house, it was just getting dark. We shook hands and she said, "Come early in the morning, I have the day planned." She had took another day off just to be with me.

I was up at six a.m. and on the way to her house. She opened the door to my knock. "Let's go," she said. "We're going to spend the day at the Eiffel Tower, mother has passes for us."

We walked for awhile, I wanted to get a taxi. She said, "No, I have a surprise for you." She took me to a French bakery. We had the most delicious pastries I had ever eaten. The coffee was good, too. Afterwards, I did hail a taxi and we got to the Tower before the crowd got there.

At the top, she pointed out so many things I couldn't remember half of them. She told me Paris was eight miles long and six miles wide, you could see the Seine River cut right thru the middle of the city. "There are six million people living here," Lily told me.

We had lunch with her mother on the third floor at the café where she worked. After lunch, we went back to the top. It got breezy and cold, I had to put my jacket and arms around her that way I could hold her tight. She rubbed her face against mine and whispered, "I like you, Frank." That made my day. We took a taxi home with her mother. She fixed supper again for us. Wow, that ended a perfect day for me.

The next morning, I was knocking on their door early. Marie invited me in and announced we three were going to the International Exposition of 1937. It was over at the Palais de Chaillot. Lilly told me America had an exhibit there. "We may meet some of your countrymen. Almost all countries have an exhibit there."

We took a taxi to the Eiffel Tower, and then walked across the Seine River to the Exposition. We visited the American exhibit first. There were some American college students working there. We drew a crowd right away. All the guys, there were a half dozen, came over to meet my lady companions. The American girls wandered away. Several of the guys got me alone and wanted to know where they could meet French girls like the ones I was with. I turned them off and got Lilly and her mother out quickly and to other Exhibits.

At noon, we had lunch and then visited Germany's and Italy's exhibits, it was a fun time. That evening, we had supper at Marie's café in the Eiffel Tower. Lilly asked me why I never drank wine? I said I didn't care for it. She and her mother laughed and Lilly said, "You will never make a Frenchman."

We took a taxi to their house again. There we had coffee and talked about America late into the night, I walked home. It was a cool evening. I was a very happy nineteen year old American boy, soon to be twenty.

That night, I had a hard time getting to sleep. How very lucky I was to have met such wonderful people as Lilly and her mother. I lay awake that night feeling really proud of myself.

I slept late, got up, dressed and was about to leave when my land lady stopped me and made me have some breakfast. She was so nice I couldn't refuse her. Before I finished, Lilly came in and sat talking with me. The land lady knew Lilly and said she and her mother were lucky to have me as a friend, my day was made. Lilly took my hand as we walked down the street the morning air was crisp and clean. It was good to be in Paris.

She wanted to take me to the Arc de Triomphe. We hailed a taxi and he dropped us off on the Avenue des Champs Elysees, within a short walk to the Arc. We walked all around the Arc several times. What a sight it is, she told me that the Tomb of the Unknown Warrior was under the Arc and that Napoleon had the Arc built. We walked back down the Avenue des Champs Elysees and had lunch at a sidewalk café. There are many cafes on this street. Lilly was a joy to be with, she talked about her growing up in Paris.

After lunch, we walked to the Place de la Concorde. She said we were standing in the heart of Paris. I told her she should be a tour guide. "You are so great, I can't tell you how much I enjoy your company."

She just smiled, took my hand and said, "Let's walk." We walked to a street along the Seine River where artists painted and sold their work. We visited with several and watched them while they worked. At a footbridge, the Pont des Arts, we strolled over and stopped in the middle. She leaned over the railing, I was behind her, and a sightseeing boat was passing below. I couldn't control myself, I spun her around, took her in my arms and kissed her ruby red lips, she kissed me back. The people on the boat gave us a big hand. We both waved to them and they all waved back and gave us a big cheer. One of the men on the bridge said rather loudly, "Paris is full of lovers." I waved to him.

Lilly said we should take a boat the next day, I agreed. We spent the afternoon walking and talking. We had supper at the Eiffel Tower with her mother again. During supper, Marie asked how we two were getting along. We both told her "Just fine." She shook her finger under my nose and said, "Frank, I want no monkey business with my Lilly."

I told her I was getting pretty fond of Lilly. "She's a joy to be with; if I was going to fall in love, it would be with her."

Marie said, "I know you Americans." She had her arms around Lilly and said, "I have my Lilly." She laughed and we all laughed.

"I promise no monkey business."

She took my hand and Lilly's and said, "Sometimes we make mistakes but I have my Lilly." I knew what she meant. We took a taxi back to their house. We had coffee and talked late into the evening. Oh, how I liked these two women. That night, I wrote a long letter to my mom and Uncle Bob and Aunt Helen.

You know, the taxis we take are very inexpensive, I mean cheap. I thought about getting a motorbike, but Uncle Bob sent so much money and the taxis were so cheap, I wouldn't need a bike.

The next morning, I was up early and had breakfast with my land lady. She was so nice, I couldn't ask for better.

At Lilly's, Marie opened the door and said Lilly wasn't up yet. "You kept us up late, Frank. I don't know what we did before you came." I had only known these beautiful ladies a few days and already I couldn't wait to see them. What Marie had said made me feel very comfortable.

Lilly and I spent the day on a sightseeing boat going down the Seine and then returned that evening. I asked if she would go with me to the foot bridge. She said she didn't trust me on that bridge. I told her I didn't trust myself there either, we both had a good laugh. We took a taxi to her house. Marie was home and had a great dinner fixed.

After dinner, Marie asked if I would like to see where the two of them were born.

"Sure," I replied. "It would be a pleasure to see such a place."

Marie said she had a few days off. We could take the train to the town they were born in.

Early the next morning, we were on a train bound for the town of Tours, a small town on the bank of the Loire River. We three sat together, I had asked Marie a question, nothing personal. For some reason, she started to tell me about Lilly's daddy. He was an officer in a truck transport company. She was dancing in a troupe at the Moulin Rouge night club. He was waiting at the stage door one rainy night. He wouldn't take no for an answer and he refused to go away. He was tall and very handsome. He had black eyes, wavy black hair and he spoke so softly. "I fell in love that very night." Tears ran down her beautiful face.

She continued, "We spent several months together in Paris. When the armistice came, he was ordered home. He wanted to marry me first but wasn't allowed to. We wrote all the time for awhile. When Lilly was born, I quit writing. I was afraid he might come and take her away. He wrote many letters and they were so sad I quit reading them, I would just burned them." She was now crying hard, so was Lilly.

"When Lilly was about eight years old, a lawyer came to my house and asked a lot of questions. A few weeks later, I got a letter from her daddy. I wouldn't reply. Then the lawyer came back and told me Lilly's daddy wanted to give me money. I refused. He asked why. I told him my fears. He said her daddy had a family of his own and just wanted to make sure we had plenty of money. He wanted her well taken care of. I said it would be alright. He had sent money for years now. I still love him." She was crying again.

Lilly told me she wrote her daddy now. "As soon as I could write, I started to write him all the time. I have two half sisters in America. Rose is ten and Clare is eight. I have pictures of them." She handed me a picture of two little girls sitting on a handsome man's lap. The envelope the pictures were in had an auto dealership heading. It was in a town in California. "That's my daddy," she said. The tears streamed down her face.

Marie said his wife had tried to stop Lilly from writing. "She wrote me and said if I didn't stop, she would sue me. Can she do that Frank?"

"I don't think she can," I told her, but what do I know? I'm no lawyer.

We arrived in Tours in the early afternoon. A fine looking man and three young girls met us at the station. He was Marie's brother and the girls were Lilly's cousins. A lot of hugging and kissing went on that day. We stayed at her brother's house, a fine French cottage. Tours is wine country; I got to taste a lot of wine the next day. I mean a lot of wine. Most of the people I met thought I was some relative of Lilly's daddy. No one told them any different. This was a very fun and pleasant time. I enjoyed the trip. So did Lilly, she said.

Back in Paris, we arrived just as it was getting dark. Paris is truly beautiful at night. We had dinner at Marie's café in the Eiffel Tower. We took a taxi to their house and had coffee. I told them how much I had enjoyed the trip and walked home. I wrote Mom and Bob about the trip. I had money in a letter from Bob. I was one lucky boy.

In the morning when I went down to breakfast, there was Lilly. Smiling and all dressed to go with me. She was more beautiful than ever. She announced that we were going to see some of the churches of Paris. My landlady said Lilly had been there almost an hour. "He's not only a funny boy, he's a sleepy boy." The landlady and Lilly both got a laugh from Lilly's words.

The first church we visited was Notre Dame, then the tiny St. Jilien-le-Pauvre, then over to the Dome des Invalides. I asked Lilly if she was trying to get religion for me, seeing all these churches. "No, I hoped you would like them." She seemed sad that I would ask. She turned on me and said, "Let's go walk the Poin des Arts footbridge." I was ready and we did. I got a wonderful kiss from her there.

We had dinner at my boarding house. All the inmates were happy to meet Lilly. They told her she should come more often. She promised she would. The next day being Sunday, I had one more day before school started.

Sunday we went to Napoleon's Tomb and walked thru the Tuileries Gardens and Place du Carrousel at the Louvre. We ate supper with Marie at the Eiffel Tower and then had coffee at their home. I told them both this was the best time I had ever had. They said they enjoyed my company, too. That night, for some reason, I had bad dreams. It must have been a foreboding of things to come.

I spent two weeks at the school doing nothing but drawings and more drawings. In the evenings, I had to do homework of drawings. I had no time for Lilly. I was bored of this work and went to see my professor. "Do I have to do these drawings?" I asked. "I have a portfolio full of drawings." I tried to make it clear I was not happy doing drawings. "Can't I get in a more advanced class?" I asked.

"Not here, you must follow our curriculum. If you want more advanced work, you must go to another school."

"Where might that be?"

"You could go to the University of Munich in Germany. They have advanced classes you could apply for." Uncle Bob went there, I remember he said so. "How can I apply?" I asked.

"I will give you a letter of recommendation to give to my good friend, Professor Hoffmann. He can get you right in." I made my mind up right there to go. The only thing that might stop me would be Lilly. "Frank, you will make a good architect. I can't blame you for wanting to advance faster." I said I would let him know tomorrow.

I went to see Lilly that evening. She and her mother were busy packing. "I'm so happy," she said. "My daddy has sent for mother and me. We have our papers all ready to go. Mother has seen the American consulate and our papers are all ready. We go to the coast in the morning and sail day after tomorrow." Holy cow, what could I say, but how happy I was for them. She said her daddy's wife had died over a year ago. He would be waiting for them in New York City. I spent the evening with them and said my goodbyes.

I walked home one sick American boy to have lost those two wonderful people. That night, I lay awake until morning. I made up my mind I was going to Munich, Germany. It would soon be a new year, 1937.

Chapter 4

Munich, Germany

The following Monday, I went to the money exchanger to have my French money changed into German Marks. I went to the school and spent four hours talking with my French Professor.

"Frank," he said, "It may be a little sticky for you going to Germany at this time."

"Why? I'm just a student. Why would anyone care about me?"

"The Nazi party has taken over Germany. The country is changing rapidly. I don't think for the better for some people."

"Why should I care? I'm not political, why would they bother me?"

"I just want to warn you, you may not be received well there."

I thanked the professor for his concern. I told him goodbye, and thanked him for all he had done for me. "I'll be fine," I told him and went on my way.

Uncle Bob had sent me way more money than I would ever need; God bless him. I wrote him and the folks of my decision to go to Germany. They could write me, in care of general delivery Munich, Germany. The man at the exchange told me to hide most of my Marks as the German Government didn't like foreigners bringing a lot of money into the country. That seemed strange to me. Anyway, I hid my money in the lining of my overcoat, trunk liner and my suit coat.

The following day, I was on a train bound for Munich, Germany. I was missing Lilly and her mother so much; just thinking of them brought tears to my eyes. I sure hoped they would like America. I think I remember the letter Lilly let me read had a return address of an automobile dealership in California. His name was on the heading as the owner.

From now on, I would be speaking German, at least the best I could. Bear that in mind as you read my story. An older German man sat next to me and asked, "Are you an American?"

I laughed and said, "How can you tell?"

"Your clothing gives you away. Are you a tourist? You look awfully young to be one."

"No, sir, I am a student. I plan to study architecture at Munich University."

"Son," he said, "I'm afraid you have picked a bad time to come to Germany."

Puzzled, I asked why he would say that. He replied, "Germany is in a really bad turmoil at this time. The politics of the dictator who has the power over the people has made life in Germany impossible for people like me." I still I didn't know what he was referring to. The look on my face must have given me away.

He shook his head and continued, "This man, Adolf Hitler, has made life a living hell for me and my people. I am a Jew and he has sworn to drive us all out of Germany, I have had enough. I'm on the way back to sell my factory, get my family and leave Germany."

This man seemed so positive of the situation, I had too ask, "What does he have against Jews, you look the same to me as everyone else? In my city in the United States we have many families of Jews."

"We really haven't the slightest idea. He makes us wear the Star of David on our clothes to identify us as Jews." This man looked as harmless as a man could look. He was well dressed.

He was wearing a well-tailored grey pinstriped suit, a black vest and a well-groomed grey beard. He wore horn rimmed glasses. He had a pleasant smile and laughing eyes. All together, a very distinguished looking gentleman. He acted like a very nice gentleman. In the next several hours, we got to know each other a little.

Now the train was slowing down. The man told me, "We're about to enter Germany. We will change engines here. An all German crew will take over." When we stopped, a uniformed man entered our car and said all foreigners must get off and report to the immigration office. My traveling companion said, "That's you, my boy."

There were twenty people standing with me on the station platform. A little old lady was the first to go in the office, I was the last to go in. All the other people could get back on the train as they came out of the station. In the office, a very stern looking black uniformed individual with a skull emblem on his billed cap gave me a hard look. He sat back in the chair with his hands folded and said very loud, "Papers." I handed him my passport. He started thumbing thru the book. He asked "Are you a student?"

"Yes sir! I'm studying architecture. I plan to go to the University in Munich."

"How much money did you bring to Germany?" Now he had his elbows on the desk, hands folded and staring into my eyes. "Let me see all your money," he insisted. I took out my billfold and handed him all the Marks I had in it. He counted the money then said, "One thousand Marks, not much to go to school on."

"My people will send me more as I need it; I plan to get a job in Munich." That seemed to satisfy him. He handed back my money and passport, turned in his chair and said, "Go." He also motioned with his hand. I hurried back to my seat in the train car. Soon the train started to move. I sat silently watching the countryside pass by. It was a very sun shiny, cloudless pleasant day.

Soon, my elderly traveling companion spoke, "Now, my boy, you have got a glimpse of the new Germany."

I asked, "Who was he? Why do they need soldiers in that job?"

"He's with the SS, they use men like him because they will be tough."

I changed the subject. "You said you were going to sell your factory. What do you make?"

"Buttons," he said. "All kinds of buttons, metal, bone - like the ones on your shirt and coat. We make all the buttons the Army, SA and SS wear on their uniforms."

"You have to sell your factory?" I asked.

"No, I don't have to, but I think it's wise that I do."

"Do you have a buyer?"

"Yes, I'm selling to my old sergeant I had in the Army."

"You were in the German Army?" That surprised me for him to be a veteran of the first war.

"Yes, I was in six long years, from 1913 to 1918. I was an officer in the artillery on the Western Front."

I just couldn't understand what he was telling me about the conditions in Germany. As we talked, I surmised he loved the Fatherland. This thing he told about Jews didn't make any sense to me.

As the train pulled into the station at Munich, darkness was falling. I asked my friend if he knew where I could get a hotel. "The Dressen Hotel is two blocks east of the station." I thanked him for being such a good traveling companion and hoped his plans would work out to his satisfaction. He shook my hand and said he would pray for me to have a healthy and safe time while I was here in Germany. He told me his name was Max

Steiner. We parted company on the platform.

I went into the station to check on my trunk. I was told it would be in the baggage room until I came for it. I carried my suitcase and proceeded to the hotel. There I saw the room clerk and rented a room. He asked many questions about America. He said there hadn't seen many Americans for some time. He gave me a key. I asked if the dining room was open. He told me it would be serving until nine p.m. I took the elevator to the third floor to my room. I washed my face and hands and returned to the dining room for supper.

In it I found a very nice room with many tables covered with the most beautiful white laced table cloths, I sat at a table. There were twenty or so people having dinner. A young man came and gave me a menu and a glass of water. In a few minutes he returned and I ordered my dinner. I sat back to observe the room and the people. There were six uniformed men and their ladies eating and laughing. All the rest were very well dressed men and women civilians, busy talking and eating.

The desk clerk came thru the big double doors with a very attractive middle-aged lady and pointed me out to her. She immediately approached my table, I stood to welcome her. She asked, "Are you an American?"

"Yes, ma'am, I am."

She asked, "May I sit and talk with you?" She spoke perfect English.

"I would be happy to talk to anyone at this time," I said laughingly. "I hate eating alone."

She sat down and asked if I had ordered my dinner. "Yes ma'am, I ordered the roast beef."

"You will enjoy that, we have the best chef in Germany, he makes the most delicious roast beef you will ever taste." Then she started telling about the Americans she had met before. "I have a delightful American friend you will simply have to meet. She is a real treasure and she is my best friend. She lives here in Munich. Would you like to meet her?"

"Yes ma'am, it would be a pleasure to meet someone from home."

"She has had a bad time lately. She has just divorced her husband and needs cheering up. Would you help me do that?"

"Yes ma'am, I'll try to help her if I can."

"Let me introduce myself. My name is Frau Dressen. My husband and I own this hotel. Have you come to Munich as a visitor or a student?"

I told her I was pleased to meet her and I would very much like to meet her friend. I had come to Germany to study architecture at the University. She said that Germany had the finest schools in the world. She asked the waiter to bring two glasses of white wine. As I ate my meal, she started telling me about Munich; Oktoberfest was in full swing. "We have many exciting things to do during this time of year." I told her I had to find a room to rent as I couldn't afford to stay in her fine hotel. "I'll have a bell boy find a room for you, there's many to be had in Munich."

I finished my meal and thanked her for her kindness. She walked me to the elevator, wished me good night and said she would look forward to seeing me in the morning. "Call my room when you are ready to find a permanent room."

In my room, I undressed and took a hot bath. This was the finest hotel I had ever been in. It had everything, the best bed I had ever slept in. The radio that played nothing but sleepy time music. I turned in and had the best night's sleep I had since leaving France. I dreamed I was back in Paris with Lilly and her mother. When I woke up it all seemed so real, I had to look to make sure I wasn't in Paris. I sure missed Lilly and her mother; I hoped they could find happiness in America.

I dressed and hurried down to the dining room to have breakfast. The dining room was filled with uniformed officers and their ladies. These were handsome and very good looking men and women. They impressed me with their well tailored uniforms and the ladies in their beautiful dresses. There were children in various age groups scattered throughout the room. I found an empty table next to the back wall. Very soon, a white coated young man came and left me a menu; I ordered eggs, sausage and coffee.

After eating, I went to the front desk and asked for Frau Dressen's telephone number. Reluctantly, the desk clerk gave me her number. I called to tell her I was in the lobby. She came down to meet me in the next few minutes. "Have you had breakfast?" she asked.

"Yes, ma'am. I need to find a room as soon as I can."

She took my arm, led me to the bellhop's station and introduced me to a young boy whose name was Franz. He looked the part of a bellboy with a red bell cap, red coat, blue pants and a friendly smile; he looked to be an older teenager. Mrs. Dressen asked him if he knew where I could find a room in this neighborhood. He said he did and the lady told him to take me there. Before we left, she asked me to come back to the hotel at seven p.m. to meet her American friend. I promised I would. She called after us that I would be having dinner with her and her friend.

As we walked down the street, we encountered many uniformed soldiers. I asked Franz why so many were in town. He said Oktoberfest was a big celebration for the German people and most soldiers got leave to come to town. Most of the soldiers had a pretty girl with them. They all seemed to be having a good time as they were laughing and acting foolish as most young people do when they're out on a date. We turned south for several blocks, and turned down a narrow street with small shops on each side. The sidewalks where curiously empty of people, I asked Franz why this was.

He almost whispered, "This is a Jewish section of town. I hope," he said, "You don't object living with Jews?"

"Why should I?"

"Some people here don't care for them. There's a move on in this country to rid Germany of the Jews, I myself like them; I have many friends who are Jews. In fact, I have some of their blood in me. My grandfather was Jewish."

I told him I had heard of this movement and I didn't understand it at all. He stopped and said that the bakery shop ahead was where there was a room for rent. He said goodbye, turned and hurried back up the street the way we had come.

I walked on and entered the bakery shop. A very attractive young lady behind the counter asked if she could help me. "I understand I might find a room for rent here, I need a place to hang my hat," I said with a big smile.

She frowned at me and obviously didn't care for my manners. She said in a very sober voice, "I'll call my grandfather, he owns this building." I want to tell you the smell of fresh baking bread was wonderful. I would like living here, I said to myself.

An elderly gentleman came back following the girl. A very pleasant looking man with a full gray beard and twinkling eyes, he reminded me of Santa Claws. He said very curtly, "Can I help you young man?"

"Yes, sir, I'm looking for a room to rent. I understand you have one."

"Yes we do, just above this store, come I will show you." We went outside and up the stairs beside the building, thru a door at the top. It opened into a hallway with four doors; we entered the first one on the right hand side. It took us into a one room flat; there was a bed, a night stand, a chest of draws and a bureau. There was also a table with two wooden chairs, a rocker and a counter with a hot plate. It was a furnished flat with bedding, towels, a few miscellaneous cooking utensils and a few dishes. The bathroom was a community one at the end of the hall.

The old man said he would furnish a pitcher and pan for water. For the price, I could not afford not to rent the room. It had two windows, one looked down on the stairs, and the other overlooked the street below.

We returned to the shop and I paid a month's rent. He introduced himself. His name was Karl Golden, his Granddaughter was Jennifer Golden. They both became much warmer toward me and made me feel welcome. I told them I had a trunk at the railroad station I had to go get. He loaned me a cart to carry it back to my room. I took the cart and hurried to the station and retrieved my trunk.

Back at the bakery, Herr Golden had a middle aged man help me carry the trunk to my room. He struck up a conversation right away. He asked, "Do you know you're in a Jewish neighborhood?"

"Yes, is there any reason I should not be here?"

"Things are getting tough for Jews in Munich. Did you notice all Jews wear the Star of David on their clothes?"

"Yes I saw that. What's the reason?"

He didn't reply to my question, but he did continue saying, "My advice to you is be careful where you go and who you go with." That seemed a strange thing to say. He went on saying, "This is my last day to work at the Golden bakery, I've been told to quit or else. You see I'm an Aryan and a new law has passed that I can't work for a Jew anymore."

"Whoa," I said, "That's one hell of a bad law."

He agreed with me and said, "I've worked for Herr Golden every since I came home from the army. He's treated me like a son." With tears in his eyes he said, "I love that old man and his family, but there's nothing I can do." He started to leave and I asked his name. "Alfred Ruche."

I checked my watch and it said it was noon. My stomach agreed. I went down to the bakery shop and inquired of Jennifer where I could get a meal. She came from behind the counter, stepped outside and pointed to a restaurant on the next corner. This was a very attractive young girl, I asked her age. "I'm eighteen and will be nineteen next month. How old are you?" she asked.

"I just turned twenty," I said with a smile.

"You're not a German. Who are you and why have you come to Munich?" She seemed concerned.

"I'm an American and I have come to study architecture in the Munich University," I said proudly.

Without hesitation she said, "You have come to Germany at a bad time."

I told her I had heard that before. I thanked her and walked down to the restaurant. At the restaurant, a large word in white was painted on the glass window. "JUDE" it read. I entered and sat at a table near the door. There were ten people eating and talking. A comely middle aged woman came and took my order of a brunswager sandwich, a kosher pickle and a glass of beer. All the people there had the Star of David on their clothes. After finishing my meal, I wished everyone there a good day. None of the people even looked up at me.

When I got back to the bakery, I went in and talked to Jennifer. I told her the people at the restaurant were very cool to me. She whispered, "They probably thought you were an SS spy."

"Holy Cow," I said. "Could that be true?"

"Yes, we have spies here all the time. You haven't told me your name."

"Frank," I said. "I must go up and take a nap. I have a dinner date at seven at the Dressen Hotel."

"With a young lady, I bet." Jennifer smiled and asked, "Is she pretty?"

"No, not with a girl, with Frau Dressen and an American lady by the name of Hellene Hanfstaengl. Frau Dressen said I would like this woman Hellene."

"Oh my!" she said, "You're moving in fast company. The Dressens and Hanfastaengls are big friends of the German Fuhrer, Adolf Hitler." That was the first time I had heard that. It scared the dickens out of me. Jennifer continued, "You must be very careful what you say to those people. You might get in serious trouble if you say anything against the Nazis. Be careful, Frank, what you say tonight."

I thanked her and told her, "I will be careful just for you."

"Be serious, I mean what I say." She had a customer so we talked no more and I went on up to my room to take a nap.

Chapter 5

Jennifer – Hitler – Helen

When I woke up from my afternoon nap, my watch said almost five p.m. I went down to the bathroom and took a hot shower. Back in my room, I dressed in my new blue suit, white shirt and new black shoes. I had used a man's deodorant I had purchased in Paris; I did smell pretty darn good. With my hair slicked down, I thought I looked the fashion plate of American men. Uncle Bob would have been proud {I hoped}.

Downstairs, I stopped to look in the bakery window. There were many customers in the shop, but Jennifer noticed me, waved and smiled. I waved back and on impulse I threw her a kiss. Hot dog, she threw one back.

It took about twenty minutes to reach the hotel. I had passed and watched many young German soldiers in their sharp grey uniforms with their girlfriends on the streets. All were joking, laughing and seemingly having a good time.

At the hotel, I entered the lobby, went straight to the front desk and asked the clerk to notify Mrs. Dreesen I was in the lobby. He said he would and I should sit down and wait for her. I found an easy chair that faced the elevators and sat watching for her to come down. I had just sat down, when a very stern looking individual in a long black coat sat next to me. He asked if I was an American. Of course, I told him proudly that I was. I thought he must be a lawyer as he asked many questions. I must have answered them correctly as he got up and left as soon as Mrs. Dreesen came to me from the elevator.

She was a very attractive middle aged woman. She was

wearing a long evening gown in a silver color with much jewelry. Her shiny black hair was done up in a bun. In all,a very desirable looking woman. As she drew close, she smelled as if she had just stepped out of a French perfume bottle.

The first thing she said was, "Do all young American men look as good as you?"

I shrugged my shoulders and said, "I guess they do." I gave a laugh. She said she had picked a bad time for me to meet her friend Hellene. She took my hand and led me to some chairs off to the side of the room. I asked who the man was I had been talking with. She said he was with the Gestapo. "It's the secret service of Germany. What kind of questions did he ask?"

I told her he mostly wanted to know why I was in Germany.

"Yes," she said, "That's what they would want to know." She invited me to sit down as she wanted to talk. All of a sudden, almost as if by magic, the room began to fill with German officers in all kinds of uniforms. Almost all of them had good looking women on their arms.

Mrs. Dreesen said, "You won't believe this, but the Fuhrer is coming to have dinner here tonight. You do know who he is?"

"Only that he's the head man of Germany." What else could I say, that's all I knew.

Just then all the people jumped up and started yelling "Heil Hitler" all over the place. They all had their right hand extended right out to their front in some kind of salute {I surmised}. Soon, a rather small looking man in a long black leather coat came into the lobby. This must be him. I had never seen a picture of Adolf Hitler before; at least I couldn't remember having seen one. This man had a brown cap on and I could see brown pants showing below the coat. He had a large entourage of uniformed men following him.

Mrs. Dreesen and I had stood up and she was doing this

salute also and calling Heil Hitler. I just stood there dumbfounded at the whole thing.

He saw her and started to move in our direction. I heard Mrs. Dreesen say under her breath, "Good God, he's coming over to us." Wow, this little guy is the big man and I'm going to meet him. I sized him up to myself. Not a very big man in stature looks to be a head shorter than I. He had a two finger mustache under his nose. Large bags under the eyes and a kind of shuffling walk.

He proceeded right to Mrs. Dreesen with his hand out to shake hers. Right away, she said, "How delightful it is to have Mien Fuhrer in our humble hotel." I thought she was laying it on a little heavy but what did I know. He was all smiles.

He said, "I always love to be in your beautiful hotel. Who is this fine looking young man?" He nodded to me.

She told him, "This is my American friend, Frank."

He put his hand out for me to shake. I took his hand and shook it; it felt like a limp rag. He then asked, "Are you a visitor to our new Germany?"

I replied, "No, I have come to study Architecture in the university here in Munich."

"How wonderful," he said. "You will be studying in the finest university in the world. Did you know that was my best subject?"

I lied and said, "I heard it was."

He had a lady on his right arm. He introduced her as his friend Mrs. Helene Hanfstaengl. "She's an American country-woman of yours. We're always glad to have Americans come and see our new Germany. I insist you two must dine with me tonight." This Helene looked at me and shook her head yes.

Mrs. Dreesen said, "We would be honored to dine with you, Mien Fuhrer."

"Fine," he said. "Go in and sit by my table." We went right

in and sat down at a table near the main table. All the tables had beautiful white lace table cloths.

I asked Mrs. Dreesen who the men with Hitler are. "The small mousy one is Joseph Goebbels, the head of state propaganda. The fat one in the white uniform is Herman Goering, the head man of the German air force, the Luftwaffe. The one with the dark black hair is Rudolf Hess and the tall one is Heinrich Himmler, the head of the SS. All these are very powerful men in Germany. How lucky you are to meet them tonight."

This lady Helene came to our table and sat next to me. She leaned over and said to me in a whisper, "I love to meet Americans when they come to Germany, I guess you know you are a very attractive young man? I love American men."

What could I say? I did say, "I find the German women...." I didn't get to finish as the women who were accompanying the Nazi men sat at a table just to our front. I said "My, my, what good looking ladies they are." They all turned to us, smiled and nodded their approval. All I could do was smile and nod back. The whole place filled up with well dressed civilians, uniformed men and lots of beautiful ladies.

We must have sat there at least ten minutes. The place was quiet, not a sound was made. It was eerie, to say the least, to be in this big crowd and no one talked.

Then a bugle sounded, drums started to roll and a large group of young good looking boys entered dressed in brown clothing. Their pants were shorts, with long socks; they all had Sam brown belts on. They started down the aisle between the tables carrying huge red flags with a white circle and a black cross of some kind in the center. There were thirty boys in all marching side by side. At the head table, they split and marched around and stood behind the table like statues. All the men who had been with Hitler came down and stood at the table. All the people jumped up and started calling, "Heil Hitler, Heil Hitler." They all had their right hands in the air and kept this "Heiling Hitler" going until Hitler reached the table. All the time he had his right hand up and a big smile on his face. He reminded me of a Bantam Rooster about to take on a hen, I thought the whole thing was funny; was that a mistake? Hitler told everyone to sit down. He started to make a speech. He talked for over an hour. No, he yelled, screamed and made all kinds of motions with his hands for over an hour. When he finished, I had a bursting headache, I sure paid dearly for that meal.

There were many white coated young boys serving the meal of roast turkey, mashed potatoes and gravy. A mixed vegetable was also served. I noticed Hitler ate only the vegetables. After the main meal, we had a delicious apple pie and coffee.

When it was all over, Mrs. Dreesen, Helene and I went into a small sitting room off the lobby and had a long talk about my America. Hitler and his group milled around the lobby for some time and then they all just left. I asked the ladies about the black cross symbol in the flag. I had seen it before on American Indian art. They told me it was called a Swastika. It was the symbol of the Nazi party. I had seen it on all the men's arm bands and on flags hanging from buildings, now I knew what it was about. This night was pretty confusing to me.

I told the ladies I was very tired and I must get to bed. I said, "I had a good time and enjoyed meeting Helene, but I must say good night." They said we must meet soon and have a real talk, and wished me a good night and a restful sleep.

As I walked home, the fresh air was great. It was a cool fall evening, you could feel winter coming in the air. The heaven was full of stars and I had a homesick feeling. How in the world did I get into that mess this evening? I wondered how all the folks were at home and why I had been so quick to make this journey to go to school. I assured myself everything would be okay. I promised myself I would write the folks tomorrow.

It was almost midnight before I finally got to bed. Tomorrow would be Saturday and I would have to try to locate the university.

After a sound sleep, I got up early and took a shower. The people in the rooms had not gotten up so I had the place to myself. I stayed in the shower longer than I usually did. It felt good just to stand under the hot water and relax. I dressed quickly and went looking for something to eat. The café I had eaten in the day before was closed. All the shops on this street were closed. I had to walk over to the next street to the north to find one open.

After having breakfast, I decided to walk around a bit, sightseeing before going back to my room to write a letter. I had walked past a department store and stopped to window shop when I saw the reflection of Jennifer in the window. She had crossed the street and was coming toward me. As she approached, I stepped out to block her way. "Good morning," I said in my best German. "You look radiant this morning. Where are you going?"

"I'm on the way to the bakery. I have to do a little work on the books. Are you going my way?"

"Yes, ma'am, may I walk with you?"

"Okay. I'd like that."

We walked together to the bakery. I asked if she would show me around when she finished. She said she would be pleased to. I asked why all the shops were closed. "It's our Jewish religious day, we all close on this day."

I told her I would be in my room. I had a few letters to write. "Call me when you're finished." She said she would.

In an hour, she called thru my door that she was ready to

go. I had finished my letters and we walked together to post them. This girl was a real pleasure to be with. She asked what I would like to see. I wanted to find the university and a Lutheran church.

"You must be a protestant if you go to the Lutheran church."

"Yes all my people are."

She said that my church was not far from her home. "It's on the east side of the Isar River."

We had to make quite a walk to reach the Englicher Garten Park. We cut thru the park on a well used path. We had just entered the park when we saw three Hitler youths in their uniforms running our way. Jennifer grabbed my arm and told me we must get off the path to let them pass. I said, "No way." She insisted. So we did.

As they passed us they yelled, "Death to all Jews."

"What a terrible thing to say," I yelled back at them. Jennifer pleaded with me to be quiet.

"We hear that all the time now." The boys had run and we continued on our way.

We crossed a bridge and there on the other side was my church. We walked north up a street called Thomas Mann. She said we were in the Bogenhausen neighborhood. "Thomas Mann, I know who he was. I read a book he wrote. It was required reading in my English literature class." I was proud I had remembered his name.

"Yes," she said, "He is a very famous German writer. He received the Nobel Prize for literature. He attended the University of Munich, we're passing his house now." I could see a beautiful two story red brick house that was all boarded up.

"How come his home is boarded up?"

"He is living in Switzerland now. He moved his family

three or four years ago," she told me.

"Why would he leave this wonderful place?"

"He was a very outspoken opponent of Nazism and Adolf Hitler." She was very positive in her words.

"I think I would be, too, after listening to him last night." I shook my head as I spoke.

She said she had heard just yesterday that Thomas Mann had moved his family to the USA. I told her he would be well received there.

We walked on down the sidewalk. The next house she said belonged to a Doctor Max Wolfe. "He's a real nice man. He told my grandfather we should leave Germany." She started to cry as she spoke. "Many wealthy Jews have already gone."

We were passing a short wall; I asked her if she would like to sit down for a few minutes. We did and I told her, "This walking I'm not used to. At home I ride a horse all the time and I had a motorcycle for a while, maybe I should get a bicycle or a motor bike."

"Yes, maybe you should get a bike." She was still crying.

I put my right arm around her and took her left hand in mine and told her, "I can't stand to see pretty girls cry. Why are you crying?"

"I was thinking of my father. He's been gone almost two months now."

"Where is he?"

"He was told to report to the Gestapo on a Monday morning and he hasn't come home. We don't know where he is." Now she was really crying. I felt helpless, I gave her my handkerchief and did my best to hold her tight. Finally, she stopped sobbing and told me her mother and sister had moved into their Grandparents' home. "My father is the Rabbi of our Synagogue. The Synagogue has been closed since he left. You know, Frank," she said, "We can't go to our place of worship, we Jews can't go to the swimming pools, we can't go to the parks or gather in any public place. We can't even go to the Cinema."

"What? I can't take you to the movies?"

"That's right,"

"I had no Idea things were this bad for Jews in Germany. I met a man on the train coming in who told me he was selling his factory and leaving Germany. I thought he was overstating his feelings. Now I see he wasn't."

She stopped crying and told me she enjoyed my company. We sat on the wall talking for almost an hour. She said I should come home with her and meet her mother, sister and grandmother. I must have looked reluctant as she said, "It's just a few houses on down this street. We can go and have lunch with my Mother and Grandmother. I'm positive they would like to meet you."

"Okay."

We walked on to her home and walked up the driveway to the rear of the house. In the rear of the house, there was a two car garage filled with two automobiles. The house was a two story red brick structure built in the same type of architecture as the other homes in the Thomas Mann neighborhood.

We entered thru a screened porch and into a friendly kitchen. The smell of cooking food filled my nostrils and reminded me I was hungry. Jennifer introduced me to her grandmother as the handsome American renting a room at the bakery. Her Grandmother in her broken English said she had wanted to meet me and now she knew why Jennifer had spoken so much about me. Jennifer turned beet red and told her Grandmother she shouldn't tell family secrets.

I took the grandmother's hand and said, "Now I know why Jennifer is so pretty."

The Grandmother said, "I am going to like this American."

The Grandfather came thru the swinging doors from the dining room and when he saw me, he seemed to be aggravated that I was there. I had met him when I rented the room at the bakery. He told us that he had a meeting going and we should keep the talk down. "Please," he said, "I don't want my friends to leave." He returned back into the dining room. As the doors opened, I could see several men sitting around the table.

Jennifer, in a hushed voice, said, "Jews can't congregate anywhere, even in our own homes. Grandfather is afraid his company will be scared you might tell the authorities and get them sent to jail."

"Good grief that is a terrible way to have to live."

The Grandmother told us to sit down and she would fix us lunch. We had sat for a few minutes when Jennifer's mother and sister came into the kitchen. She said some Hitler youth had been following them and calling them bad names. The sister was in tears and I could see Jennifer's mother had been crying. Jennifer went to her mother and tried to console her. There wasn't much I could say but that I was sorry for people like those kids.

At the introduction to the mother and sister, the mother said she wanted to meet me and could see why Jennifer had made so much over me. Again Jennifer turned beet red and said with anger in her voice, "Mother, please!" I just laughed and so did they, all except Jennifer.

We all sat at the kitchen table and had a good lunch of cream cheese, fresh baked bread from the bakery and milk. Several times, as the dining room door opened, I could hear a few words. Once I heard the Grandfather say, "Leave, the sooner the better." I surmised the men were planning something.

We sat and talked for the next hour. Heir Golden came in, sat with us and talked awhile. I told them all I had better go as I wanted to walk around downtown Munich and get to know my way around. All the Golden's were very gracious to me and the Grandfather said something very strange to me when he said that he wished I would have a safe and healthy stay while I was in Germany.

That afternoon as I walked home alone this whole thing of anti-Semitism in Germany was puzzling. Why were the Nazis so against the Jewish people? Somehow I must find out, maybe as a Christian I could help the Jews. I decided I must go to church tomorrow, it being Sunday.

Downtown, I walked passed an auto repair shop and went in to ask the man there if he knew where I might purchase a bicycle or motor bike. This walking was getting old. The man said his name was Hans and just by chance he had a BMW motorcycle for sale. He took me into a back room and there sat the beauty. A black and white BMW with a side car. "She's a 1929," he told me.

"Does she run?" I wanted to know.

"Like a top," She was all covered with dust and cobwebs.

"How much you want for her?"

"Four thousand marks."

"Too much for me, how about three thousand?" I wanted her, but I didn't want to spend all my money.

"Okay, you can have her; I'll get her out, clean her up and have her ready for you Monday morning."

"I'll be here with the money." I walked to my room one happy American motorcycle buyer of a German motorbike.

At the bakery, a big black Mercedes car was waiting for me. The driver said that Helene Hanfsaengl had sent the car for me and that she was waiting for me at her apartment. I found out later that this car was the Fuhrer's own automobile and the driver was his chauffeur, Emil Maurice, one very talkative individual. I went with him to her apartment, had dinner and a lot of interesting conversation.

She wanted to know what I thought of the new Germany and if things in America were getting better with Franklin Roosevelt in office? I told her as far as my family was concerned we were getting along fine and most of the people I knew were too. I had a lot of serious questions to ask but held them for another time. I didn't want to make her mad as I could see she was impressed with the Fuhrer.

Around ten o'clock I asked if I could go home. She called the chauffeur. He came to drive me home; I found he is a very talkative individual.

Chapter 6

Hitler's Chauffer – Rose

On the way home, the Chauffeur started telling me about his life with the Fuhrer. He was proud to be the man's personal chauffeur. I wanted to ask a lot of questions, but was afraid until he started to say negative things about Hitler. He opened right up and told of a girl he had been in love with. A niece of Hitler's who Hitler had stopped him from seeing. This girl was in love with him but Hitler wanted her for himself. He made so many demands on the poor girl and kept her almost locked up. She had committed suicide right in the Fuhrer's apartment with his own pistol.

As he spoke, tears rolled down his cheeks. I heard him say faintly, "God, how I loved that girl." For some reason, I asked her name. The poor man really began to sob; I told him I was sorry to have asked.

We had parked in front of the bakery. When I started to get out, he stopped me and said he would like to talk for awhile. He said his girls name was Geli Raubal, a daughter of Hitler's half sister. He said he had loved her so much he almost committed suicide himself. I didn't know what he expected me to say. I thought he just wanted to talk to someone outside of the people he worked with.

I asked, "Why do you keep working for the man? You don't seem to like him."

He sat quiet for a minute before he answered. "The boss is good to me and besides, I wouldn't know what I could do. They would probably put me in the army, I sure don't want that."

I asked if Hitler had a wife.

"No," he said, "He'll never marry; he's married to the Nazi party and Germany. He has a girl friend; she lives in the apartment house you just visited."

I had to know, so I asked, "What's she like? Is she pretty?"

"Not bad," he answered. "Not as pretty as Geli, but a very nice girl, too good for him. He treats her badly; he won't take her out in public and gets mad if anyone talks to her."

"That's a terrible relationship."

"Yes, I agree. If you ever meet her, stay away, he doesn't like men talking to her."

"I'll never meet her," .

"You never know. You live here in Munich. She shops all the time. He gives her all the money she wants. He's a very wealthy man." He seemed concerned about me, I told him I would heed what he said if I ever meet her.

We sat talking for more than an hour, but I never got up the nerve to bring up the Jewish situation. It started to rain and I told him I had letters to write and I was very glad to make his acquaintance. I said, "Good night," and went up to my room.

I wrote uncle Bob and the folks. I told them I had plans to buy a motorcycle, this was a very large city and I needed some cheap transportation. I liked this bike that I had looked at and thought it would be a good one.

That night, I dreamed I was back in Paris with Lilly and her mother. It all seemed so real when I woke up; I thought I was still in Paris. My bubble burst, I was here in Germany in this lonely room. It was Sunday morning and I had the feeling I had to go to church. After a hot shower, I dressed in my brown suit and headed for the Lutheran Church.

It had rained almost all night and the clear blue cloudless sky was a welcome sight. Most of the gutters in the city were still running with water. At the church, I found a seat near the rear. The service was like ours at home. I could see many young people, quite a few my own age, in the congregation. I said to myself this will be a good place to get to know people. The pastor, a Mr. Emil Cramer, welcomed me with enthusiasm as I left the church. He knew right away I wasn't a regular German. He invited me to Sunday evening worship. He said he could introduce me to lots of people my age and many who went to the university. I told him I would be there for sure.

I hadn't eaten anything that morning, so I looked for a café on the way home. I found one on the Maximilan Strasse downtown and stopped in. The place was filled with soldiers and some girls, all seemed to be having a good time. I got looked over pretty good as I entered and sat at the counter. The waitress who took my order was as friendly as any I had ever met. She looked to be in her late teens. When I went to pay, she told me I was welcome to come back anytime.

"If you're here, I will."

She smiled and said, "I work here every day."

"Ha, things are looking up," I said to myself.

I walked back to the bakery and to my room. I spent the rest of the afternoon writing letters home. Then lay down and took a nap. When I woke, I was as lonely as I had ever been. I was feeling sorry for myself and said so out loud.

I went down to the bakery; Alfred was there alone.

I asked "Where's Jennifer?"

Alfred kind-a hung his head and said "She has gone to Switzerland; the Golden family have all gone. It's been planned a long time. I now own this bakery. Jennifer asked me to tell you good bye and she said she will miss you.

There I go again Jinxed with women. Find one I like: she's gone I hope they will be safe.

I said a silent payer to God to keep the Golden family safe.

I felt hungry, so decided to go back to the café I had been at this morning. There I saw the young woman I had talked with this morning still working. I took a table by the window. She came and took my order. When she came with the food, she sat down and asked questions about me ; I told her my story. Right away, she became friendly and told me her name was Rose. She said she had never met an American.

"It's time for me to go home; would you like to walk me there?"

"You bet I will." Walking her home, I told her I had planned to go to church this evening. "Will you go with me?"

"Yes, I don't belong to that church, but I'll go anyway."

I left her standing on the porch of her home. I said to myself, "I feel better meeting this good looking girl." I could hardly wait to see her again. It was not far to my room from her house. I took a short nap.

On the way to her house, I stopped at the bakery and had two donuts for supper. As I approached her house, she met me on the sidewalk. She asked, "Do you go to church much at home?"

"Most of the time I go every Sunday." We walked to the church and went down to the basement where the young people were meeting. It was a little strange, to say the least. There was little talk of Jesus or of God, a lot of talk of the new Germany. One girl asked Rose why she was there. "You don't belong to this church." Rose only looked away.

I told the girl, "She's with me." That's all that was said.

After the meeting, Rose and I walked on the way to her home. She had said very little, I was afraid I had offended her somehow. We were passing a short wall of a house. I asked if we could sit and talk awhile. She sat right down, took my hand and said, "Frank, you are the most pleasant boy I have ever met. You must know that I am Catholic, do you care?"

"No, I think that's swell; you are the kind of girl I am

looking for. Rose, would you leave your country and come live in America if you fell in love with me?"

"I can't answer your question, only if I fell for you."

We stood, I took her in my arms, she looked up at me, and her beautiful round laughing eyes looked straight into mine. Her dimpled cheeks and long brown hair made a perfect picture in the dim moonlight. I could not help myself, I kissed her soft lips. She pulled away, then came back and kissed me hard on the lips.

"I've never been kissed by a boy before."

"I hope I'm the first and the last."

She was smiling as she spoke, "You speak German very well, did you learn it in school?"

"No, my grandparents are German, they speak it all the time, so does my Father. My mother is French. She made my brothers and I learn as we grew up. We also speak Mexican, as that's about all the cowboys on our ranch speak."

"That's wonderful, Frank, to have command of so many languages."

"I wish I was better."

By then we had reached Rose's home. As we climbed the steps to the porch, her mother opened the door and said, "It's late, Rose, past your bedtime."

Rose turned to me and said, "Thank you, Frank, for a swell evening."

Her mother pushed her through the door and gave me a hard look, never saying a word. As I walked away, I said to myself, "I don't think that woman cares for me.

I had a fitful night, I dreamed of Lilly and her mother, somehow Jennifer and Rose seeped into my dreams also.

It was Monday morning; I had a bike to go get. I sang all the way to the auto shop. The song was {Bicycle Built for Two}.

At the shop, she sat out on the sidewalk all polished and shining. Wow! She looked better than I expected, I asked if she ran. Hans said, "Like a top. She's full of fuel and waiting for you, I checked her out complete. She is ready to take you anywhere you want to go."

I paid him, got on and kicked the starter. She fired right up. "Thank you, Hans!" I yelled over the engine noise and rode out on to the street.

It was an hour before I had to be in class, so I took a ride around town, and then parked in the lot at school. Several guys came over and told me the Army had many bikes with side cars like mine. After class, I drove around some more. Hunger got to me, so I went to the café Rose worked at. She wasn't there. I asked the boss about her.

He told me she only worked part time now, she had studies to do. She worked a few hours in the mornings only.

I rode passed her house with no results. I went on home to the bakery and parked in the shed at the rear of the building. I went in the shop to see Alfred to tell him about my bike. He gave me some strudel for my supper. I retired to bed after writing letters home to Mom and Uncle Bob.

The week fairly flew by. I had heard more disturbing words about Jews from my classmates. I tried to defend them, saying we had many well known Jews in America and no one said anything bad about them.

One smart ass boy said to me, "You don't know the Jews in this country. They own everything, all our trouble was started by them."

"The Jewish people I have met in Germany have come to be my friends; they don't brag or are pushy at all."

That boy didn't like what I said but he would not challenge me. After that, I didn't hear much from the students about the Jews.

I kept going to the café Rose worked at, but I had not seen her in quite awhile. I began to wonder if my kissing her turned her away from me. I thought I sure was jinxed when it came to women. I thought I should turn to God, maybe he could help me.

I hope he can find a girl I could be with awhile.

Chapter 7

Rose – Doctor Wolfe

This is what I came to Europe to learn. Professor Hoffmann was a wonderful teacher; he made the subject of architecture easy. I now see why my Uncle Bob wanted me to come to Europe. The days flew, the subjects were first rate, I loved this school. Even most of the students were becoming friendly.

Saturday morning I was up early. I wanted to take a ride on my bike and see some of the countryside. At Rose's café, I was eating breakfast when Rose came to work. My bike sat at the curb in all its glory.

From my table, I saw her stop to look at my beauty. She came in and talked to her boss, then came to my table and sat down. She said, "My boss just gave me the day off. You want to make a day of it with me?"

"Holy Cow, you bet! We'll take a ride out into the country."

She said, "We should go tell my daddy we're going for a ride." Her words took me back a bit.

"Are you sure he'll approve of me and my motorcycle?"

"Oh, yes," she said. "I told him all about you. He likes Americans. Frank, he was in the war and was captured by the Marine American soldiers. He said they treated all the captured Germans very well. He wants to meet you and see your BMW, he had one when he was young."

"I'm going to like your Father; he's my kind of man. When can we go to see him?" All my fear of meeting her father suddenly disappeared.

"He's the desk man at the main Police Station; it's in the

heart of Munich. We can go see him now." We went out to the bike. I gave her a leather helmet and goggles. She put them on, I told her she looked just like Amelia Earhart.

She asked, "Who's that?"

"Only the greatest woman American flyer. You could pass for her." She got a big laugh out of that. She gave me the cutest smile I ever saw. I pulled my helmet on and fired my beauty of a bike up. She climbed in the sidecar and we were off to the police station.

At the station, I backed the BMW into the curb where there were several police bikes parked. Rose jumped out and strolled right into the station. I had to hurry to catch up with her. She went right to the policeman behind a desk. He got up and came around the desk to meet us. What a good looking man her dad was. He saw me and put his right hand out and I shook it.

"This is Frank, my American friend," Rose said proudly.

"Who else?" her father said looking at her with the helmet and goggles on. He asked, "Are you going flying?" he was laughing as he spoke.

"Don't you laugh; Frank told me I look just like Amelia Earhart? You know who she is?"

"Yes, pet, I read the papers. She's a great American woman flier." I liked her dad. "Where are you kids going?" he asked.

"For a ride in the country," Rose answered with lots of enthusiasm.

He turned to me and asked, "Do you have a sticker for your bike?"

"No, sir. I didn't know I had to have one."

"Come to the desk, I'll issue you one." He went to a drawer and gave me a large red sticker with a black swastika on it. "Put it on your front wheel cover, it will take you anywhere you want to go, almost."

I thanked him and said again, "I didn't know I had to have

one."

"You bought the bike from Hans. He should have told you, you had to have one." Rose's daddy was a nice guy. I'd met many good people like him in Nazi Germany. He asked again where we were going.

"For a ride in the country," Rose told him.

Her daddy told us not to go north. The army was having some kind of war maneuvers that way. "Go southeast. I'll give you a pass to go thirty meters, no farther."

"I would like to take her to the movies when we get back." As I spoke, I gave him my best eye to eye look.

He said, as he gave me a hard look, "You have her home by midnight."

"Yes, sir, I will, I promise."

On the way to the bike, she was skipping and kind of dancing, she jumped right in the side car. She was as cute as a bug, just as cute as a girl could be. I'm a lucky guy, to have met her. It seemed I'd been very lucky meeting nice girls.

I got on the bike and looked across the street at a huge flag hanging from the building; it was red and had a white circle with the black swastika. I asked what the place was.

"It's Gestapo headquarters. A place you don't want to go," she said. "From what I've heard, no one wants to go there. My daddy says people go in and never come back."

I fired up and we headed southeast to Roseenheimer str., across the Isar River and on to the road going to Salzburg. It was a clear, cloudless fall day; the blue sky was never bluer. There was a bit of a cold nip in the air, my jacket felt good. I rode slowly, the fresh air in our faces made you glad to be alive.

Rose was having a great time with both hands in the air making them float. She was smiling and laughing until a big bug hit her square in the face. I pulled over to see if she was hurt. "It hurts," she was almost crying. A big red round welt appeared on her left cheek.

I lifted my goggles and said, "Come over, I'll fix it." She leaned over and I kissed her cheek. She got out of the sidecar and climbed a small rise and sat down. I climbed up and sat beside her.

I was looking her hurt over when two German soldiers pulled up on motorcycles. Both men came around my bike and stood before us. Both had rifles slung over their backs. The older one demanded our papers. She went to the sidecar and got hers. I gave him my passport and the pass Rose's father gave me. The other one was looking Rose over pretty good. He was about our age. The one with me made me take off my helmet and goggles he made me stand and raise my hands, he patted me down. The other started to do the same to Rose.

In no uncertain terms she said, "Don't you dare touch me." He didn't.

The older one said, "They're just kids. What's a nice German girl doing with this American?" he was addressing Rose.

"That's none of you business." She came over and stood next to me.

He threw my papers on the ground, gave Rose hers and told the other soldier, "Let's go," in a gruff voice. They fired up and left.

Rose said, "Two nasty men. Let's go, I know where there's a village we can get something to eat."

We rode a little farther. She had me turn off on a dirt road. In a few meters, we entered the village of Miesback. A beautiful little village set in a mountain meadow. There was a small café and we had a sandwich and a beer.

Back at the bike, we had drawn a crowd of youngsters. They were looking the BMW over. Rose climbed in the sidecar and put on her helmet and starting telling them all about the machine. More kids came. Rose told them I was an American. One little girl touched me. She said I looked like everyone else. Rose told them that some of my people were from Germany.

One girl came and gave me a St. Christopher medal on a chain. "It will keep you safe in Germany," she said.

I tried not to take it but Rose said I should. "This village is Catholic, see the church?" She pointed to a beautiful little chapel, I hadn't noticed it before. Rose said, "I'm a Catholic, too."

"I guessed that," I told her.

We wished all the kids good luck, good bye and drove back to the main road. We drove a few meters on to the east and stopped by a big lake. We sat talking for a while. The shadows began to get long. We had to head back to Munich before it got dark.

In town, we stopped at the Carlton café and had supper. Now it was after dark, I wanted to take her to a movie. She wanted to see a German film called {Triumph of Will.} It was showing at a local movie house. She told me her Father didn't want her to see it until she grew up. "Do you think I'm old enough to see an adult film?"

"Is it a dirty film?"

"Oh no, it's about Germany, the Fuhrer, the Nazi party and all that. I would like to see it."

"Okay, let's go have a look."

What a letdown that film was, I wasted my money on that awful movie. You would think by that movie that the Nazi party was the second coming of Jesus Christ. What a phony, I think half the people in that movie house thought that Hitler was the German Messiah the way they were applauding at every mention of Hitler's name.

I got Rose home around eleven o'clock. We sat on the front

porch until her mother came out and told her, "It's time for bed." I wanted to meet her mother again. I could see where Rose got her good looks. I told her mom that, I got a great smile from her. I told them good night, drove home, put the bike in the shed and went up to bed without a shower, I was dead tired.

I was awakened by the sound of glass breaking. I jumped from my bed, looked out the window down at the street below. What a terrible sight, two men in brown clothing were beating an old man with a club. Others were breaking windows out of all the shops that I could see. What was going on? I asked myself.

A young man came from one of the shops across the way. He tried to run up the street. Three of the hoodlums knocked him down and beat him with clubs unmercifully. The poor guy never had a chance.

It was all over in a few minutes the street became quiet. It was Sunday morning. What a way to greet the Lord's Day. I got dressed as quickly as I could and went down on the street to see if I could help these poor people. Other people had come out to help. The man beaten so savagely was dead; Good God, what a mess all the shops had their windows broken out, all accept the bakery. All the windows were broken that had the Star of David on them.

I was helping an older man when Alfred came to help me to get the man into one of the shops. His wife was there. She was crying uncontrollably. When she saw we were trying to help, she led us to their rooms in the back of the shop. This old man was a clock maker. The hoodlums had broken both his hands; at least he was alive. We laid him on a bed, she said she would take care of him now.

Alfred said we should get over to the bakery. "The thugs may come back. We better be off the street." I followed him over to the bakery. Inside, he said, "This kind of savage beating of Jews and destroying their property has been going on all night. The radio has named it {Pogrom}, the Destruction of Jewish Property. The Nazis are calling last night {Crystal Night}, the breaking of Jewish glass. I would feel bad to be a German today."

"Surely the police could have stopped these men?" I questioned Alfred.

"No, they just watched. I saw it time and time again as I came to the shop. The police just stood by and watched."

"How can that be? The police are supposed to help the people." I was more confused than ever.

Alfred suggested we should stay off the streets today. "I have food in the ice box and a hot plate in the rear room. We can fix our meals here." He said he was concerned for our safety. "These thugs running the streets may jump anyone they find out there. Let's not take the chance." I agreed to his suggestion.

We stayed all day in the bakery. I got to know Alfred a little better that day. He told me if I ever needed him he was more than ready to help me. Jeepers, what a nice guy he was.

That night, I stayed in my room and had a fitful night's sleep. I wrote Mom and Dad a letter but said nothing of the trouble I had seen. If my incoming letters were being opened, I was sure outgoing ones were, too. I played it cool.

Monday morning, I got the bike out and rode to school without breakfast. There was a buzz going on about Crystal Night. I didn't hear many students condemn the brown shirts' actions against the Jews.

At lunch, I went to the school cafeteria to eat. A young lady came to me and told me Professor Hoffmann wanted to see me in his office. I hurried to finish my lunch and went to his office. He was having his lunch out of a brown paper bag. He asked me to sit down as he wanted to have a talk. "You had trouble in your neighborhood where you have rooms?"

I replied, "It was a terrible Sunday; worst I ever had."

"Frank," he said, "I want you to move from that place. Your safety is my concern. This kind of trouble is just the beginning."

"Sir, I don't know where I can find another room in such short order."

"I have already procured you a room if you want it."

"Yes, sir, I would like to have a room closer to the university."

"Fine, a friend has a home very near here. He said he would be proud to have you live in his house."

"Sir, I can't thank you enough for your kindness."

"The man's name is Doctor Max Wolfe."

"I know his house; it is very near the Golden house." I was surprised to hear I could live close to Jennifer's old house.

The professor told me that Doctor Wolfe would be at home waiting to meet me this afternoon. I couldn't be more pleased. I rode my bike and parked at the curb. At three thirty, I was at the doctor's home ringing the doorbell. This was the most beautiful red brick house. It was a three story structure, with a steep roof and many cupolas. A young lady answered my ring.

"I would like to see Doctor Wolfe," I told her.

"What about?" she asked.

"It's personal,"

She looked me over pretty good, then said, "Come on in, I'll see if he's in."

I followed her down a hall into a huge living room. On the way, I got a good look at this girl. She was a blonde with a gorgeous suntanned face and sky blue eyes. She had a magnificent body that showed even in the full dress she had on. As she walked, her hips swung from side to side. A real pleasure for a man to look at. When she stopped and turned around, I could tell she had enjoyed my looking her over.

She knocked on a door. A man's voice invited us in. This very distinguish looking elderly man got up from a desk and welcomed me with an extended hand. "You're Frank, I presume?"

"Yes, sir, Doctor Wolfe?"

"Frank, I have wanted to meet you for some time. Professor Hoffmann speaks very highly of you. Did he tell you why I wanted to see you?" He had taken off his glasses and was rubbing his face with his left hand.

"Yes, sir; he did. Professor Hoffmann was kind to say that. I like him a lot."

"Well, Frank, would you like to live in our house?"

"Yes, sir, I would be most happy to live here."

The young girl spoke up and said, "Father, when have we started taking strangers into our home? Especially foreigners."

"Helga, this young man is in need. We can fill that need. So hush yourself and go get your mother. I want her to meet Frank."

"Doctor Wolfe, I can pay for my room and board."

"Frank; that will be between you and my Mrs. I like having young people around."

The young girl did as her father requested and left the room.

"My daughter Helga is a spoiled young woman and a problem, it's my fault, I have never corrected or punished her in her lifetime. I have three children, Helga and two sons."

A very neatly dressed woman came into the room. She looked younger than the Doctor. She had graying blonde hair, blue eyes and a beautiful smile. All in all, a tall, slim, very good-looking woman. She put out her hand, "You must be Frank, the American boy we've heard so much about."

"Yes, ma'am, I am. I hope you've heard good things of me?"

"Yes, nothing but," she said with a smile. "My husband has the highest regard for Americans."

"Yes, I do, Frank. I was in the war and captured by your Army. They treated me very well." He was very gracious as he spoke.

The daughter was entering the room and had overheard her father. "Father; that can't be true. The enemy is always the enemy."

"Helga, you've been listening to the Nazis too much. I was treated well as anyone could be."

Frau Wolfe asked if I would like to see my room. "Yes, I would. I can pay for my room and board just let me know how much."

"Don't worry about that. We have a housekeeper and a cook. You can pay anything you want. Now come with me, I'll show you your room."

We went thru the living room into the entrance hall. A large staircase on the right took us to the second floor. A smaller staircase led to the next floor. She opened a door that led to a nice comfortable bedroom. It had a large four poster double bed, a night stand, a desk and a rocking chair, it is well lighted with lamps, a very nice room. It was on the front of the house and had a large window overlooking the front of the house and the street. I asked Frau Wolfe if I could pay for my room and board.

"Please call me Bette; I want to be your friend. Do you like the room?"

"Yes, ma'am, it's a wonderful room."

"No one stays on this floor. The bathroom is at the end of the hall. Will you move in today?"

"Yes, ma'am, I can go get my things now." I wanted to

make the move as soon as possible.

Downstairs, I told the Doctor I found his home as nice as I had ever seen someone's home. "I'll go for my things and be back shortly." I was really impressed with the doctor and his family.

Chapter 8

Rose – Helga

On my way to the bakery and my rooms, I stopped to see Rose. Her father answered my knock. "Is Rose home?" I asked. "No, Frank, she has gone to Berlin to go to school."

"When did she decide to do that?" I was very frustrated and puzzled. Why would she do that, I asked myself.

"She had been trying to make her mind up for some time. She had applied to the Sisters of St. Francis to become a Nun. She had applied when she finished high school. They accepted her yesterday."

"Holy cow, she never mentioned that to me." I was completely taken aback.

Her father said, "I think you helped to make her mind up. She left a letter for you, I'll go get it." When he returned, he handed me the letter. He apologized for Rose not telling me her plans.

I thanked him, said goodbye and rode my bike over to the bakery. I had that old empty feeling again. Why every time I found a girl I really liked she left me? I must be jinxed when it came to the fair sex.

I went in and told Alfred I had a new room near the university. He said that was fine. "I'll help with your trunk when you're ready."

I went up to my room and sat on the bed. I started to open Rose's letter but decided to wait. I guess I was afraid of what she would tell me. I packed my trunk and suitcase. Put my letter from Rose inside my shirt and called for Alfred to come and help. We loaded the trunk and suitcase into the side car. I told Alfred how much I appreciated his help, I said goodbye and told him that I would see him soon.

He reminded me, "If you ever need me, I'll be here." What a great guy.

At Doctor Wolfe's, I parked in the rear of the house by the garage. The Doctor came out of the back porch with a young man. He introduced him as his son Marius. He said Marius would help me take my trunk up to my room. Marius looked like he really didn't care to do that and said so.

"Come on Marius," his father said, "It won't hurt to be helpful."

We set my trunk on the porch and as I went to get the suitcase it started to rain. The Doctor opened the garage and helped push my bike inside. He told me to keep the bike in the garage. There was plenty of room. There were two nearly new autos there. One looked like a Ford that was made in my country. The Doctor told me that the Ford Company had a factory in Germany.

"This is great to be able to park my bike in your garage. I can walk to school from here."

Marius helped take my trunk to my room. He said nothing as we did the task. I thanked him for the help. He said not a word in return. He was a strange boy to say the least. I took my suitcase up and returned to the living room.

Bette called for everyone to come in the dining room for supper. I was introduced to the youngest son Fritz. They said he had just turned ten years old. He wasn't friendly at all. He never said a word or smiled. He just looked blank. The Doctor made a point to tell me the others kids ages. Marius was seventeen and Helga nineteen. The doctor said a short prayer; I noticed none of the children bowed their heads. All three looked bored.

After supper, we retired to a solarium on the back of the

house. It was raining hard outside. Bette served coffee to all but Fritz. Strong black coffee. The two house women came in and said they were leaving. Bette introduced me to them as their new student boarder from America. "Gera is our good cook and Anne is the best housekeeper in all of Germany." The two women looked to be fifty or a little older.

I told them I was happy to meet them and I would try not to make any more work for them. Both seemed pleased to hear that. They said good night. I saw them leave by the back porch. Both had umbrellas. I asked Bette where they lived.

"Across the river in the south part of town. They travel by trolley. Both ladies have sons in the army."

Helga spoke up and said, "One of the sons went to high school with me and now he's in the Waffen SS. He looks marvelous in his uniform, he's very handsome."

Marius interjected, "I'll join the SS when I get out of high school. I'm a leader in the Hitler youth."

I said nothing to their remarks. The Doctor and Bette looked dejected; neither said anything to discourage the children.

We sat talking until after ten p.m. They all asked about my home in America and why I had come to Germany to study. My answers about my studies seemed to satisfy all the children. Fritz really got friendly when I told them I was raised on a cattle ranch and had been a cowboy. I could tell Fritz had seen our Hollywood movies about cowboys. I sure didn't want to break his fantasy about cowboys. He asked if we all carried guns.

I told him, "Only during the roundups." His face really lit up at that talk.

I said goodnight and how happy I was to be in their beautiful home. In my room, I unpacked, I sat down to read Rose's letter.

Oct. 1938

Dear Frank,

When you read this letter, I will try to make you understand why I couldn't see you again. You see, Frank, I have wanted to be a Nun all my life. When I met you, I started changing my mind. When I found out I was accepted to the Sisters of St Francis, I just had to go.

Frank, I was afraid if I stayed in Munich my heart would belong to you. You are so handsome, kind... a wonderful person. I did enjoy your company.

Please forgive me.

Your friend, Rose.

I want-a tell ya, it was all I could do to keep from crying. I did shed some tears. Damn. I liked that girl. I said a prayer and asked God to take care of her. I went down and took a hot bath and I did shed some more tears just thinking about her. The jinx remained.

The next morning, I had breakfast with Helga and her mother. I found she and I were classmates. In my social studies hour, she said she had seen me before. I had never seen her there. That's one class I couldn't stay awake in if I wanted to. It's all about how great Germany has become since the Great War and under the Nazis. It's all propaganda. It was a dead class for me. She said she had seen me there. "All my girl friends would like to meet you."

Hmm, maybe things would get better. I felt a little better already. There were many pretty girls in this Munich University. I liked pretty girls, as anyone could tell.

That morning, Helga and I walked together to school. I found this girl was a lot of fun to be with as she joked about everything we talked about. She was tall and pretty darn good looking. She even told a joke about the Nazis. The way she had talked the night before I kind of figured she was impressed about the Nazi party. Anyway, she introduced me to a half dozen of her girlfriends and a couple of boys she called good friends. All these young people were good looking and were friendly.

The school day flew by. I skipped lunch and spent the time in study hall. When I came out of the building, there sat Helga on the steps. I passed her by. She jumped up, grabbed my arm and said she was waiting for me.

"Why?" I asked.

She said, "I want to protect you. I heard some of our boys say they were going to see what an American was made of."

"They want to fight?" I asked her.

"Aren't there bullies in your country?"

"Sure, there will always be bullies anywhere you go," I told her. "I'm not going to fight, but if they think I'm afraid, they'll be surprised."

"Some of these fellows think they're tough, at least they talk tough," she said. "Come on, let's hurry, maybe we will miss them."

I asked her to let me carry her books. She did.

We had walked for several blocks when four brown uniformed young guys blocked our way. "Why are you with this American, Helga?" the one who acted as the leader asked.

"It's none of your business. Go away and leave us alone. Frank's not bothering you."

I was real brave. I guess because Helga was there. I said, "If one of you brave guys want a fight, step forward and I'll do my best to accommodate you." I showed a doubled up right fist and a set jaw. I didn't get any takers. These guys were all bluff, I said to myself. "Now get out of our way and let a lady pass." I was mad and figured I would hit the leader in the nose first, but they all backed away and let us by.

Helga put her arm thru mine and as we walked away she said, "Do you know you're a very handsome young man?" She smiled and rubbed her cheek on my shoulder.

"Go on, Helga. You're just saying that because it's true." She got a big kick out of my saying that, she was laughing hard. "You're not too bad to look at either," I told her. Now she was really making up to me.

She asked if I would take her for a ride on my bike. I told her I would if her folks said it was okay. "Can we go this weekend?"

"I'll look forward to it," I told her. She rubbed her cheek again on my shoulder and was smiling all the time. She was a very attractive girl and not a bit shy. I liked that in a girl. She reminded me a lot of Gloria, my first love.

At the house, Bette said, "A Jewish man shot a high ranking Nazi official in Paris, France. It was on all the news. Your father is really upset. He's afraid the shooting might start a war like it did in 1914."

"When will father be home?" Helga asked.

"He called and said that Professor Hoffmann and Father Green are coming to dine with us this evening. He asked that Frank should be offered an invitation to be with us. Will you, Frank?" Bette asked me.

"Yes, ma'am, I'll be pleased to have dinner with you and your guests."

That evening, we had a delicious meal of stuffed turkey, mashed potatoes, brown gravy and green beans.

The three men and I retired to the Doctor's study. A room filled with a large bookcase, a big desk and pictures on the wall of famous German writers, mostly men and one woman. There we men had coffee and an apple strudel for dessert.

After eating, the three lit up a cigar or a pipe and began to talk of the shooting in Paris. I was most interested in what these learned men had to say.

The Doctor asked, "Do you think this shooting will start a war with France?"

Father Green said, "No, Hitler wants something bigger than a Jew killing a Nazi."

Professor Hoffmann agreed. "I think he's looking to the east. He wants more land for his new Germany. He implies this in all his latest speeches."

The Doctor talked directly to me and said, "Frank, what you hear here, let go no farther. We have known men to disappear for having talks like this. Please keep our talk to yourself." I promised I would.

The men started to discuss the good things that Herr Hitler had done for Germany. I was very interested in what they had to say and asked, "If Germany is in such a state of depression, where does the money come from to make all the improvements he's making?"

The professor said, "The Treaty of Versailles is not being adhered to. Germany and the Nazis have refused to give any more reparations and France, England and your country are not going to challenge them. The Fuhrer is using that money for social reform and to build up the military."

Bette came in with more coffee. German coffee is much stronger than ours at home.

Father Green said that the Fuhrer was doing wondrous things for the country. "If he died soon, he would go down in history as the greatest German leader of all time." This talk really puzzled me and I asked why this was? Father Green elaborated, "The Fuhrer has started old age benefits. In your country it's called Social Security. It's been well received here. The old folks are happy to have it. His economic policies have awakened our whole economic system."

"Yes," the Doctor said. "I like what he has done with the autobahns. When it's all finished, it will unite all the nation in a way never before."

The professor agreed. "He's making life a lot better for the most of us. Too bad he dislikes the Jews so much."

Father Green said, "I think he blames the loss of the war on the Jews, and I understand he says the Jewish doctor who treated his mother contributed to her death. He was in love with her so much it almost killed him when she died."

The Doctor said, "I think that's the most irresponsible notion I've ever heard. Why would anyone even suggest a doctor would kill a person on purpose? I just don't understand his feelings?"

The men kept talking about the Fuhrer. I could tell they had a lot of pent up anxiety about the Nazi party and its leader. "Herr Hitler is doing his best to put all the people into an auto with this new people's car. He calls it the Volkswagen. I understand it is cheap to build and anyone can buy one, even the average German. It's small and will get many meters to a gallon."

Father Green seemed impressed with the new car. Professor Hoffman said he had seen one in Berlin on his last trip. "It's small, but four people can ride in it and it's air cooled; it won't freeze in the winter. That's a plus for a country doctor. Don't you agree Max?"

"Yes, the concept is good, everyone should have an auto. The thing I like the best that he is doing is the strict pollution control and the numerous park and green areas he is developing." All three men agreed the Fuhrer was doing some good things, but the Nazis treatment of the Jews overshadowed the good.

The men decided to meet again in a few weeks and we bid each other good night. This was a very enlightening evening for me. I went up to my room and wrote Mom and Uncle Bob a letter saying I was having a good time. If someone read my mail, they would get the idea I liked it here in Germany.

The next morning, I walked to school with Helga. She invited me to join her the next day, Saturday, November the ninth. A parade would be held in Munich to commemorate the martyred dead who gave their lives in the 1923 putsch. She said that the Fuhrer and all the head men of the Nazi party would march. I told her I would go just to see what it was all about.

That day it was quite a show. People lined the way with hands held high in the Nazi salute. A band played the Nazi marching song, {THE FLAGS HIGH}. All along the route, pylons bearing smoldering urns bore the names of those killed in the putsch. I thought Helga was going to wet her pants when Hitler walked by, smiled and waved at her. She held her right arm high in the Nazi salute. She was yelling, "SIG HEIL, SIG HEIL."

I made pretty light of the whole thing. I told her I had met the man and he had the hand shake of a wet noodle. She didn't take that very well, but I really didn't care. I invited her for a ride on my motorcycle Sunday afternoon. She soon forgot all about Herr Hitler. She got all excited about a ride on my bike. Just like a woman.

After the parade, Helga and I stopped to see Rose's father and asked for a pass like he had given me before. He seemed glad to do it. Across the street from police headquarters, there was a big commotion at the Gestapo. I asked what was going on. Her father said some people had been arrested for making trouble at the parade. "Most likely, those people will get a stiff jail sentence."

"What did they do?" I asked.

"I heard they were hissing at the Fuhrer." I just shook my

head in disbelief. He said, "It's a sad day in Munich today." I agreed, then I asked about Rose. He said she was getting along fine, but didn't know it was going to be so hard to be a Nun. I told him when he writes to give her my best. Then I bid him goodbye.

As we walked home, Helga wanted to know all about my relations with Rose. I could see she was worried about it. I passed it off the best I could. That evening, we had a wonderful meal and a good time playing cards, late into the evening. It started to rain hard around the time I went to bed. It sounded great beating a tattoo on the roof. It put me fast to sleep.

The next morning, Helga woke me up at six a.m. by knocking on my door. I invited her in. She came, sat on my bed and said she was excited to go for our ride. I asked if the streets were wet. She didn't know. "Does it matter?" I told her it was a little scary to ride on wet pavement. All she said was, "I'll chance it." I told her to leave so I could get dressed. She did.

At breakfast, I asked if her mother had given her permission to go for the ride. Her Mom heard and said it was okay as long as I was careful. "I will be," is all I could say.

We pushed the BMW out onto the drive and I fired her up. Helga hopped on the back, with her arms tight around my chest. I wanted her to ride in the sidecar. She said she wanted to ride on the seat with me. I gently rode the bike out onto the street. The streets were damp but not wet. The going was okay.

We went out the same road Rose and I had gone and stopped at the same lake. There we sat on the grass and had a long conversation about Germany and Hitler. She told me her father had taken the family to the 1936 Olympics. "We were there for the opening ceremonies. It was the most wonderful day. The sky was clear and blue, and all the people were having a good time. The Fuhrer lead a parade into the stadium and trumpets greeted his coming. A large chorus sang

{Deutschland uber alles} and also sang "Horst Wessel Lied," then they sang the Olympic Hymn. It was written by Richard Strauss. All the athletes from the different nations paraded around the stadium. Then the games began. We had to go home. I would have liked to stay and watch the Germans win the most medals. Germany won the whole thing," she said so proudly.

"America won a few." I was going to say something about Jesse Owens but she blabbed on so I gave up. We got back home just in time for supper.

November passed so fast I couldn't believe it was December already. We had lots of snow. It was a real white Christmas. We heard very little news in Germany now. The Doctor's family was so good to me I hardly missed not being home that Christmas. The Doctor gave a big party for New Years. I had never drunk champagne before; I found it to my liking. I had a Merry Christmas and a Happy New Year 1939!

Chapter 9

Helga – Nazis

Springtime in Munich was beautiful. The snow was gone, the birds and bees were singing and humming everywhere. All the flowers were in bloom, a sweet smell of new mown grass filled your nostrils. The sky was a beautiful blue, big puffy clouds drifted lazily across the heavens. Everything seemed alright in the world for me. My school was going great and my home life was looking up.

Helga and I were becoming good friends. So much so, her mother took me aside to have a friendly heart to heart. "Frank, our Helga is falling for you. All she talks about is you. Do you have any feelings for her?"

Holy Cow, what could I say? "I like her very much. She has quit talking about Hitler and the Nazi party. She asks a lot of questions about my home in America."

Bette said that she was glad Helga had stopped talking about Hitler. She said she was afraid Helga had a crush on the Fuhrer like a lot of other young girls in Germany. "Now she never says a word about him anymore. I think she is putting her attention on you, Frank. Her father and I approve of that. You are a very nice boy. We're proud to have you in our home." Then she shook her finger in my face as she spoke, "We don't want any funny business out of you two, if you know what I mean."

"I get your drift." What could I say to a girl's mother? I'm not that kind of guy? She wouldn't believe me anyway. You know all kids our age have a bee in their bonnet, or so I've heard. Sometimes my bee gets pretty big. Anyway, I told her I wouldn't try anything with her daughter. That seemed to satisfy her.

It was funny to me; the very next day Helga invited me on a trip to Nuremberg to attend Nazi Party Day. It was the biggest day of the year for the Nazis. Helga told me that was where Lei Riefenstahl made the movie Triumph of the Will. She wanted to know if I had seen it. I said I had. Then she asked, "How did you like it?"

I said it was okay. What could I say? I didn't want to make her mad by telling the truth, it was a sorry film. I turned the subject off as soon as I could. I asked if she would go for a ride on my bike. She jumped at the suggestion.

I rolled the baby out of the garage, fired her up. I gave her helmet and goggles. She put them on and jumped into the sidecar. We took off and cruised around town for a while. She was having a great time. She waved to her friends as we passed by. She really got a kick out of the ride.

When we went by the police station, I saw Rose's daddy standing in the door. He waved and pointed to the Gestapo headquarters across the way.

I looked where he pointed and saw a group of black uniformed men giving us the once over. For some unknown reason, I felt uneasy over that. We circled around a while longer then went to Theresienwiese; it's a park where a big Oktoberfest like celebration was being held. I guessed it is a new year's party. I parked the bike and we walked around awhile.

Helga was a pure pleasure to be with. She liked me to tell her about America. Of course, I liked talking of my home. When she got off on Hitler and the new Germany, it was another story.

We found a bench and sat awhile talking. She really got to talking about the Fuhrer and the Nazi party. How wonderful it was that he had made living in Germany for German people better than it had ever been. "Your President should take pointers from our leader."

This made me mad. I told her, "We have the best type of government there is. Your Fuhrer is a dictator. I don't want one man having life or death in his hands. I don't want to live the rest of my life under a dictator. In America, we vote and have a little bit to say how the government is run." Boy-o-boy did I hit a sore spot.

She answered curly saying, "Your country is a pot of discontent, all the papers in the world say so. Your government treats the minority badly. Your black people are going to revolt one of these days, they're under the heel of bad people, and all our teachers say so. Why they can't even drink at the same water fountain and use the same bathroom you do."

"Yes, we do have some bad things going on, but I never saw a policeman beating or killing our citizens."

She came back with, "Your country will never be a world power. Germany will rule the world some day. You just wait and see."

Now she made me real mad. "This man of yours, Mister pompous little Hitler, is just a wimp. He wouldn't even congratulate Jesse Owens, the world's greatest athlete, when he won at the Olympic Games in Berlin. What kind of man is like that?"

"Frank," she said, "We can argue all day and neither of us can be proven right. I like you too much to go on with this conversation."

I told her she was right. "I like you very much. You have all the things to make any man happy. A beautiful face, lovely hair, a desirable body and a great personality, I could fall for you." That seemed to make her happy. I added, "You also have great looking legs." We both laughed at what I had said.

"Thank you, Frank, for the kind words. Will you go with me to Nuremberg next week? The Nazi party has a big celebration every year. I think you would like to see it. Will you go? Please?"

What could I say? She asked so nicely, I said yes without thinking. My afterthought was why I had agreed to go. Holy Cow, I don't give a rip about the Nazi party or the things they celebrate.

I told her we must get permission from her parents before we make any plans. I was hoping they would say no. We rode on home. She went straight to her mother. She told her mother I wanted to take her to the Nuremberg doings. I stopped her and said, "This is all Helga's idea, I just agreed to go with her if you said it was okay."

Bette gave us both a hard look. Then she asked, "How do you plan on going? Not on the motorbike I hope."

Helga said "No mother, we can take the train and stay at Uncle Ludwig's house. He lives in Ansback; we can take the train to the party celebration."

Her Mom looked to me saying, "Frank, if I say okay, no funny business."

"No funny business from me, I promise."

Helga spoke up, "We're going to watch the celebration. Don't you trust us mother?"

Bette's response was, "I was young once. I know how your hormones work. Helga, you leave Frank alone, I'm sure he'll leave you alone." She knew Helga, that woman was smart. She knew Helga pretty well. Bette gave us permission to go.

We started to make plans to go to Nuremberg. Holy Cow, I really didn't want to see a bunch of Nazis parade around waving flags and listen to their propaganda. I'm into it now, I'll have to go.

That evening, I had a long talk with Doctor Wolfe in

private. It was about the Nazi party celebration. He said they do it every year at this time. He told me to go and see how bad the people are brainwashed about Hitler and his crowd. "Go, but say nothing. Talking bad about them can get you in trouble." I said I wouldn't say anything. Doctor Wolfe was one smart guy. He had my respect.

On March 11th, Nazi Germany troops crossed the frontier of Austria and occupied the country. I told Helga that America would never do such a thing to another country. She said nothing and just shrugged her shoulders. She made a funny face, I gave up.

As the weeks passed, I regretted telling Helga I would go to Nuremberg. I couldn't think of a way to get out of going. Some girls can get a guy into something he doesn't want to do. I wouldn't go if I was paid. Oh well, I must go and make the best of it.

When Helga and I were preparing to go, Doctor Wolfe could see I wasn't very happy about the whole thing. He took me aside and said, "Last year, the Nuremberg rally was rained out, maybe you'll get lucky and it will rain again."

I sure liked the Doctor. "I hope it will rain again. I hope there's a flood at the rally," I told him. We both had a good laugh.

When it was time to go, I packed a bag. Bette drove Helga and me to the train station in their Ford auto. It was a cloudy day and it was misting a little. Bette turned in the front seat to talk to the two of us. She shook a finger at us and said, "No funny business out of you two."

I told her in loud and clear words, "Yes, ma'am."

Helga got huffy and terribly mad. "Mother," she said, "We are two adult people. We can make decisions on our own without advice from you. What we do is our business not yours. I've a good mind to join the army so you can't tell me what I should do."

I thought Bette was going to blow her top. She said in anger and very loudly, "You two behave yourselves."

Helga pushed me out of the car and headed to the station waiting room. I told Bette we would be on our best behavior. She told me, "I'm not worried about you Frank, it's my daughter that's the problem, I can tell what that girl's thinking, I don't like it one bit. She has sex on her mind all the time, I can tell."

I tried to console her. "It will be okay, please don't worry." She nodded yes to me.

I went into the station waiting room. There sat Helga with her legs crossed, so anyone looking could see up her dress, I pulled her leg down, that made her even madder. She said so loud everyone in the room could hear, "My mother made me so mad. If we want to have sex, we can, without her permission."

Holy Cow, I was so embarrassed, I covered my face with my hands. When I looked around, all the people in the room were looking at us and smiling. One old fart gave me a big wink. I said loud so everyone could hear, "Helga, you and I will not do any such thing."

Thank God the train pulled in about that time. We got on board and into a compartment with just the two of us there. I told her how bad she had made her mother feel. I told her we were not having sex now or maybe never.

This was some girl; she proceeded to move next to me, put her arms around my neck and said while tearing up in a little girl's voice, "All our teachers say we women should have children for our Fuhrer. I don't see a thing wrong with that."

"Helga, I'm not having a child for your Fuhrer, now or ever. I won't live under a wimp like him." Boy did the S— hit the fan. She got all curled up in a corner and started to cry. I told her, "Helga, if you're going to act like a little cry baby,

I'm getting off at the next stop." She turned it around in a second, sat up and dried her tears and acted as if nothing had happened.

She said, "Everything is fine." She really turned on the charm. "We'll have a good time at the rally." In her sweetest voice she said, "I love being with you."

I said to myself {this girl is not for me, if she can act this way.}

She came over and put her head on my chest, arms around me and told me how much she liked me. "Wouldn't you like to make love to me?"

"Helga, get off that stuff. If I want a woman, I'll make the moves. The way you act, you just turn me off."

She looked me in the eyes and said, "We will see."

Holy Cow, this girl was not easy to discourage.

The train stopped at the village of Ansback. Only two other people got off besides us. Helga told me her Uncle Ludwig owned a beer hall. It was not far from the station. In a few minutes we were in the hall. She introduced me as her friend Frank, "Our American boarder." He was Bette's older brother, a man of immense stature. He was a jolly and friendly man and almost shook my arm off.

He said he was happy to have us in his home and hoped we would enjoy our stay with him and his wife. We then walked a few blocks to his home. The house was in an upper class neighborhood, a beautiful red brick two story structure. I thought to myself {the beer hall must be a good business.} I found out later he also had two new autos in his garage.

Inside, he introduced me to his wife, a rather heavy set woman with short blond hair, a ready smile and a pretty face. She told us to make ourselves at home. Right away, she showed us pictures of their children, two daughters and a son. Both daughters were married to German soldiers. Both girls had children of their own. We got to see loads of pictures of grandchildren. Their son had just turned twenty-one. He was in training to be a Luftwaffe pilot. I could see the parents were proud of their offspring.

Helga and I were shown separate bedrooms on the second floor. I was told my room was their son's. I could see the boy was an airplane enthusiast as there were pictures of German military planes on all four walls. It was a beautiful room, overlooking the front yard. It even had its own bathroom. It would be a comfortable and pleasant room to be in.

That evening, we were treated to a wonderful meal. The wife was a great cook. After supper, Helga and I took a walk downtown. This was a really nice clean small town. She took my arm as soon as we started to walk. There were many small shops, reminding me of my home town. We window shopped awhile. The girl was really hanging on me as we walked. I tried not to pay much attention to her.

At a coffee house we went in to have some. The place was full of young people having fun and talking silly. There were quite a few soldiers and their girlfriends. No one paid any attention to us.

Helga and I found a small two person table. We had several cups. We then headed for Uncle Ludwig's. On the way, this girl got all over me, I mean all over me. I did my best to discourage her. No go. She kept running her hands over me, if you know what I mean.

At the house, we sat in a porch swing to enjoy the cool evening air. She began to try to kiss me. I did my best to turn her off. Finally, I gave in a little and gave her a good kiss on the lips. Shouldn't have done that. She was a heck of a good kisser. Thank goodness her Uncle came out and insisted we come in and listen to the Fuhrer making a radio speech.

Hitler was saying how good it was to have all his friends

and old army buddies coming to the rally. He went on and on for two hours. Boring, boring. The three of them hung on his every word. I was ready to blow my stack and throw up. I was glad when he finished and everyone wanted to go to bed.

Up in my room, I took a long hot soaking bath. Hitler's words rung in my head. I thought how anyone could fall for his bulls–t. I put on my pj's and slipped into bed. Before I could turn off the light, Helga came thru the door, wearing the sheerest night-gown I had ever seen. I could see all she had and then some. God, she was a well built woman. I told her in my harshest words she should get the heck out of my room. "I promised your mother, don't make me break it." She paid no mind at all. The gown dropped to the floor. She slipped right into my bed stark naked. What a deal! It took all I had to resist. It was a hard time, if you know what I mean.

I asked, "What if your Uncle and Aunt found you in my bed?"

"They sleep downstairs and I don't care what they think." She sounded positive, so I jumped up, went into the bathroom and locked the door. I filled the tub with cold water and sat there for what seemed like hours, I will never know how long I sat there. It was the hardest time I had ever had, turning down this beautiful girl. It was a real challenge. When I peeked into the room, she was gone. Thank the Lord; I locked the door, fell into bed and fell asleep after awhile.

I didn't hear a thing until she was knocking on my room, calling for me to come to breakfast. "Hurry," she called, "We will miss our train to Nuremberg." I could care less, but I did get dressed, went down and had a great meal. The four of us caught the train to the rally.

You should have been there. I never saw so many uniformed people, young and old alike. There were half a dozen bands playing as loud as they could. They played the

Nazi marching song over and over. I thought I would lose my hearing. Flags were everywhere. All had a big black swastika in a white circle on a red background. There were Iron crosses on long poles carried by the Hitler youth, so Helga said.

This whole horde of people was marching around what seemed like hours. They sang the Horst Wessel marching song too loud, I thought I would go deaf, and then things got really bad, the speeches started. There were six speakers; Heir Hitler came to the podium. The whole place jumped up, gave the Nazi salute and yelled "Heil Hitler" over and over again. Finally, he made them stop, I was dumbfounded at this display.

The man talked for hours. When he wasn't talking, he was yelling. He yelled and screamed like he did at the Dreesen Hotel, like he did when I met him before. He kept telling how much he loved the Fatherland and the German people. How he would never let them down and would always take care of them. By the time he finished, I was sick, sick of the whole thing. Wishing I had never come. The people went crazy when he finished. How they carried on, I could not believe.

We four walked back downtown and went to a café Uncle Ludwig said served good meals. Indeed it did, we had a most delicious sauerkraut and franks supper. It did take some time to get served as the place was a little overcrowded

After supper, we returned to the rally to see a night time exposition. I never had seen anything like it. All these people came marching in carrying flags, banners and torches. The marchers pranced around for over an hour. Again, there were more speeches. I want-a tell ya, I had had it by the time it was over.

It was well after midnight by the time we got back to Uncle Ludwig's house. I was dead tired, so were the rest of my companions. We all said good night and off to bed. Helga stopped me and said in a sweet voice, "I'm not too tired to see you later." Holy Cow, didn't she ever give up.

"No," I said, "I'm going to bed." I locked my door, took a hot bath and hit the hay. I slept until Uncle Ludwig woke me calling me to breakfast.

At breakfast, Helga said nothing to me. She did say in a sharp voice, "Let's go home." On the train, she didn't talk at all, at least not to me. At the station, she rushed off and called her mother to come for us. On the way home, Helga said nothing to me or her mother. I tried to make some conversation to no avail. Helga said nothing to me or her mother. At the house she jumped out of the car and into the back porch slamming the door as she went.

Bette knew Helga and I were not speaking. "What happened between you two?" she asked.

"Nothing, absolutely nothing," I replied.

"Ha!" she said. "Helga tried something and you turned her down. Isn't that right, Frank?"

I told her, "All I wanted was to be friends with her."

Bette was one smart woman. She told me Helga would come around and we would be friends again.

That did not happen; Helga would not even talk or look at me. She kept bringing men home to introduce to her folks. One was an SS man. She told her folks she was going to live with him. Her Mother and Father took her news very sadly. Helga moved in with him in an apartment uptown.

Summer came. I looked for a job for the summer while school was out. I found one at Mrs. Dreesen's hotel. She put me to work as a bellboy. I got to really like doing the job. Everybody said I was good at doing bellboy work.

I had worked there about a month when I got a letter directing me to come to Gestapo headquarters the following Monday. Wow! I wondered what the heck this was all about. I went on my bike to see Rose's father to see if he could shed some light on the situation. He had no idea. "Frank," he said, "Come see me just before you go over there. I'll try to find out what they're up to. I want to see how long they keep you." What a good friend he was to worry about me.

"I guess they will ask a lot of questions about the people you have come in contact with while living here. If they ask about me, tell them all you know. I have nothing to hide." I was really puzzled by his remarks.

I told him, "All the people I know are good Germans. Most of the Jews I know are leaving or are already gone."

"They may be looking to see how your friends feel about the Nazi party and what they have told you." I just stood there shaking my head. I couldn't believe this was happening to me. "If anyone has confided to you, try not to mention it to them." I said I would keep a closed mouth.

I thanked him and rode my bike on home. I want-a tell ya, the next few days I had bad feelings of things to come. Doctor Wolfe and all the family gave me a cool time the next few days. I had told them all where I had to go. I guess they were worried I might say bad things about them. Heck, I would never do that. I hoped all would go well for me and my friends.

At Gestapo Headquarters, the whole thing did not amount to much. A big burley guy in a black uniform asked a lot of questions about my being in Germany. He said in a rather nasty tone, "We don't want you Americans here. Why don't you go home?"

I said nothing in return. He told me in no uncertain words to get out of his office. I obliged.

At the hotel, Mrs. Dreesen told me to get my money out of the bank and close my account. She also told me to write my Uncle not to send any more money. I took her advice.

At home, I found the Doctor and Bette in a sad situation; both their sons were taken to a Nazi youth camp. Doctor Wolfe said very sadly, "I have lost all my children."

I've never felt so bad in my life for anyone before. It got a heck of a lot worse for me, more than I could ever imagine.

Chapter 10

Escape from Germany

As the train chugged along, I could tell we were moving in a northerly direction. The sun was coming in on my right shoulder. All the men were having a high old time. All the occupants were singing, laughing and acting as if they were bound for a party. I kept asking myself how in the world I had gotten into this mess. My dad's words drifted back saying, "Frank, you don't want to get caught in a war over there." Here I was, drafted into the German army. I didn't want to be in any army, especially not the Germany army.

By my pocket watch, we stopped at ten a.m. and got off the train. We were made to stand in two columns facing a very stern looking Sergeant. He told us we were going to a basic training camp and would be sworn to the allegiance of the Fuhrer and the Third Reich. "You will swear to die for the Fatherland and the Fuhrer, if necessary." I sure didn't like the sound of that. The men all started "Seig, Heiling" and "Heil Hitler, Heil Hilter." This went on for several minutes until the Sergeant made them stop.

He left-faced us and we started marching on a dirt road leading off to the east thru a forest of large trees. I asked the boy beside me if he knew where we where? "We're near the Danube River, I think. My father took me hunting in this forest when I was a small boy." A soldier passing told us to shut up and quit talking. Singing broke out again.

We marched in step for over an hour, then entered a camp of long low buildings. We stopped in front of one. A road went between this building and the one across the way. It looked to me to be about thirty feet between the buildings. All the structures looked new and built like tar paper shacks. We were told to break, go inside and get ourselves a sleeping cot. I found one in kind of an isolated area. It was off behind a tall green screen. It suited me just fine. We got to rest about an hour, then were told to form up outside to go to noon meal.

Outside, a long line of young girls was lined up and moving toward the food counters across the way. I was in the very rear and I spied an attractive blond in the rear of the girl line. I finally caught her eye and gave her a big smile. She turned away. When she looked back, she looked very sad in the face but it was a lovely, beautiful face.

While filling my plate, I asked the man serving, "Who are these girls and what are they doing here?"

"You don't know?"

"No," I replied.

"They're your entertainment as long as you're here."

"What do you mean entertainment?" I couldn't understand what he meant.

"You dumb duck; they are here to make babies for the Fuhrer. You boys are to be the fathers. Go find one you like; she'll be yours until you leave."

"Holy Cow," I said to myself, "What kind of deal is this?"

I got my food and returned to where everyone had sat down and started eating. I saw the girl who had caught my eye and moved across the road and sat beside her. This was a very attractive young woman. Her shiny blond hair was in two braids wrapped around her head. Her light blue eyes fairly sparkled and when she smiled she had deep dimples in her rosy checks. She looked at me, then turned her head away. When she looked back at me, sadness filled her face.

I poked her with my elbow and asked how she was. She didn't look at me, but I heard her say she didn't belong here. I told her, "I don't belong here either and I don't know how in the hell I got in this mess." She brightened right up and said she was Swedish and had come to Germany for the summer and got put in this baby factory. I told her I was an American and all I wanted was out of here.

She leaned over, put her face next to mine and said, "I know how we can leave, if you will help me."

I was all ears. "How?" I asked.

"Meet me behind this building in ten minutes and I'll show you."

"Lady," I said, "I'll be there." I hurried to the barracks and got my jacket. I returned to where she had sat and finished my meal. I slowly inched my way around the building. There she was waiting. I asked what the deal was?

"We go right out into the forest, I know where we're at, follow me." She took off into the forest, I followed. The trees were fairly thick with a lot of heavy bushes. We were about a hundred yards out when she stopped and told me to lay down beside her. I did as she asked. "A patrol is coming. If they see us, I'll tell you what to do."

She rolled over on her back and said, "Get on top of me quick, I think they can see us." I did as she asked. "They have stopped, they can see us. Pretend we're doing it. They know what we're here for. They won't interfere with us."

I asked, "Can they see us?"

"Yes," she said. "Keep doing it, they're pointing at us and laughing." We kept the same position for a few minutes longer. She said, "They're moving on, get off me and let's go." She took off in a stooped over long run, I followed.

In thirty minutes, I was winded and had to stop. She came back and told me to rest a while. I sat down and watched as she disappeared into the forest. Soon she came back and told me she knew exactly where we were. What a relief. "The Germans are building the Autobahn road a few hundred yards ahead." I could hear equipment working if I listened intently. "We must not be seen," she said.

We moved to where we could observe the workmen and lay hidden until they quit for the day. As we lay there, she told me in a whisper about her life. She was so pretty I had a hard time controlling myself, if you know what I mean. The day drug on and around four p.m. the workers started leaving; by five p.m. all of them were gone.

We emerged from our hiding place and crossed the road into the forest on the other side. We moved south for perhaps an hour, all the time staying alert for vehicles coming down the road. We would hide when one came our way. Finally, we could see a village off to the left. My companion said this was the place we were looking for.

"We'll wait for darkness, then I'll go look for my friends." We found a good spot to observe the goings on in the village. We sat for over an hour. In this time, I found out her name was Inga Swanson. She said she was from Stockholm, Sweden. She was as bright a person as I had ever met. The friends she had in the village had come to Germany to work on the Autobahn road project. The man was a heavy truck driver and his wife had come with him to Germany. Inga had spent some of the summer with them.

We waited for total darkness to set in before we moved closer to the houses. We found a spot where I could wait while she looked for her friends. She left and was gone for several hours. When she returned, she told me to stay put as there were soldiers in the village looking for men who had left the army camp. She said twelve men had taken off.

I asked, "Did you hear if the soldiers had any names?" She said they had all twelve names and there was no Frank among them. Boy, was that a relief. Now all I needed was papers that I could use to get out of Germany. It was well after midnight when she came for me.

We went straight to her friend's house in the construction camp. Inga introduced me to her friends. The man looked to be around thirty. A big strapping guy, blonde hair, blue eyes and he had a smile that lit up his face, a friendly kind of guy. His name was Erik. His wife Olga was a tall dark haired beauty. She had a smile that covered her entire mouth showing her snow white teeth, a most attractive young woman. Anyone could tell right away these people were kind and friendly types.

They spoke with Inga in the Swedish language. Inga related to me that they were ready to help her and me in any way they could. They both said that what the Germans were doing to young girls was wrong. I had Inga tell them I was an American student and was drafted into the German Army. I told Inga all I needed to do was get back to Munich. There I had people who would help me get the heck out-a Germany. Inga translated and the couple nodded their heads in agreement at my words.

Inga told me Erik was a truck driver and went to Munich often to pick up supplies. He said it would be no problem to get me there. Boy-O-boy was I relieved to hear that.

That night, Inga and I were bedded down in the front room on a pallet of blankets. I only took off my shirt and shoes. Inga stripped down to her underwear. Wow! Did this girl have a body, a firm, round, shapely body. As tired as I was, it was hard for me to sleep with this beautiful girl lying next to me. Her smell and presence made my blood rise. When she rolled over, her long blonde hair fell across my face.

A Street light sent a shaft of light thru a crack in the window curtain. The light fell across her face in a way to emphasize her dimpled cheeks and full lips. She lay there looking like a true GODDESS. I just could not contain myself. I pushed myself up on my hands and arms and as gently as I could dropped my face down and kissed her beautiful full red lips. To my surprise, she was awake and said, "Frank, you can kiss me again." This time I took her in my arms and proceeded to kiss her hard on the lips. Boy, did she retaliate in a most wonderful way. Her kiss made my desires respond as they hadn't in a long, long time. That was one night I didn't mind losing sleep. This was one sensual woman. I'll never forget that night as long as I live.

Before it got daylight, Olga came in, woke us and told us we must go out into the forest and hide until it got dark as soldiers were coming to check out the village. She fixed us a food sack and Inga and I went out deep into the forest. We found a nice hiding place and spent the day, talking, hugging and kissing. We had a lot of fun with each other, just being ourselves. I could really fall for this girl.

Several times we spotted soldiers poking around in the forest. Luck was with us and they never came close to where we were hiding. Inga came deeper into my arms as we watched the men. She would shake and tremble as they poked around thru the trees. "I want to go home," she kept saying.

Well after dark, we returned to her friend's house. The night flew by as Inga and I again spent the night on the floor on a pallet. We had to hide in the forest once more the next day.

After dark, we returned to the house. Erik told us he had to go to Munich the next morning for supplies, that it would be easy to take me. I asked Inga if she wanted to go with me. She said she wanted to go home. Erik said he would take her to the north coast, there he could find a boat to take her home. "You both will have a better chance going alone." I knew he was right.

The next morning, I said goodbye to Inga and Olga. I told Inga I could fall for her if we stayed together. She told me she had a heart ache parting from me. We both shed a tear when I left with Erik.

We had no trouble on the road. He dropped me off several miles out of town. Well after dark, I made my way to Doctor Wolfe's house. I slipped into the back yard. Looking thru the kitchen window, I saw Bette working there. I gently tapped on the window. She saw me, turned the lights off, then hurried to let me in.

"Frank," she said, "I'm so glad to see you. How did you manage to get here?"

I quickly told her my story. In the dark, we went upstairs. "You must not be seen here. The Doctor will see you safely out of Germany."

Was I glad to hear her say that? When Dr. Wolfe came home, he told me my policeman friend would help get me out of Germany. He said he had talked with him several times about coming to get me free of the army. Now I knew I would be okay. Gosh these people, my friends, were good to me. I was to hide at Doctor Wolfe's house until arrangements could be made for my leaving Germany. I stayed in the attic room for over a month. Doctor Wolfe or Bette would bring food and drink once a day mostly in the evening hours.

On one evening visit, Doctor Wolfe wanted to talk. "Frank, there's bad news. Germany has invaded Poland. War has started. The United Kingman, Canada, Australia, New Zealand, South Africa and France all have declared war on Germany. I and your friend the Policeman have made preparations to get you out of Germany. Your policeman friend has Nazi papers making you a messenger for the Fuhrer; no one will dare try to stop you. Here is a letter he gave me for you from his daughter Rose. A military truck will come for you and your bike early in the morning. You will be taken to the Salzburg road, go to Budapest and see the American Ambassador. I'm sure he can see that you will get safely home. Bette and I are leaving for a medical conference in Switzerland, we won't be back. Bette's mother has some Jewish blood; it will be trouble for all my family when the Nazis find out. Go with God, Frank, and all our blessings."

Doctor Wolfe gave me the papers and the letter from Rose. How could I ever thank these people, my friends? Frau Dreesen had sent me an envelope of money, God bless her. Doctor Wolfe left, I was on my own.

Early the next morning, the truck arrived. Two men helped load my bike and I was on my way to the Salzburg road. I was dropped off just before it got daylight. One of the men gave me a map and said, "Good luck." The truck turned back and drove away.

I thought of Jennifer and the Golden family. Surely God had helped them into safety. How sad it is people have to leave their homes. I hope it will never happen in America.

Little did I know the mess Germany had coming. I would bet if the people in Germany could see the future, things would be different. A terrible world they have made for themselves.

Chapter 11

The Long Road Home

Watching the truck disappear back toward Munich, I had never felt so alone. I felt tired. I found a side road, took it for a ways, found a safe place and took a short nap. After my nap, I looked my bike over and discovered I had new tires all around. "Thank you, Doctor Wolfe." What a nice person he was. I also looked behind the seat in the sidecar and found to my surprise four cans of meat, four cans of fruit, a leather jacket, a blanket, a light green tarp, a tin box with a knife, a small compass and some matches. Doctor Wolfe thought of everything.

I passed the checkpoint going into Austria with no trouble. I passed through Vienna late the next day, refueled, drove to the border and crossed into Hungary.

I found a spot just off the main road to take a rest. I opened the letter from Rose. She wrote that she was happy at the convent and had applied to go to the Vatican to study nursing. She finished with, "I pray for you each night at Vespers." Her letter made me sad as I missed her a lot.

The next day, I continued on my way to Budapest. It was late in the day before I found the American Embassy. The place was a hubbub of activity. A staff member told me they were pulling out for home. There was no room for me to go with them. He said, "You'll have to find your own way home; maybe you can get help in Rome at our Embassy. Goodbye and good luck."

How's that for help from your country? The only thing I could do was start for Rome...a thousand miles or more away. I found the road to Yugoslavia that went west. I looked for and found a spot to spend the night. The next day, I saw I was traveling along a large body of water and railway tracks. On my map it was Lake Balaton. Late that day, I crossed the tracks, parked in some bushes, spread the blanket, laid down and went to sleep.

The next morning, being close to the water, I decided to take a bath or really a swim. After my swim, I felt clean again. I had just finished dressing when I heard a large splash, a big fish or someone else taking a swim I thought. I crept along through the bushes. To my surprise, I saw a person was having a swim. I watched for awhile and the person swam to the bank and stood up to walk out. HOLY COW! It was a bare-naked beautiful woman. I watched her get dressed. She put on men's pants, a shirt and an old torn dress coat. She put her long blonde hair up under a man's cap. She started to cross the tracks toward the road.

I yelled at her, "Who are you?" For a minute I thought she was going to run.

She called back, "Who are you?"

"I'm an American; on my way home." I hope, I said under my breath. At my call, she ran straight at me and into my arms. I thought for a minute she would knock me down, instead she ran into my arms and put her arms around me.

She yelled at me, "I'm hungry, I'm hungry. Do you have food? Did my guardian send you?"

"No one sent me and I have some food, please follow me."

I lead her to my bike and handed her an open can of meat. She ate with her fingers as fast as she could. I stopped her as I was afraid she would get sick from eating so fast.

Looking her over, she appeared to be a tramp. I started asking questions. "Who are you? Why are you in Hungary dressed like a tramp? Where do you come from? Are you really an American?" She sat down on the blanket and started to cry.

I tried to console her by saying, "You're ok now, you're with me. Please answer my questions." Gosh, this was a pretty girl, big round blue eyes, dimpled cheeks and kissable full red lips. I saw her body as she came out of the water. She was a real beauty.

Through here tears she told me her story. "My name is Laura Brownell; my parents were killed in auto accident near our home in Dallas, Texas. My Father was an oil man. He had a partner that my Father had willed to be my Guardian. He took a job in the oil fields in Rumania and made me come with him. A week ago, I told him it was my 18th birthday. He came to my room that night and said I would have to sleep with him to pay back his kindness and money he spent on me. I was shocked. I told him I was in my period. The next day when he went to work, I took what money I could find in his room, took these clothes. I stole these shoes from another room. I have hitched rides and walked to be here. My feet are so sore I can hardly stand it."

"You poor kid, that guy is a dirty rat, let me see your feet." She had big blisters on both heels. "We'll get something for them in the next town."

We pushed the bike over the tracks; I gave her goggles from a side pocket. I fired it up and turned west on the road. We could not talk over the noise of the engine. I stopped early and found a spot to stay the night, just a few kilometers from the Yugoslavia border.

I couldn't do much for her blisters. I put some grease from the bike on them. She said that made them feel a little better. We finished another can of meat and tried to sleep.

The next day back on the road, we got in line with cars, trucks and busses crossing the border. We were waved right on through. I guess the guards were lazy or didn't care.

We arrived in the town of Zagreb, found a small hotel and

rented a room. I went next door to a café, purchased a basket of food, and took it to our room. We had our first good meal. We both fell into bed and went to sleep. In the morning, we found a shop and bought boys clothing for Laura. We went looking for a doctor and found a female doctor. She lanced the blisters and put some kind of salve on Laura's heels.

With Laura's feet in stockings, we went back on the road going west. I pushed the bike hard all day. As evening set in, we came to a small town called Rijeka where the road turned south. Without any trouble, we found a café in a hotel with rooms and a bar. The owner was a Frenchman, a very friendly and talkative guy.

His business was far from booming. He wanted to talk with us; he introduced his wife, a dark good looking woman about thirty. He told us she was an Albanian he had met and married four years ago. She gave us a big smile and spoke perfect English. I could see his wife was taken with Laura. We ordered a meal and the two of them sat down and talked with us. I asked about the news of the world, as we had been out of touch awhile. He told us that Germany was occupying France. France had surrendered. England was taking their troops by the Channel from a place called Dunkirk. He was really upset over the situation.

He said he had gotten into trouble in France and had to skip out of the country. "I'm still a Frenchman." The tears rolled down his cheeks. He told us that Italy had joined Germany as an ally.

"What bad luck! We're on our way to Italy and the American Embassy in Rome."

The Frenchman told us his name was Jon. He asked us to stay awhile to see how things would go in Italy. He said he could find jobs we could do for our keep. Laura and I decided to try it for a few days. Heck, we chopped wood and stacked it for him. I even repaired a water line that had broken. Jon found jobs we could do all the time.

Laura and I stayed in the same room; we even slept in the same bed. I never tried anything, she was such a sweet girl. She told me she was a virgin and she was saving herself for her husband to be. It was tough but that was the way I left it. Some nights, the way she dressed and smelled, I want-a tell ya, it was a tough deal for me having her so close. She looked like an angel when she slept.

The Frenchman's wife, we called her Sis, took Laura shopping several times and purchased clothing for her. One time she purchased a beautiful Yugoslav dress and scarf. In it, Laura looked like a native. I became more attached to this girl with each passing day. Having her sleep next to me every night added to my frustration. I had fallen in love with beautiful Laura.

Two months passed so quickly I had hardly noticed the time passing. Laura had something to do with that. She and I were doing odd jobs out back. I stopped, turned to her and asked, "Laura, honey, will you marry me?"

She turned her head away, walked a few steps away. I thought, "Damn, I've spoiled my chances for her."

She turned to face me and said LOUD AND CLEAR, "Let's get married today." She rushed into my waiting arms: I planted a passionate kiss on her beautiful full red lips.

She said loudly, "I've been waiting for you to ask. I love you, Frank."

We hurried in to tell Jon and Sis we wanted to get married. He told us to get ready; he would go get a Priest within an hour. A quick bath, a change of clothing, with Laura in her new dress, we were ready.

Sure enough, Jon returned with a Priest and a big group of people. To tell the truth, neither Laura nor I understood a word the Priest said. Anyway, there were papers to sign and we were legally married.

After the ceremony, a great time was had by all. A band started playing and dancing broke out, singing, too. I'll tell one thing, the Slavs are kissing people as we both got kissed many times by old and young alike. That night, I had the most enjoyable time I ever had. To love someone as I do Laura is the best you can have in this life.

The next day, Jon told us he thought we could continue on to Rome. "The Italian Army is having a bad time in North Africa. I'm sure no one will bother you."

Early the next morning, we thanked Jon and Sis for their kindness and loaded the sidecar. We took the coast road south along the Adriatic Sea. Our destination was the town of Dubrovnik where we could get a ferry to cross to the Italian town of Bari. It was on the east coast of Italy.

The weather was clear and cool making traveling by bike pleasant. As we rode, we traveled south and the country was beautiful. It was hilly, wooded, with ocean views. Once in awhile, when we could get close to the water in a secluded spot, we took a swim. Laura looked so cute in my boxer shorts with no top. I told her that there would be none of that topless stuff when we got home. She laughed and laughed, saying, "What's the matter, Frank, afraid the boys will look?"

In one small village, we stopped for an overnight stay in a hotel where we were invited to join the festivities of a wedding party. Laura put on her native dress and we danced and had a wonderful time. The food was great, the people gracious and friendly. It was a fun time.

Traveling on, we reached Dubrovnik late in the afternoon. The ferry was still in Italy. We had a three day wait. Again, the people were friendly and kind to us. The trip by ferry made us pretend we were on a cruise for our honeymoon. Another most enjoyable time. We arrived at Bari, Italy, early morning and got directions to Naples. We had to travel all the way across the Italian boot. The scenery was beautiful; Italy is truly a beautiful country. The bike ran like a top, it was burning a little oil, no problem though. My speaking Spanish learned from the Mexican cowboys at home helped with conversing with the natives. The two languages have many similar words.

We took a lazy time going from Naples to Rome. In Rome, we found the American Embassy. We had to do some tall talking to get the Marine Guards to let us in. Once inside and meeting the Ambassador, we had a really friendly welcome.

I sent my folks a cable to let them know where I was and that I was okay. I got back a message of that said they were relieved to know of my whereabouts. My Dad even sent money. I received a cable from the folks telling me my brother Tom was in England with the RAF. The bad news was we could not get transportation to the States right then. We would have to stay in Rome a while. The Ambassador put Laura and me to work, she could type and I became a chauffeur. I got to find my way around Rome pretty well.

On one of our days off, we borrowed the car and took a ride to the Vatican on a chance Rose was there. A guard we spoke with was nice enough to summon a Sister Superior. I asked the older Nun if there was a Student Nurse, a Sister Rose living there.

"Are you a relative?" she asked.

"Yes, may we see her now?" I flat told a lie.

The older Nun left without saying a word. We waited. In a few minutes, a Nun in a white habit appeared at the top of the steps of this building. As she came down the steps and toward us, I knew it was Rose. I felt like crying she was so beautiful. I had told Laura about Rose. I embraced Rose and told her how beautiful she was.

Laura told her, "You are a beautiful person, I'm glad you became a Nun."

"I love being a Nun. If I hadn't, I would be where you are now."

Laura replied, "We both love the same man."

Rose agreed and we three hugged. I kissed Rose for the last time. She turned, walked back up the steps and into the life she had chosen.

We drove back to the Embassy in silence. Rose was never mentioned again.

It was two months before we could get air service to Madrid, Spain; railway passage to Lisbon, Portugal; air service to Cuba, and airline service to my home in the Southwest.

We had a marvelous homecoming with my family. Uncle Bob was great about my not getting a degree in Europe; he sure spent a great amount of money on me. All the folks fell in love with my Laura. I went back to architecture studies at a local university and worked *for* Uncle Bob again until December 7th. I spent four years in the Marine Corps and went island hopping from Guadalcanal to Okinawa. Didn't get a scratch; I received a battlefield commission on Saipan.

Back home, I finished my degree on the GI Bill and went to work once again for Uncle Bob. Sometime later, my Aunt Helen and Uncle Bob willed the business to me.

Laura and I have one daughter, two sons. I became an architect of some renown, designing building and homes for developers.

Someday I hope to write about my time in the Marine Corps. At present, the men I served with and the memory of them and their faces are much too vivid.

Our Father's Generation

Book 3

Brother Albert, The Infantryman

Our Father's Generation

Chapter 1

Albert Tells His Story

Albert's story is dedicated to the men of the 90th Infantry Division {both living and dead} and to all Infantrymen who served this nation in war and peace. {GOD BLESS THEM ALL} Any reference to real people or places is strictly coincidental.

Somewhere on the French Coast, Normandy Beach, the day after D-Day, June 7, 1944 - 6 a.m.

I could feel the LST hit ground. Standing on the port side of the boat, I was more than ready to get the heck off this tub. We had been cooped up on her for four days waiting orders to move out. We crossed the English Channel in the night. The sling on my M1 was cutting into my sore shoulder. We had been waiting for orders to disembark for over an hour. My combat pack felt too damn heavy. We had just been issued a bandolier of ammo for our M1's, it weighed a ton. All in all, I felt sick all over. The trip over from England was rough to say the least. I was sick to my stomach and had a busting headache, so did everyone else. Some of the guys were puking, this tub smelled pretty damn bad.

Looking down at the water below on the way in, I could see our infantrymen who had been killed on the first landing, floating face down in the surf. The sight made me even more sick. I said a silent prayer for the dead men, if there's a heaven surely they're there.

I could see all kinds of equipment in the water...there were packs, mess kits, canteens, MI rifles and M4 tanks just under the water. I hoped the crews had made it out before they sank.

Human body parts were floating and washing up on the shore. The beach was a mess of burned out tanks, halftracks and jeeps. Our infantrymen lay dead in every position you could imagine. I could see the steps being lowered on the side of the LSD. We started to move in a single line down to the beach. We had to wade the last ten yards or so in the water to get on to the beach. Our sergeant was yelling for us to double time up the beach to a path leading up to the top of the cliffs to our front. It was a steep climb.

Our Sergeant Billy Joe kept pushing and yelling, "Get top, get top." As soon as we reached the top, the Sergeant spread the platoon out and yelled, "We'll take five. Smoke'em if you got'em."

I took off my pack and took a swig of water from my canteen. I was thirsty after the steep climb. A lot of the guys had slipped and fallen. I had gathered mud and sand on my wet shoes and leggings which made them weigh a ton. I managed to make the top without falling. Even in good shape, I was out of breath. The training in England was not that tough to prepare us for this, although we did a lot of PT while on our stay in England. Lots of push-ups, etc.

After our five minute rest, we moved thru deep grass. There were dead German and American soldiers lying in the grass everywhere. I passed one, his head was gone, the body was twisted in a grotesque way. For a southwest want-to-be-cowhand, this was one place I didn't want to be. I've many times seen and helped to butcher cattle and slaughter hogs, this was different to see human death. I had never seen this before. God all-mighty it was horrible. The smell of death and blood was in the air everywhere. Gunpowder has a smell of its own and the air reeked of it. The fighting was over just a day ago. It must have been damn tough; it was not a pleasant place to be.

As we moved along, I saw graves registration men

collecting dog tags. I pulled on my neck chain with mine to make sure it was still there. Now my neck hurt from this damn steel pot on my head. The mud had kept collecting on my leggings and shoes, making walking a little more difficult. I had to keep adjusting my rifle sling as it kept biting into my shoulder. My canteen bounced against my butt. This was a dog's life; no wonder we're called dog faces.

In a half mile we reached a dirt road running parallel to the ocean. We were split into two columns on each side of the road. We moved in a southerly direction. I could see smoke in the distance. The sound of artillery was coming from that direction. I knew a battle must be ongoing.

My buddy Hank was in front of me, our squad Sgt. in front of Hank. All of a sudden the sound of aircraft broke into my thoughts. The next thing I knew I was hugging the ground for all it's worth. When I looked around everybody else was on the ground, too. Our Platoon Sergeant, Billy Joe, starting yelling for us to get back on the road. "They're friendlies," he hollered. Then he yelled, "Fall out, we'll take a ten minute break here. Smoke-em if you got-em."

About this time, we were told our platoon leader Lieutenant Griffin had been killed. He had stepped on a mine. He was with the platoon runner looking for the Company CO. Sgt. Billy Joe was now our platoon leader.

A jeep came down the road and stopped. An officer in the jeep talked with our Sergeant and then drove off. Our Sergeant told us to chow down. I got out my c-rations and opened a can of peaches. I drank the juice. It was so good I ate the peaches with my fingers. The sergeant came over and sat down with me and my buddy Hank. He asked for our cigarette packs. He knew we didn't smoke. I tossed him my Camels from the c-rations.

We were all watching and could hear the P47 fighter planes

dropping their bombs and strafing their objectives. I asked the sergeant what was there. He said in the port of Cherbourg the Germans were holding out. "You boys may have to get in the fight. How about it? You ready?"

"Hell yes," Hank reported loud and clear. "I'm itching for some action." Hank was the kind of guy who sharpens his bayonet all the time. He was from Macon, Georgia. He talked with a Southern drawl.

"Bull shit, Hank, I ain't ready to fight nobody," I told the two of them. "When it comes to kill-en people, I can't tell if I'm up to it. Hank, you were a real tough SOB in New York City when them two sailors wanted to fight."

Hank changed the subject, turned on me saying, "Al, what in the hell did you join the infantry for? That's what we do. Kill people and shoot up things. In New York City, that was different."

The Sergeant asked, "What happened in New York?"

I told him. "Ha-ha, two good looking girls walked pasted and old Hank called to em… 'How's about showing two lonely GI's the city?' The girls turned around and smiled. Before we could say another word, two sailors jumped in front of us. Hank said in a mean voice, 'Shove off Swabs.' The sailors turned on us, fists up ready to fight. 'Come on ground pounders.' Hank grabbed me and we walked away. Hank put his arm around my shoulder and said, 'Who the hell wants to spend a pass in the stockade? There's more fish in the sea.' He was right there sure were."

"Yeah, Hank, you're one tough SOB," I repeated with a big laugh. We three had a big laugh.

The Sergeant ordered us back on the road. Hank was walking in front of me. What a guy. Hank and I had been together a long time. We met the first day of basic training. He was my bunk buddy and we just fell in with each other. Ya gotta like the guy. He was full of it all the time. He attracted women like flies to honey. He got lots of letters from girls. He was real good looking, kind-da the Clark Gable type. Everywhere he went, girls seemed to be there. In Louisiana, New Jersey, New York City and England this guy was never without a girlfriend for very long. What a smoothie he was. He knew I wasn't old enough to be in the army, but he never let on. He had just turned nineteen, I had turned seventeen the day we shipped out.

At a turn in the road, I saw a sign that read {Valognes} and in the distance I could see houses, it must be a French village I surmised. Hank turned back to me and said, "Where's all the French babes, I hear they're good in bed. I'm ready to get laid."

Our Squad Leader, Buck Sgt. Tommy Smith, was in front of Hank. He yelled back at Hank, "If they ever open your head, all they'll find is pussies."

"Hell yes," Hank yelled back, "What else is there?"

The roar of an aircraft engine got all our attention in a hurry and the rattle of machine gun fire drove us face down into the bar ditch alongside the road. When I looked up, I could see the bullets kicking up down the road. The German was right on top of us. When he passed over us, he wasn't more than fifty feet off the ground. I could have spit on that sucker.

I heard more aircraft engines. Standing up, I saw two P-47's coming in after this boy. Guns blazing, all three turned out over the Atlantic. Smoke poured from the German, the two American fighters had scored hits. All of a sudden, the German just blew up in a fire ball.

Hank was up yelling, "Kill that son-of -a bitch, he's trying to kill me." I was laughing so hard I couldn't stop. Then the laughing was over.

The German fighter had hit some of our boys. Sgt. Tommy

Smith was trying to stand up but his left foot was gone. He was a high school fullback. He was only twenty and made Buck Sgt. because he showed leadership. Jack Grimes had taken one in the back. He lay dead. Never knew what hit him. He had been a band member in high school, a drummer. I could see several more of our boys had been hit. I thought it was one hell of a way to die. They never got one shot at the enemy. Now I was ready for a fight, I wanted to kill. War will change a guy in a hurry. I never thought I'd feel this way, I was mad as hell.

Hank and I tried to help Tommy off the road. I couldn't say a word to him. We helped him into the ditch. He never said a word either, he was in complete shock. A medic came and started administering to him. He stopped the bleeding and gave him a shot of morphine. Platoon Sergeant Billy Jo had us move the dead guys off the road. We carried and put them side by side across a ditch. Some villagers came out to help. Altogether we had five dead and six wounded. Two Medics showed up and took over for the rest of our wounded. I thought at least they're out of the war for the time being.

We went back on the road, sadder, but a hell of a lot wiser. We hadn't gone very far when the officer in the jeep came back. He and our sergeant talked a few minutes. The sergeant ordered all of us to the left side of the road and put us in a patch of trees. "Take five, smoke-em if you got-en," he yelled.

Soon, the officer with another came back and got out of the jeep, they came to talk to us. One was a First Lieutenant, the other a Captain. I had never seen either of them before. The Captain told us he had two details for us. We were all going to join the Division fighting to take Cherbourg. He needed ten men for a detail to go take a French farmhouse where some Germans had holed up. He asked, "Anyone here speak German?"

I watched. No one spoke up. I raised my hand. "Sir, I speak

a little German."

The Captain asked, "Can you carry on a conversation in German?"

"Yes, sir. My folks at home spoke a lot of the language. I picked up some."

He pointed to me and said, "You, get over here."

We were all privates except Billy Jo our platoon sergeant. He was an old career soldier. He said he had been in the Army over twenty years. He looked and acted like it, too. The captain picked nine more men. A buck sergeant came from the jeep and told us to follow him. I motioned for Hank to come on with us. The guy just shook his head, no. He always told me don't volunteer for anything. Damn that Hank all to hell anyway, to be separated this way, I didn't like it.

The sergeant from the jeep took us back up the road a ways, a hundred yards or so and took us into some trees just off the road. He told us to sit down, "We may be here awhile." This sergeant had on a tanker jacket, and a soft cap, he carried a Tommy gun. The sergeant looked to be about twenty-one. I took off my pack and laid down still cussing old Hank. I thought it was a damn shame to be separated this way. We stayed there for an hour. I looked at my watch, it was one p.m.

A duce and a half pulled up and the First Lieutenant we had seen before got out of the cab and came over to talk to us. "Listen up you men. I've been put in charge of this detail and I want it to go smooth, I want it to go easy, I want to do a good job. Do you all understand?" We all shook our heads, yes. "Who's the one who speaks German?"

I raised my hand, "Here, sir."

"What's your name Private?"

"Al, Sir."

"Look, Al, I want to talk these men out of that house. We need to talk to them. You know, interrogate them."

"Yes, sir, I know what you mean."

He turned to the Sergeant and told him to move us out. The Sergeant ordered us to load on to the truck. He sat on the rear with the Thompson lying across his lap. The Lieutenant got in the cab. Most of the officers rode in the cab.

There was a lot of traffic on the road and it took awhile for our truck to get turned around. We were traveling in a southwest direction. In about two miles, we turned left onto a dirt road. Dust poured over the back tailgate making our breathing hard and dusting our weapons. The sergeant hurried to the back of the cab and started banging on the back glass of the cab and yelled for the driver to slow down. "We're suffocating back here you asshole, slow down."

We had gone a couple miles. I could see some farmhouses and fields along the way. Finally, we stopped and the order came to dismount. The Lieutenant and Sergeant led us into a thick patch of trees. Two soldiers met us there and informed the officer that all was quiet.

"We ain't seen no movement in the last two hours, Lieutenant," a PFC reported.

"Good. They must all still be in there." The officer seemed happy about that. He gave orders, "Sergeant, take five men and watch the back of the house. You two," he said to the two who had just joined us, "take that side." He pointed to his left. "You men," he pointed to three men, "Take the right side. Al and the rest of us will take the front. Remember no shooting unless you have to. You people got that?" All agreed we had. "In ten minutes we'll start walking. Move out. Remember we need prisoners." Everybody went their way.

The Lieutenant took out a cigarette and lit up, took a deep breath and blew a large amount of smoke out. "God, I hope this goes good," he said out loud. His hands were shaking a bit. We waited the ten minutes. We moved into position.

He ordered me to call for them to come out. "Tell them they're surrounded. Come out and no harm will come to them."

I called as loud as I could in my best German and repeated his orders. Not a sound came from the house. I called again and said, "It's no use, we're bringing up a tank, it will run right thru this house. All of you will die, if you don't give up and come out."

The Lieutenant asked what I had said. He gave me holy hell for saying that about a tank. Before he finished giving me what for, a white flag appeared from the front door. I called again for them to throw out their arms and come on out.

Slowly, the front door opened and a young woman came out followed by another young girl. An older woman and an older man came out; all had their hands in the air. This was the French farmer and his family, I guessed. The group came right to us. The young woman started pleading for us not to hurt the Germans as one was her husband. I told the Lieutenant what she said. "He's the father of my baby. Please not to kill him." I could see by her little round tummy she was pretty far along to being a mother.

"How many Germans are in there?" The Lieutenant wanted me to ask the French farmer. I did in my best high school French, and asked the question. He told us there were four Germans in his house. I asked if he could get them to come out? "We don't want to kill them, just ask some questions." He turned on his heels and went back into the house. Soon he came back and the four Germans followed him out.

Our Lieutenant was one happy officer about this turn of affairs. All our men surrounded them and disarmed them. We were all damn happy about the situation. Our guys were busy taking souvenirs off the Germans. The French wife ran to and was hugging a young blond guy for all of her might. Just about then, all this happiness came to an end.

From out of nowhere, the whole lot of us were surrounded by French Partisans. There were about thirty men and five women. ALL HAD GUNS AND ALL THEIR GUNS WERE POINTED AT US. This was damn scary I'll tell ya.

The leader stepped forward and ordered all of us to throw down our guns. The sergeant started to swing the Tommy gun around, the leader shoved a pistol in the back of his head. He laid the gun down pronto.

"These Germans are our prisoners now," the leader said in no uncertain terms. I protested that we captured them and we needed them for interrogation. I kind of stammered in my French.

The leader pushed his pistol in my chest and said, "These Germans are the men who killed ten young men in the village yesterday for no reason, now they are ours."

I protested again. "We captured them, they're ours."

The leader wasn't paying any attention to me at all. "This girl is a traitor to France. This entire family is traitors, we should kill them all." He was steadfast and determined. I could see he meant business. All the French partisans began cheering. The four Germans and the wife were pushed and shoved off into the thick woods south of the farmhouse. We could hear the young wife was begging not to be killed. Two women and three French men went with them. Both women told her, she had made her bed. In just seconds, the gun fire of a machine pistol sealed the fate of the five people. There was nothing we could do.

The Lieutenant reluctantly told all of us to go load on to the truck. He told me to get on the Jeep with him and the Sergeant. I hopped up on the side of the rear of the jeep with my feet hanging over the rear wheel with my M1 lying on my lap. We went out to the main road and turned south. We had traveled only a short distance when we met several trucks coming our way. Our jeep driver pulled over to the right side of the road.

All I heard was a loud explosion. I was thrown head over heels into the air. I landed some distance from a blown apart jeep. I was lucky to be alive. I couldn't hear a sound. My M1 was still in my hands. The explosion had taken my hearing. I couldn't feel my legs and when I tried to stand, they wouldn't work, so I just lay there for what seemed like hours. I slowly regained my hearing and the feeling in my legs. I then could see my right foot angled off in an unusable direction. Looks like my ankle was broken I thought. The pain hit about this time and a medic found me at the same time. Right away he started cutting my pant legs.

"Hey! Why are you cutting my pants?"

"You got blood pouring from both legs." I hadn't noticed that before. Cutting away my pants, I could see steel fragments sticking out of both my thighs. God almighty, I was in terrible pain. The medic gave me a shot of morphine. It helped a little. He said he would go find a litter to carry me up to the road. He left and disappeared up on the road. I lay back and looked up at the clear blue French sky and said a prayer, "Thank you, God, for sparing me."

A black GI came over to look at me. A convoy of trucks had stopped on the road. He said, "Boy, you sure look in a hell of a way. You were in that jeep over there?" He pointed to the overturned jeep.

"Yeah, I was in it."

"All them boys are dead. I done see-d some boys picking their pockets. Hell-of-a-way to treat the dead." He acted mad that would be going on. I agreed. He asked if I wanted him to help me up to the road. "No, a medic went to get a litter, I'll be ok." I thanked him for his concern. He went back up to his truck. Soon the convoy moved on. What a nice guy he was.

I lay back again and watched a cloud pass; it hid the sun for a minute or two. What a beautiful day, I said to myself. I saw some GI's dragging the men from the jeep and laying them side by side. Now that sight made me sick. I could be dead just like them. I had only known them for an hour or so. I threw up and got sicker. I took out my canteen and took a big drink and threw up again. Boy, was I sick all over.

The medic came back with another GI and they rolled me on to a litter. Up on the road he hailed an ambulance. The driver told him he had no room for another casualty. "I'm full up," he said. Soon, several more ambulances came along all with wounded from the fighting at Cherbourg. The last ambulance stopped and I heard the driver tell my medic he had a dead GI on board. They unloaded the poor guy and put me in his place. Holy Cow, I'd taken a dead man's place. I saw them put the dead guy over by the dead men from the jeep. I had so much pain I really didn't care.

The ambulances all stopped at a collection spot on the cliffs above Utah Beach. One of the medics told me where we were, I really didn't give a shit, I was hurting bad. More wounded came in. I saw Sergeant Billy Joe. He had a head wound. They laid him near me. I called to him and somehow he recognized me. "How you doing Al?" he asked in his deep familiar voice. He was up on his elbows looking at me. "I guess you heard your pal Hank got it this afternoon. Took one right between the eyes from a sniper. He had done a lot of kill-en just before he got his."

Now I was in bad shape. I started to sob out loud and couldn't stop. "Hey, don't take it so hard, Al, I heard he was gonna get the big one, the Medal of Honor."

I yelled back, "WHAT THE HELL!? I would rather he be here with me than getting a damned old medal." Billy Joe wasn't making me feel any better. I loved that son of a gun, my buddy Hank. Just like old Hank, the people in Macon, Georgia, will probably name some big government building after him and all the girls he knew will come around crying cause he's gone. Damn old Hank anyway. I sure am gonna miss him.

Now it was getting dark. A lot of artillery could be heard in the distance. All the wounded were being loaded onto a waiting LST down on the beach. Within an hour, we were on our way to England. My time in Normandy was over.

"I'll never have a friend like Hank again, and I'll be damned if I ever want one. I loved that guy. I'll never forget him."

Chapter 2

Wounded At Normandy

All the wounded were loaded into the hole of an LST. God almighty, I was hurt-en. The place stunk like blood and puke. I couldn't see old Sergeant Billy Joe anywhere. The boat started moving. The groaning and moaning were terrible. When I looked at my legs, the steel was sticking out as before, but at least I wasn't bleeding anymore. My ankle was killing me. I was hurting something terrible. My only hope was the time would pass quickly. There were medics and nurses moving around the wounded giving what care they could.

I saw a nurse come toward me. She looked like an angel. She passed right on by and started to administer to a GI a few litters away from me. She was beautiful even in the half light in the hole of this LST. I don't ever remember seeing or meeting a better looking woman.

Even in her OD coveralls and her hair tucked under a cap, I could see this was a real good looking woman. She had moved past me going away. I called to her, "Hey, Miss, I need some help." She turned back and came toward me. God, this was a real beauty. She stood over me smiling, her cheeks had big dimples. I had never seen a better looking woman in my whole life; even in my pain, she was beautiful.

"What can I do for you, soldier?"

"I need a shot!" I was desperate. "I have a lot of pain."

"Yeah, yeah, everybody on this boat wants another shot."

I motioned for her to lean down. She did. I grabbed her by her shirt and pulled her face down to mine. Her smell almost made it all worthwhile. Her perfume was a real treat for my nostrils. God, she smelled good. "I need a shot bad," I demanded.

"Let go! Let go!" she begged.

"Not till I get a promise you'll give me a shot." I was getting more desperate.

A medic saw what I was doing, came over and told me, "Let her go."

"Get the hell away before I shoot your ass off." I told him in no uncertain terms. He left, he didn't know if I had a gun or not, he wasn't taking any chances, smart fellow. She was struggling to get away. I hung on with all my might. "You going to get me morphine or not?"

"I can't do that, only a doctor can do that." She was still struggling to get away.

"Look, lady, either I get a shot, or you and I are gonna have some kind of bad trouble here and now."

"You're in no shape to have trouble with anybody." She was looking at the steel sticking out of my legs. "Let go and I'll try to get you some help."

"You promise you will?" I pulled her face down almost touching mine. I told her, "I have a lot of pain in my legs." I brushed her cheek against mine. I think she liked that.

She gave a big smile and said, "I promise, I promise." I let her go. I was more forward than I had ever been in my life. Pain must have done that for me. In a few minutes, she returned and showed me a big syringe full of a clear liquid. She gave it to me in my right arm. "Soldier boy, you will sleep now," she was smiling.

"Thank you, sweetie pie." That's all I could say.

She leaned down and said, "I want to get to know you." She turned and strolled away. I enjoyed watching her walk. She hadn't gone very far, I went out like a light.

When I came to, I was in a building I recognized. It was

the same building we had stayed in waiting to board the LST several days earlier. I was still on a litter with a blanket covering me. I was thirsty and hungry. I peeked under the blanket and saw I had bandages on my legs. My ankle hurt like the dickens. As I looked around, I saw I was with a bunch of other GI's on litters. Now I remembered the good looking nurse. She was nowhere in sight, damn.

A young guy in a white coat came over and stood over me. "You're awake, I see. How you feeling?"

"I need something to eat and drink."

"I'll see what we can do. I took the steel out of your legs and gave you a few stitches last night."

"What about my ankle? It hurts like hell."

"I could do nothing, you must have an x-ray. Your ankle looks like it will have to be broken again to fix it right."

"Holy cow, just what I need."

"Don't worry, you have a nurse looking after you. She's been asking about you all night. Here she comes now." I turned to see sweetie pie coming toward me. Good God, she looked good.

"I have food and drink for my favorite soldier." Boy O Boy, did she make me feel better. She had a tray with a sandwich and a coca-cola in a bottle. I sat up as best I could. She pulled up a stool and sat watching me make short work of the food. I don't think I was ever this hungry in my life. It all tasted so good. What a nice dining companion I had and I told her so.

She told me I would be going to a hospital shortly. "The more seriously wounded had gone on to hospitals last night. We will leave soon. The doctor fixed you up pretty good. I'll be going with you wherever you go." That was the best medicine I could have gotten. This was one beautiful girl, how lucky can a guy be? I asked if she could find out about Sgt.

Billy Joe. She said she would.

More wounded started coming in from France. Many had terrible wounds. Buses with Red Cross painted on them started arriving. Me and the others in the building were loaded on the buses. My personal nurse got on my bus and we were off to some unknown destination. All night and into the next day, we traveled in a convoy of a dozen buses. I slept on and off all the way. When we were unloaded, my nurse came and told me we were at a hospital somewhere in Scotland. She said not to worry she would see me later that evening. We were all put in a good bed and had a good meal. There were more nurses here than I had ever seen.

My nurse came to me just as the darkness set in. She pulled a chair up and sat looking at me. "How are you feeling?"

"Now that you're here, I couldn't be better. By the way, what's your name? Where do you come from in the states?"

"My name is Jenna Watson and I'm from Dallas, Texas."

"Holy Cow, my brother married a girl from Texas. I hope it runs in my family." Then I saw it, the Silver Lieutenant bar on her uniform. Holy shit, me a private mooning over an officer. I told her, "I can't be your boyfriend, it's against regulations. Officers and enlisted people can't mix."

She said, without missing a beat, "I don't care, I never follow rules anyway, do you?"

"Well, I never had occasion to break any before."

She took my hand and said, "If I'm to fall for you, I must know something about you. All I know is your name is Al. You're darn good looking and for some reason I'm attracted to you." How do you like that? This girl was making a move on me. Old Hank would be proud.

"Tell me about yourself first." I wanted to know all about her.

She started right in talking. Her father was a Texas

National Guard Army Officer. "He's over here somewhere in Europe. He commands an Infantry Rifle Regiment in the 36th Division. My Mom is one Texas beauty and she teaches school in Dallas. My brother is in the Marine Corps and is in the South Pacific on some island called Bougainville." She continued, "I started studying to be a nurse in high school. I went into training right after graduation. I joined the Army as soon as I finished and here I am. Now I want-a know about you." How can I be so lucky? I thought to myself.

The GI in the next bed overheard us and asked, "Can't you love birds knock it off and take it outside and let a guy get some sleep?"

I called back, "Blow it out your butt, Mack; I'm talking to my lady here."

He yelled, "Drop dead, dog face. I'm gonna come over and clean your plow."

"Yeah," I was yelling, "I'll kick your ass with my cast foot."

An orderly came over and told us, "Knock it off, people are trying to sleep." He told her to go get a wheelchair and take me out in the hall. "You guys can talk all night." The whole ward was up in an uproar saying they all wanted to hear us. Holy cow, all these guys had been listening. We both started laughing, so did the GI in the next bed. Anyway, she put me in a wheelchair and we went out in the hall.

In the hall, I started telling her about myself and my family. "I was raised on a cattle ranch in the Southwest. My grandfather homesteaded the place in the 1890's. My Dad was born on the place and so were I, and my two brothers. Tommy is the oldest, he's an airplane pilot. Frank is now in the Marine Corps. He came over to Europe to study architecture in the late 1930's. My Dad met Mom when he was in the Army during the First World War. My mom is French and was raised in

Louisiana, that's where dad met her. My uncle Bob, my mom's brother, was a flying Ace in the war. He stayed in Europe and studied to be an Architect. He married an English girl. They live in the city near our ranch. They're great people. They never had any children of their own, so they took us kids on like we were theirs. I love them both dearly, almost as much as mom and dad." Can this girl listen! She just sat there and never said a word. She was smiling all the time. How very cute she was. I had to ask, "How old are you?"

"I just turned twenty, how about you?"

I couldn't lie, so I told her the truth. "I'll be eighteen in December."

She kept on smiling and said, "I knew I would fall for a kid." She laughed the most wonderful laugh I had ever heard.

"Does it make a difference?"

"Not one bit. Tell me more about your family. I want to know all about you and yours."

How could I be so lucky to find this beautiful girl? I continued, "Tommy became a pilot at seventeen. Uncle Bob taught him, much against Mom's wishes. Tommy was a natural, or so uncle Bob says. Tommy became a barnstormer at eighteen. Flew all over the west doing stunts and taking people for rides. He met and married a girl pilot. She's with the Ferry Command and Lockheed, she delivers airplanes all over the globe. She's the most beautiful girl you will ever meet."

Jen said, "I'd love to meet her."

I continued, "Tommy joined the Canadian Air force when England went to war with Germany. He flew with the RAF and is now in the Army Air Corps here in Europe. We've been told he is an Ace."

"What a family you have." Jen seemed impressed. I'm gonna try to keep her that way.

I began telling her about Brother Frank. "My brother Frank

was a real problem for Mom and Dad. In fact, the whole family worried about him for two long years. He wanted to be an architect. He worked in Uncle Bob's office all the way thru high school. My Uncle Bob sent him to Europe to study. Frank got messed up with the Nazis while he was going to school in Germany. He got drafted into their army. We didn't hear from him for over a year."

"I'll bet your Mom and Dad were worried sick." Jen had a real worried look on her face as she spoke.

"When we did hear from, him he had met and married a girl he met in Bosnia. She was a Texas girl, Laura is her name. She was working in Romania in the oil fields for her Uncle, her guardian. Frank said her uncle was trying to put the make on her. She took off. That's when she and Frank got together. They fell in love and got married in Bosnia. It took awhile, but they finally made it back home. She lives with Mom and Dad while Frank serves in the Marines."

"That's a real love story," Jen said.

"Yeah, Frank and his wife's story should be made into a movie."

"Maybe someday it will be a movie." She's so cute. I just had to pull her to me and give her a big old wet kiss. She kissed me back.

She said, "I think I'm in love." She was gasping for breath. When I kiss-em, they get kissed.

"Tell me about you. I must know all about you," she insisted.

"Not much to tell." That's the truth, there's not much to my life yet. I started anyway. "When I graduated from high school, I needed a job to save money to go to college. My Dad had a friend who was a big boss of an aircraft factory in Wichita, Kansas. With his help, I got a job there running a drill press. I met a guy who wanted me to join the Army with him. He was some smooth talker. He got me a fake birth certificate and I joined with him. The dirty rat went with the Air Corp. He had told me he was going into the infantry. I did, he didn't. That's how I got here." It was close to midnight when we finished our talk.

The next morning, I was wheeled into an exam room and had the cast cut off. When told to stand, I couldn't straighten my foot. Back to x-ray. I had to have the ankle broken again. Six more weeks in a cast. When I woke up, I was in my bed in the ward, it was dark. It was a moonlit and windy night. The tree outside my window threw a shadow of dancing leaves on the wall across from my bed. I watched for some time as the leaves waved at me on the wall. For some reason, I wandered back to the time I was inducted into basic training at Camp Polk, Louisiana.

When my group got off the bus, a Sergeant came and introduced himself to us after putting us in line. "My name is Sergeant Billy Joe Williams. You give your soul to God, but your ass is mine." And he meant just that. "This is the formation you will always be in, look at the man in your front, back and each side. This, you dog face, is how you will line up from now on. FALL OUT!" he ordered rather sharply.

That's the day I met old Hank. We became buddies from then on. I don't think I would have made it through basic without him. He braced me up every time I got low. He was a true, true friend, I'll never forget him. The next three months were a living hell, but when Billy Joe was done, we were soldiers. I had to give him credit for that.

He gave us all a hair-cut. He cut all our hair off, that's what I mean. We got issued personal serial numbers, a rifle and even it had a serial number. He told us, "The next time I talk to you, you better know the numbers by heart." We got a cot and a new mattress, a foot locker and a wall locker.

In the first formation, I stood by old Hank. We became buddies that very day. The first day was easy. We got uniforms, our field packs and personal stuff like shaving kit, towels, wash cloths, sheets and blankets. The Sgt. taught us how to salute and stand at attention. The biggest thing was how to make up a bunk. It had to be just right, hospital corners and all. We were given the Ten General Orders all soldiers must remember. Then the training began.

The next morning, at five forty-five a.m., we were in first formation dressed in a T-shirt, fatigue pants and high top shoes. One hour of calisthenics, called PT in the army. This was every morning. That day, we learned how to do close order drill. The Sgt. taught us good. Soon, we were the best platoon in the whole dang camp. He said so. Hup-two-three-four, to the rear march, to the right flank march, hup-two-three-four. He had us doing it all. Then came the Manual of Arms. Right shoulder-ARMS-left shoulder-ARMS-Order ARMS. He said we did it right the first time, the man was a teacher.

We played Simon says and sang Jody was there, "Jody was there when you left, your right. Your baby was there when you left, your right. Your Momma was there when you left, your right. Sound off, one-two, sound off, three-four. Cadence count, one-two-three-four, one-two-THREE-FOUR. Ennie-meene-minni-moe, let's go back and count some-mo." As I say, he was a teacher. The next subject in our training, I got to shine.

My Dad gave us three boys a 30-40 Krag carbine on our twelfth birth day. He was a rifle instructor during the first war. He spent a week with each of us teaching us how to shoot. By the time I was fifteen, I had taken five black tail bucks. We spent a week taking the M1 Grand Rifle apart and putting it back together. We knew every bit of nomenclature of the rascal. We could take her apart and put her back blindfolded. A week of dry firing, then out to the range. I qualified EXPERT RIFLEMAN the first time. I was ordered to help the others. At the ceremony giving out marksmanship medals, only two in our platoon got EXPERT, me and Hank.

Basic over, we went to Fort Rucker in Alabama, to go into advanced Infantry training. We got weekend passes to go into the town of Dothan. Hank fairly shined with the girls everywhere we went. What a guy. At Rucker, we were taught squad, platoon and company tactics, both offense and defense. We learned all the common stuff, like hand and arm signals, the EE-8's telephone, walkie-talkies and the sound power telephone. We had all kind of maneuvers both dry and live fire.

After the training, we were on our way to Fort Dix, New Jersey, by rail road. The war in Europe was heating up and we were told we were needed. At Dix, we took more advanced infantry training and got more three-day passes.

Hank and I went into New York City on one three-day pass. What a great time we had. The USO Cantina was across the street from the bus stop where we arrived. How good we were treated there. Girls, girls and more girls were everywhere. The New York girls were good looking, exciting and desirable. We made many friends in a short time. Against regulations, a couple took Hank and I for their very own project. They escorted us to the Statue of Liberty and to the top of the Empire State Building. Two nicer girls you would never meet. I was sorry to say goodbye to them. Darn if I can remember their names. We only saw them for one day. We had a chance at two others, but that's another story.

Back at Dix, we knew we were close to shipping out as the men leaving the post were in full field equipment and they had their duffels. Sgt. Billy Joe was letting up a bit, if he did that we were pretty darn certain something was up. Then the word came, no more passes.

Sunday morning, the first of April, we were ordered to march to some trucks with all our gear. In two hours, we were processed and embarked onto a waiting troop ship. Stuffed in a hole, four bunks high, we left the docks and were on the way to England. I would soon be eighteen.

The crossing was uneventful to say the least. Sgt. told us the German subs were pretty well out of the war, or at least that's what he was told to tell us. We got to take turns to go up on deck. Hank and I always went up together. I really liked to watch the other ships and to see the Navy protecting us. The Atlantic Ocean is one cold mother even in the spring time. I always took my field jacket on deck with me. We docked at Liverpool, England, on a bright sunny afternoon. It was good to have my feet back on solid ground again.

Back at the hospital, I hadn't slept a wink that night in the ward. I didn't hurt, but I didn't like to be in a cast again. Oh well, I would have to suffer my way thru another time. I had Jen to make my time a little easier. How lucky can a guy be to find a girl to love in time of war?

The next morning, Jen came in and told me some awful news, Sgt. Billy Joe Williams had died in this very hospital. "He had an infection the Doctors couldn't control. I'm sorry to be the one to tell ya." I could see tears in her eyes.

I couldn't say a word, I was so shocked. I tried to hold my tears, it was no good. "Jen, I really loved Billy Joe." I cried to myself on and off all that day, I couldn't help it. I prayed Billy Joe and all the others would be in Heaven this day.

God Bless all our men. Jen said it was all right to cry. "All men cry over people they love." I was so glad she understood. I think that's when I really fell in love with her.

That night, I thought a lot about my going back to duty. I had mixed emotions. I didn't want to leave Jen and at the same time, I wanted to get back in the war. Paris had been liberated and our troops were moving on toward Germany. I wanted to be part of the winning team. I hoped most of the real dirty fighting was over. How wrong can a person be?

Chapter 3

Return to Duty – The 90th Division

After six more weeks in a cast, I finally got the dang thing off and my ankle was good as new. A young officer came thru the ward that very afternoon and threw a brown leather case on my bed. He said I had earned a Purple Heart with an oak-leaved cluster. Every man in the ward got one.

After a full physical, I was classified fit for duty. Me and three other GI's were moved to a cottage just off the hospital grounds, there to wait for orders to return to duty. I got a whole new issue of clothing.

A new OD wool Ike jacket, this jacket had just been issued for the first time to enlisted men. Two pair of new OD wool pants, two khaki shirts and a tie, an overseas cap with blue infantry braid and low cut shoes; plus a heavy wool overcoat, something I had never had before, as well as a set of wool long-johns. I was given enough fruit salad to fill my chest. I liked the Infantry combat badge the best.

The first day in the cottage I got a three-day pass. So did Jen. We took a bus to a coast town on the west coast of Scotland. The village was called Mallaig. We checked into a small hotel. It was in fact the only one in town. The people there were so nice. If I ever moved to the British Isles, this town was where I would want to live. What a great place!

Jen and I stayed there for three days and I proposed to her three times a day. She turned me down each time, saying if we were meant for each other we could wait for the war to end. I knew she was right. Why would she want to be a young widow? I will never forget those days. We took long walks along the beach and had wonderful meals at the hotel. The best was we made love at nights. Jen was the most wonderful person I had known, bar none. What a lucky guy I am to have met and fallen in love with her. I hoped this time would never end. All good things come to an end sooner or later. Our leave time did. All the way back, I know we both must have looked like some kind of sick puppies.

Back at the cottage, I got my orders to go to a replacement center on the east coast of England. What a sad sack I was to leave my Jen. I got on a bus with twenty other GI's returning to duty. Our goodbyes made me sad for days. She said she would ask for a transfer to France. "Hopefully, we will meet over there soon." She had tears streaming down her beautiful face as she spoke. Then and there I knew she loved me.

As the bus pulled away. I began to sniff and sob a little. The guys on the bus must have thought I was a chicken. What is matter with me or was my thinking of old Hank. I hated the thought of going back into combat without him. I kept thinking of the song that Gene Autry sang, {My Buddy…Nights are long since you went away, I think of you all thru the day, my buddy, my buddy, your buddy misses' you.} I cried out loud. I didn't give a shit what they thought. I loved old Hank, I missed him. Oh how he would envy me over my Jen.

We traveled to the east coast town of Plymouth and onto an LST. We crossed the English Channel, landed at the French port of Cherbourg. The port we were trying to take before I was wounded. This is where I got it. We were trucked to a replacement center somewhere south of Paris. The air was getting cold as October was almost over. I had nearly lost track of the time of year. At the center, there must have been a hundred men waiting for orders. I'd never seen such a complete mess that they were making, trying to assign us GI's to units. It was almost three weeks before I got my orders sending me to the 90th Infantry Division.

The outfit was in a rest camp northwest of Paris. I reported to the Division Adjutant. He assigned me to the 359th Regiment, 1st Battalion, Infantry Company B. The First Sergeant sent me to the 2nd platoon, 1st Squad. The whole division was staying in squad tents. This outfit had stormed the beaches of Normandy on D-day. The division nick-name was the T-O, "Tough Ombre." Shoulder patch is a TO in red on a green background. How about that? It's a Texas National Guard outfit.

These GI's had a high rate of casualties when they stormed the beaches of Normandy. They were glad to get us as replacements. My being in combat before made me a special member of the squad. About all we did waiting for orders was close order drill and digging latrines. The cooks were good and I liked my new platoon Sergeant. He was a Staff Sergeant, a man named Rocky Stump has to be good. My squad leader was Buck Sergeant Jimmy Good. He was just promoted to the job. I found he was a hair trigger and all who knew him said he was a fair man.

The platoon had no officer. The only one they had had been killed at Normandy. This Sgt. seemed good enough for me.

The CO of Company B was a Captain who had been killed on Utah Beach during the landing on D-day. Sgt. Rocky had been the leader ever since. One old time GI said Rocky was one hell of a man. "I'd follow him into the gates of hell." The new CO was a Captain; his name was Cook. I was told he had been an enlisted man for a lot of years before the Division got called to active duty. He looked to be a man who could handle himself. Tall dark and handsome, he looked like a man who meant what he said; I liked that.

We were all waiting for a pass to go to Paris. A USO show came one cool evening. The star was Marlene Dietrich. WOW, what a women! She had beautiful legs and boy did she show them to us. She wasn't bad all over. It was great to forget the war for a few hours. I'll never forget her. She danced and sang in her sultry voice. What a gal. I dreamed about Jen that night. I also had a dream about Hank. Damn-it, I sure missed him.

I was with this outfit almost a month before I got my first pass. All this time, we did a lot of close order drill and took classes about Infantry Tactics. Sgt. Rocky was one hell of an Instructor.

Hot-Dog, I had three days to spend in Paris, France. I spent Christmas day in Paris. We loaded on trucks for the trip to Paris. Sgt. Good sat beside me and we got acquainted. He asked if I would like to be the squad BAR man. I told him I would think about it. I would rather be just a rifleman. He didn't seem to care either way.

On the way, I got to thinking about Hank and me on our three-day pass in London. I just couldn't stop thinking about him. That time we went most of the way on the rails, then bussed on in. We weren't there more than ten minutes when Hank had two girls, one on each arm. What a guy! We took or were taken to a pub in downtown London. Hank was having a high old time. To me, since I didn't drink, it was a bore. Anyway, we were shown around town by the girls. I can't remember their names, but I think one was called "B" and the other "Smart."

We had a good time until a buzz bomb was reported coming our way. We all headed to a shelter pronto. At the shelter, I learned to admire the British people. They all sat there laughing and having a gay old time as if nothing was happening. Many just lay down and went to sleep. Even the children took it all in stride. Me, I was scared out of my skin. One of the girls told us if the thing made a direct hit we were all gone. When the all clear was sounded, I'll tell you, I was relieved, real relieved. That's no BS. Hank took it all in stride. I'll never forget Hank, he'll always be my friend and he will be twenty to me even if I live to be a hundred.

After that, we went to another pub. This time it was full of English servicemen. If we heard it once, we heard it twenty times, "You Yanks are over-paid, over-sexed and over-here." I guess it was true. We did have more money to spend than they did. Oh well, such is war.

We sure got along with the girls. We saw a lot of London or at least what was left of it. The city had taken one heck of a bombing during the Blitz. Bombed out houses and buildings were everywhere. It all made me sad. I was ready to get back to our training camp.

When we first got to England, the camps were so full we had to be billeted in private homes. Hank and I sure got lucky as our English family was tops. The Wells, Edward and Marge, were two of the nicest people I ever met. They had two kids at home, Harold and Mary, and two boys in the army, Gerald and John. Both had been fighting in North Africa and now were in Italy. I could tell they all were worried sick. Gosh, I miss old Hank.

About that time, I wrote Mom and Dad to tell them where I was and I got a stinging letter back. Mom gave me Billy- H. I could tell Dad was proud of me. He said many times, he was sorry he had never made it to France during the first war. I and my brothers made up for him, I guess. At least that's the way it sounded to me.

In Paris, the trucks dropped us off slap dab in front of the Eiffel Tower. I never told any of the guys I could speak some French, as I wanted to be on my own here in Paris. All, I mean all the guys talked about was girls, girls and girls. I had my Jen. I didn't want to be a go guy for anyone.

Winter was fast approaching and my wool uniform felt

good. My new Ike jacket fit like a glove. OD wools are warm and comfortable. Our GI's looked pretty darn sharp in their OD's. I could see a lot of soldiers from many countries wandering around outside the Tower. There were English, French, American and others, all looking up at the Tower.

I went right on in and up in the tower, what a sight to see. At the top, you can see for miles and all of Paris. My brother Frank told me he had met a wonderful girl and her mother while he was in France before the War. He said the mother worked in a café in the tower. It was nice to be at a place my brother had been. I wished I had been with him while he was here. When he talked of the young girl, I thought he had fallen in love with her. Now, he's married to a real beauty, a Texas beauty. I hope he's all right serving in the Pacific with the Marines. I know he misses his wife. Dad was so proud of him in his uniform, a handsome devil he was. When I wrote Dad, I told him Frank would be an officer before the war was over, he's one smart guy.

I was told to get a room fast as the town was full of GI's and lots of military personnel, so rooms were hard to come by. I went looking pronto. I crossed the Seine River and walked south on Avenue de New York for quite a ways. I turned into a side street and continued several blocks. Across the street, I saw a building with a huge sign that read {U.S. Commission for French Reorganize Nation.}

A young French girl approached me, about this time. I stopped her to ask if she knew where I could get a room. My French seemed to delight her. She smiled the most attractive smile I had seen since I left Jen. She said she could take me to a hotel. I asked her to show me. We walked some ways and turned into another aside street. In a few minutes, I saw the small hotel sign. I thanked her, but she insisted on helping me get registered. We went in and I got a room.

Back outside, I could see she wanted to talk, so we sat on a bench in front of the hotel. She started asking about America, you know, where I was from, etc. Just then I noticed an American officer across the street watching us. In a few minutes, he came right over. I had to stand and salute him.

"I need to have a talk with you, private."

"What about?" I couldn't image why he would want to talk to me, a buck private.

"I am assigned to Brigadier General Clarke. He wants to see you and this girl you just picked up. He's waiting in his office at the U.S. Commission."

"Sir, I don't understand what you're talking about? Why would he want to see this young French girl and me?"

"Private, I was ordered to bring you and this girl to see the General. Now cut the crap and let's get to it." He seemed awful pushy to me.

"I don't have to go anywhere with you. I'm under orders of the 90th Infantry Division. So you shove off Lieutenant." I was mad and showed it. Boy-oh-boy, did he come unglued.

"I'll have you in the stockade if you disobey my direct order to you. I'll have you up for insubordination, now cut the crap and come on, the General is waiting."

"Why would a General want me? Why does he want this girl?"

"Look you dumb ass!" He was getting mad. I could see it in his face. "He's a man and he wants a French girlfriend. He thinks you can get him one. He saw the way you picked this one up. You're a really smooth operator."

"I ain't pimping for the General or anyone else."

He backed off a little and got real friendly. "I don't like this deal any more than you. Just play along a while until we can figure out what to do with this guy."

I turned to the French girl and asked her name. "Michelle,"

she said. I told her to beat it in big letters. "He wants a French girl, I will look you up later. She said she lived around the corner in an apartment with her folks. "Come see me soon."

I told her, "Stay away from some of the American officers." She smiled, turned and walked away up the street. If I hadn't had my Jennie, I would pursue this girl Michelle. What a very attractive young woman she was.

The officer really got uptight, he told me to go get her back. I said, "She's only about sixteen or seventeen and I don't date girls that young." I needed a way out and thought saying she was too young was a good way. He relented and asked me to go meet the General with him.

"I hope he won't get mad at me and you if we don't bring the girl with us."

"What the hell do I care?"

With that, we walked over to the commission office. Inside the building was a big room filled with desks, soldiers and Wacs going about their business. We went down a hall to a door with the general's name on it, {BRIG. GEN. CLARKE}. The officer smiled and said pointing to the general's name, "The general likes to see his name and for everybody to know who he is. He wants to run for a political office when the war is over." He knocked gently on the door. A harsh voice invited us to come in.

Inside, a stocky man with a large handlebar mustache sat behind a big desk. The desk was clean. I mean there was no paper work or anything else on the desk. He sat leaning back, his arms folded, with a glare on his face. "Is this my man?" he asked.

We both saluted. He returned our salute in a haphazard way. The Lieutenant told him I was the GI with the French girl he had seen across the street. "Where's the young lady?" He sat up, looked at me and in a harsh voice said, "I wanted to meet that girl."

This guy really pissed me off. I got mad and told him I didn't pick up girls for anyone but myself. "That goes double for a General." With my rank, what did I have to lose?

He could see I was mad. He tried to console me saying, "Don't get mad. I just would like to meet a nice French lady. I hoped you could help me. I just came to Paris a few days ago and I'm not very good at meeting ladies." He had a smile on his face and begging in his eyes. I felt sorry for him, but not that sorry.

By that time, the Lieutenant had worked his way behind the General and was giving me all kinds of hand signals. I could see he was about to have a conniption fit. Be cool, he signaled. I tried to comply by saying, "General, I will try to find you a French girlfriend. It may take a little time." He told me I had better get to it as he didn't have a lot of time to fool around.

Now, the Lieutenant was smiling and shaking his head: " yes, yes."

I saluted, turned on my heels, went out the door and headed for the outside door, hoping I could shake this mess.

A Staff Sergeant grabbed my arm and pulled me over to a desk where a Wac was sitting. He said, "You gotta help us boy." This was a big husky man. The Wac was a Captain.

She said, "We need your help to get rid of this big shot guy. Will you help us? This General is so horny he makes us all miserable." All the talk was in whispers.

I leaned down right in her face, "What can I do?"

This lady was about thirty years old and not bad looking. She grabbed me by my tie and said, "We have a plan." I must have looked dumbfounded as she said, "We will take you to dinner tonight and tell you all about it."

" Okay." What did I have to lose? "I'll be at my hotel. The Lieutenant knows where I'll be."

She let go and I hurried outside to my hotel. In my room, I took off my cap, jacket and shoes and lay down, asking myself how I got into this mess. I must have gone to sleep, as the next thing I knew someone was knocking on my door. I got up and opened it.

There stood the Wac Captain, the Lieutenant and the staff Sergeant. All three came right on into the room. I had backed up and sat on the bed.

"We have to get this man a girl. Since you speak French, you can help us," she said. "Get dressed, let's go to dinner." I did as she told me.

They took me to a café and we had a great dinner. There they told me their plan to rid them of the general. They wanted me to find a French whore, or some other girl, clue her in and bring her to the office. Have her make a date with him at a night club. They had a friend with the Stars and Stripes paper. He'd be there with a photographer to get a picture with her on his lap kissing the general. It'd come out in the paper. "We'll see his wife gets a copy."

"Hey," I said, "This will take time. I only have a three-day pass."

"Don't worry." The Captain said she would get my pass extended.

I had to agree to their proposal. It seemed the only way I could get back to my outfit. The Sergeant and I went looking to find the red light district. It wasn't too hard to do. We just looked until we found a taxi driver we could talk to who knew the town.

We spent time in several houses looking for the right lady, one not too old or too young. In the third place, I found a girl who would fit the bill. She was about nineteen or twenty and a real beauty.

I took her to her room and tried to explain our deal to her in the best French I could manage. She got the message and agreed to our plan for a price. I took her out and introduced her to the Wac captain. They got along really good right away. The captain, thru me, told her our plan again. The young woman said she thought it would be fun to be an actor for us.

The Captain told her that the general didn't like to use prostitutes, it made the lady mad. She said, "There's nothing wrong with my work and I'm damn good at it." She was very indignant that the general would think that way.

We made a date with her the next afternoon to meet and I would take her to meet the general. It was all set. The Captain and Sergeant took me back to my hotel and set a meeting for the next day.

I went looking for the French girl I had met that afternoon. The hotel clerk knew her family and directed me to their apartment. I knocked on the door and Michelle answered and was surprised to see me standing there. She invited me in and I got to meet her mother and little brother. Her father was at work. He was a trolley conductor in downtown Paris. Her mother and brother seemed happy to meet an American GI.

It was nice to talk with these people. Her mother insisted I stay for dinner. Guess what? They had spam for dinner. American-made spam. The way the mother fixed it, it wasn't bad. I told her so.

They all asked a lot of questions about America. When I told them I was raised on a cattle ranch, the girl and her little brother became real excited hearing I had been a cowboy on a cattle ranch. I guess people everywhere know about American cowboys.

The questions came fast. Did you rope and ride mustangs? Did you fight outlaws and Indians? All I could do was laugh. I told them, "You've seen too many cowboy movies. Ranch life is mostly hard work. You fix fences and dig post holes and cut mesquite wood to make posts. I never saw an outlaw or Indians on our ranch." I think I broke the little brother's heart saying those things about cowboys not being some kind of hero. Michelle and her mother seemed to know what I told them was the truth.

After dinner, Michelle and I took a walk to downtown Paris. The city became the place of a million lights. The Tower was lit up and you could see it for miles and miles. The girl said she was so glad the Germans were gone and that Paris could go back like it was before they came. She said the last four years crept by so slow she thought the war would never end.

She started laughing, dancing and waving to all the people we saw. She was a real joy to be with. She said she was so happy she could hardly contain herself. "You Americans are wonderful to come help France win the war and rid Paris of the German invaders." She started hugging me and kissed me over and over. Drat, I had to ask her to stop, I was thinking of my Jen. Don't think Jen would approve of my being mugged by this girl. I liked the things she was doing though.

We spent that evening together, had dinner in a sidewalk café and then I took her home and met her father. All the families were nice as could be. I liked them all. I took my leave around nine p.m.

My hotel room was nice and warm and I had a warm shower. After a good night sleep, I was up at six a.m. and had just dressed when the WAC Captain knocked on my door. She was nice enough to take me to breakfast, a good French breakfast. These women officers don't act at all like the men. She was a real lady.

After breakfast, we took a cab and picked up our conspirator. This girl was perfect. At the General's office, he was beside himself. She played her roll to the hilt. She even showed the General a little leg. The plan worked like a dream. At the night club, she sat on his lap and was smooching him as the guy got the picture. I had to hang around in Paris another two weeks. It wasn't too bad duty. The Captain picked up my bills and I got to know Michelle a little better. A really nice girl she was. Too bad I had my Jen.

Anyway, the General got orders to go home. His wife was the daughter of a Senator. I'll bet the fur flew when he got home.

The weather was getting a little chilly. It was the first of December. I felt good as I left Paris to return to my unit. Hooray!

Chapter 4

Battle of the Bulge

I was reluctant to go back to my unit as I was having a good time in Paris. I came to like the people I met there...Michelle, her family, the GI's and even the officers. I was glad to have helped rid them of the General. What a joke he was to wear the uniform of an officer. Oh well, he's on his way home to face a mad wife. I hope I never hear of the man again.

When I got back where the 90th had been bivouacking, I was told by an MP the 90th Division and 359th Regiment were on the way to help close a gap the German 7th Army was trying to escape from in the Falaise Pocket. The Germans had been trying to cut off 12 American Divisions. The 90th was sent to stop the Germans. I had to catch up to them somehow.

I hooked a ride on a supply truck headed their way. After several more hitched rides, I found a Company of the 359th Regiment, 1st Battalion, herding German prisoners down the road, taking them to the rear.

I asked a GI if he knew where I could find "B" Company. He told me the company was down the road about two miles. He said "B" had been in a tough fight and had taken a lot of wounded. I hurried on as fast as I could. I was pointed into the forest where my company was supposed to be.

I found the company off the road several hundred yards and dug in. I reported to the CO. He was mad as a hornet and wanted to know where in the hell I had been. I tried to tell him, but I could see he was in no mood to listen to my story. The 1st Sergeant grabbed me and sent me on my way to my Platoon.

He said, "The old man is upset losing so many men. This company has been shot to hell." God, how I hated to hear that.

I found Sgt. Rocky, he was unhappy with me, too. I had been gone so long. I tried to explain but he wasn't ready to listen either. He pointed me to Sgt. Good. My Platoon Sgt., Sgt. Rocky, told me to pick up a rifle, "They're many lying around. Get your ass in a hole and be ready as we may have a counter attack anytime now." I picked up an M1 on my way.

When Sgt. Jimmy saw me, he yelled, "Get in a hole. Where the hell you been? We sure as hell been needing you."

I dropped into a hole with a young guy I had never seen before. I must have looked strange as I had no field equipment or helmet. I was still in low cuts and a class a uniform. I did have a field jacket on. I had picked up an M1 and a bandoleer of ammo. The guy said, "I'm Josh. Who are you?"

"I'm Al. I'm in this squad."

"You must be the guy all the boys been talking about. You went to Paris and never came back?"

"That's me."

"You go A-WALL?"

"Hell, no." What else could I say?

He told me he had joined the squad four days ago. "Man, I walked into a hell of a fire fight. These old boys are one hell for fight-n. I'm glad I got in with this bunch." This guy looked to be in his early twenties.

I was tired. I sank down in the hole, laid the rifle against my shoulder and went to sleep. Josh woke me up and told me I had been asleep for over an hour. "Man, you must have been real tired to sleep like you did. Here's a helmet I took off one of the dead guys." I took it and thanked him. Looking at the headband, it read "J. Jones." Shit, I remember the guy. We dug latrines together before. Jones told me he was from Oklahoma City. He had a gal he wanted to marry in the city soon as he got home. Now I'll be wearing his helmet. This damn war is Hell.

After a while, Sgt. Rocky came to our hole. It was getting dark. He gave me two blankets, "I got-em in a hole over there." He pointed to our left. "Them guys won't be need-em anymore. You boys get ready, we're going to get hit any time now." He left on his hands and knees.

I took out a clip from the bandoleer and pushed it into the M1, rammed a round home, set the safety. I was ready. I had never fired this rifle. I said a silent prayer it would be okay and would function properly. I didn't have long to wait.

I could see dark figures moving thru the trees toward us. Josh whispered, "They're Germans."

I pushed off the safety and said out loud, "Baby, do your work." I squeezed off a round. I saw a figure drop. The one I fired at. "That one is for you, Hank, old buddy." All hell broke loose. The darkness came alive with rifle and machine gun fire. Tracers were flying all over. When one hit a rock or glanced off a tree, they flew up or sideways. Somehow, it looked like the Fourth of July at home, only these fireworks were meant to kill me. I fired and fired. I don't know how many times I did.

Then it was silent, not a sound could be heard for several minutes. I felt to see how many clips I had left. ONE! I didn't know how many rounds I had in the M1. The guy Josh whispered, "You got any more Ammo?"

"No, all out." We both pushed our bodies hard against the side of our hole.

It was so silent you could hear a pin drop. Then the wounded started moaning and groaning. It was terrible to listen to men you can't help, even if they're the enemy. There was no more sleeping that night.

As the morning light came, you could see the men laying to our front. A sight I still remember. Dead and dying lay all over. It wasn't very damn pretty.

Sgt. Rocky came stooped over running to us, dropped down on his belly by our hole. "I think them boys has had enough. We sure took the fight out'a them." Then he said, "Clean your weapons. Stay alert just in case." He crawled a few yards away, turned and called back, "Stay in your hole. I'll send some rations as soon as I get' em." He went on checking the other boys. Later, we found out we had not lost a man. That made me feel pretty damn good.

Josh and I started to get acquainted. He gave me a Lucky Strike. I told him, "I don't smoke." After a second, though, I took it and asked for a light. He pushed his Zippo in my face and lit my butt. I took a deep drag, inhaled and watched the smoke I blew go up and fade away.

He smiled and said, "You smoke now." From that time on, I was a smoker, at least a pack a day.

Sgt. Jimmy came to our hole and dropped in. "Al," he said, "I'm glad to have you back." He shook my hand. I really felt I belonged. He took out a pint from his jacket. "How's about a snort." Josh took one, so did I. It was Old Granddad.

"Wow," I said, "I could get to like that." They both laughed. Jimmy crawled out to go check his other boys.

Josh and I continued to get acquainted. He said he was 26 years old and had enlisted six months ago. He asked about me. I told my story in five minutes. I asked why he had enlisted.

"To get away from my old lady, she was driving me crazy."

"You're Mother?"

"No, my god damned wife. That woman was running around with any man in pants. She was giving it away to any guy she was picked up by. All she did was get on my nerves. She's a regular bar fly."

"Why did ya marry her if she was that bad?"

He took a picture out and showed it to me. Here was a beautiful girl in a swimsuit leaning against a tree. He said,

"Ain't she a beauty?" I nodded my head, yes. She was beautiful. He said, "I had to marry her. You see, she said I had knocked her up. She lied, she was never pregnant."

"You had to marry her?"

"I loved her." I asked no more questions about his wife. I did ask where he was from.

"Ohio," he told me. He had worked in a bakery on the night shift and his wife liked the bars. "She was good looking and an easy pickup. That drove me nuts." I felt sorry for him.

That afternoon, the Germans had withdrawn. We were replaced by another outfit.

The 90th was ordered back to a rest camp again. We were only about five miles from the line. The area we moved into was all set up with squad tents, latrines and mess tents. This was really living.

I got a whole new draw of equipment and clothing. The weather was really turning bad...rain, sleet, wind and some snow. Our winter gear was kind-a pitiful. I did get a new set of long-johns, wool socks - three pair - and best of all, new rubber galoshes. I also got a brand new M1 rifle.

My squad got a three-day pass to go to a town called Nancy, more of a village than a town. The French people were more than cordial to us GI's. I was told the village had been shot up pretty bad during the 1st World War. The town had been occupied by the Germans for the last four years. We GI's were asked to stay with the town people in their homes. I got a nice room with Sgt. Jimmy and we could take a hot bath.

We didn't have much entertainment, so we played with the kids. We played ball, soccer and made ourselves as friendly as possible. Our supply sergeant, Sgt. Max, showed up with a lot of food and candy. Boy-O-boy did that make a hit with the kids. We saw smiles and even laughter could be heard miles away, made me feel good to help these people.

The next thing that happened was that all our passes were canceled. We had to get back to our company pronto. Back at the company, there was much excitement. Sgt. Rocky said the Germans had launched a major attack en force and the 90th was ordered to stop 'em.

He said, "Get your gear and ass together. We're move-n out in an hour. Wear your long-johns, two shirts, two pair a pants and your field jacket. It's gonna be damn cold where we're going."

I did as he ordered. I packed my duff, tagged and took it to the supply truck. My M1 had been in the rack and needed cleaning bad. Sgt. Jimmy said we all could clean them in the trucks on the way. We were loaded on duce and half's. The trucks were packed like sardines. I had no room to do anything but sit. I'd have to clean my rifle at the first rest stop.

As the darkness came on, the truck behind us turned on his blackout lights. All the trucks that we could see did the same. It kind of looked eerie to me. It was pitch black in the truck. You could only see the guys' faces when they lit a cigarette. I'm telling ya, I could see the anticipation on their faces. Going into combat is a feeling no one can explain. God, how I wish old Hank were here, I sure would feel better if he was. God, how I missed that son-of-gun.

We traveled what seemed like hours. My butt got so sore I could hardly sit still. I tried to sleep, but the truck kept hitting all the bumps in the road. Most of the guys dozed off in spite of the tough ride. It's not fun to travel in the back of a covered truck. It was really cold. You couldn't see anything except looking out the rear. Boring, boring. It got colder as the night got longer. PFC O'Dell said out loud, "Ain't war fun." Not for me. I couldn't get Hank off my mind. Gosh, how I wished he was here. He'd make the trip a lot better just being here.

The convoy stopped in a small village just before daylight.

The order came to dismount and to get into the houses. The street was narrow with shabby looking buildings on both sides. It was snowing hard. It was colder than a well digger's you know what!. My squad filed into one of the private houses. It was nice and warm inside. Outside, the snow was coming down in earnest. We were all glad to have shelter.

The family living in this house, there was an older man wearing a shabby grey suit, a woman about thirty and two girls maybe ten or so years old. All four people acted glad to see us. Made me feel better to have invaded their home and to have the occupants friendly. All the guys found a spot and bedded down.

In a few hours, Sgt. Rocky came in and gave us each a box of c-rations. He told us we would be moving up to face the Germans soon.

"Clean your weapons!" He had a demanding voice. I cleaned my M1 as soon as I finished eating. To my surprise, I found my squad had only ten clips of ammo amongst all of us, I had but one clip {eight rounds}. It was kind-a scary to say the least…to be going into combat with no ammo.

I gave the candy bars to the girls. Most of the guys shared their rations with the family. We got a lot of Danker-Shanes from the family. Nice people, they spoke German mostly. I got along fine with them.

Sgt. Rocky said we were in Belgium. I had no idea where we were. We marched out on the road heading east. The snow was knee deep to a tall Indian. We went in single file on both sides of the road. A group of GI's came up the middle of the road. A sorrier looking bunch I never saw. You could see with one eye they had had a bad time. They were almost in rags, unshaven and dragging their butts. They looked like the sad-sacks in Stars and Stripes newspaper.

We stopped to have a little conversation. WOW, what a

story they told us. The Germans had them surrounded; they had fought their way out bringing their wounded with them. They told us to watch for MP's as the Germans had on our uniforms and were acting as Military Police. They said a bunch of our guys had been captured at a crossroads and machine gunned down. It was pure murder.

I asked one private if he had any extra ammo. He started to load me down with two bandoleers. All the other s in our outfit started getting all kinds of ammo from these men. About that time, a jeep with a trailer came along the road giving out ammo. We got all the ammo we could carry…fragmentation hand grenades, bazooka, BAR, white-phosphorus and smoke grenades. All the machine and rifle ammo we could need. My Squad was ready.

After loading ammo, we moved on down the road. In several miles, we met an MP outfit bringing a bunch of German prisoners. I spoke to them in German. One young solider started to tell us his troubles. They hadn't eaten in several days and said they were glad the war was over, at least for them.

I was never more proud to be an American that day. When I told our guys what the Jerry said about be-n hungry. Our boys started sharing our c-rations with them. You never saw such smiles and hand shake-n in your life. We gave them candy bars and smokes. I know we made a lot of friends that day.

We continued on down the road for several miles. Our company was ordered off the road to the right into deep woods. We were put into Platoon and Squad formations. 1st and 2nd Platoons were to lead 3rd Platoon in the reserve. We had to cross a railroad track and the snow was really coming down.

The forest was thick as hell and with the snow we moved slowly. All of a sudden, all hell broke lose. The Jerrys opened up with their terrible machine gun. If you ever heard one, it's a sound you'll never forget. Death lurks in its path. We all hit the ground and returned fire. I emptied my rifle and pushed in another clip.

The fire fight stopped as soon as it started. The Germans made a hasty withdrawal. Sgt. Rocky called for us to find a hole and get our butts in one. Josh and I found a hole with two dead Germans in it. We drug them out and pulled them a few yards away. The boys had dug a good hole.

I had never been so cold in my life, I couldn't feel my feet. I was afraid I was getting frost bite. Just by luck we found a small stove in the hole. What luck?! Josh fired it right up. I began to feel human again. The warmth was wonderful.

Sgt. Jimmy came over and dropped into the hole with us. "You guys trying to hog this heat?" He took off his gloves, his hands were blue. He stayed with us on and off all night. Toward morning the stove ran out of fuel.

The CO came to our hole and asked if he could have the stove. What the heck, we had no fuel, so we gave it to him. He told us to get ready. "We are going to assault hill 490." At least I was a little warm now. I was all ok, except I thought I had got a boil on my butt. Man-O-Man it was painful. I forgot my other miseries. I was afraid to tell anyone because I might get sent to the rear.

We moved out about 10 a.m. and took the objective without much trouble. We were ordered to push on and close a gap between the town of Bastogne and Wiltz. This move trapped 15,000 German troops. They surrendered without a fight. They were tired and hungry, and lost the will to fight.

That evening, we dug in again. That night turned out to be most unpleasant for me. My boil was killing me. I couldn't sit or lay without pain.

The next morning, lo and behold, the sun came out. What a day! We hadn't seen the sun in two weeks. By noon, the sky was filled with our aircraft. The Air Corp was on its toes. We got all kinds of air drops, even toilet paper. Hooray!

Our Battalion formed up back on the road. We moved back the way we had come. Some of our troops came out of the forest and joined us. One of the troops said they were the 82nd Airborne. Said they had been surrounded in Bastogne for days with no help. "The Battle of the Bulge is over," one of them said.

"Battle of the Bulge, what the hell you talking about? We ain't seen no bulge," Sgt. Rocky sounded mad. I heard him say, "We gave them Jerrys a damn good butt kicking. The 90th sure as hell got 'em on the run." That man had a lot of pride in that outfit.

We had a hell of a fight to cross the Moselle River. The river had expanded to a mile wide because of flooding. I'll tell you it took some real engineering to get us across. You got to give it to the combat engineer boys. They paved the way for us. God bless 'em.

Next, we had to cross the Saar River. No bridges at all. We got across on the backs of the engineers again. Once across, we captured the city of Metz and the Fort of Koenigsmacher. We were told Metz was the first time it had been captured in modern times.

Now, we were to start the assault on the Siegfried line. Our platoon had been lucky as we hadn't lost anyone in the fighting. A few guys had gotten sick and were sent to a hospital in the rear. I asked a private, Joel C. Stone, to see if he could find any word of my Jen. He said he would try.

Later, the company CO came by and told us the company field mess was setting up down the road a piece and the whole company would be getting hot chow this evening. You should have heard the cheers our guys made. We had hot chow that evening, shit-on-a-shingle. Boy-O-boy was it good.

The next morning, we were taken by trucks back where we had come from. We went into a quick rest camp. We were told we could get a shower and a change of clothing, then we'd go right back on the line, attacking the Siegfried Line.

The hot shower was wonderful. I felt my boil, squeezed the thing and it broke open and shot stuff all over the place. The damn thing wasn't a boil after all, just a big old ripe pimple. God, I was glad to rid myself of that thing. I had a whole new lease on life, except we had to set up pup tents.

What a miserable way to have to sleep. The rain came in sheets and us in pup tents where a guy couldn't roll over or even get undressed. All I took off in three nights was my galoshes. I'd get in the tent to change socks during the day out-a the rain. Worse yet, we had to eat in the rain. This whole deal was a little maddening.

Now I was ready for the Siegfried Line or anything else the Krauts could throw at us. Little did I know what was in store for me and the 90th.

Chapter 5

1944 – Drive into Germany

After the Battle of the Bulge, the 90th resumed its drive east. We had a short rest, a shower, a shave. Me, I shaved for the first time in my whole life. We got clean clothing and a renewed spirit by our Chaplain.

Our next mission was our old one, to take the Siegfried Line, the most dreaded objective in the war. The good thing was we had help to eliminate some of the best troops the Germans had in the Ardennes. The Battle of the Bulge did that. The Siegfried Line was held by German National Guard units, mostly old men and the real young. The bad part was we were introduced to the Jerries screaming-mimis. I never heard a sound lik-em before. Thank God the rain was over and our P-47's took out the launchers.

The Battalion CO gave the company a talk about taking the Siegfried line. What he had to say, we knew we were in for a bad time. I didn't really know what the Siegfried Line was. He told us it was a line of pillboxes covered by other pillboxes. Most of them were in a hundred yards of each other. "You can tell a lot where they are as fields of fire will be cleared of all trees and underbrush. The best time to move into an assault position will be just before daylight. Use the darkness to your advantage." He kept talking, "You men will have to take-em one at a time. Use a lot of smoke and cover your ass." He didn't have to tell us that. That came with the territory. WOW, we all knew we were in for a hard time taking those pillboxes.

The Company Commander, Captain Will Crook, gave us a talk about how we would take on this mission. "We'll attack by platoons. Here's what you're up against. The pillboxes are built, one in front, two on each side and one back a ways. They cover the flanks. A command box is further back, and it covers the two on the flanks. Men, this is a tough mission. Cover each man as he moves up. Take the apertures under fire with BAR and rifle fire, make 'em button up. The hard part will be finding these boxes before you come under their fire. They are well camouflaged. You leaders, study the terrain well before committing your men. Try to locate all the boxes in your assigned area. We have tanks and tank destroyers to help us. Their 75s should do a good job on 'em. We know there are places where a vehicle can't get in close enough to bring accurate fire on 'em. The trees and underbrush are damn heavy in places and the terrain is very hilly. In those places, you will have to do it on your own. Good luck, keep your ass down. I don't want men killed in this operation. Now let's get to it."

This little talk didn't help my feelings one bit. Anyway, I went to the Company CO and asked if he could find out anything about my brother Tom. I told him Tom had been shot down somewhere in France flying a P47. He told me he would get Battalion on it. "Al, you're a fine soldier and if your brother is half the man you are, he'll be okay. The French people are looking out for our fliers. If your brother is alive and the Germans don't have him, he'll be just fine."

I thanked the Captain and returned to my platoon. He made me feel a lot better. In the morning, our platoon got its assigned area and we moved out to do the job just before it got light.

Holy cow, when we got where the pillboxes were supposed to be, I couldn't see anything. Sgt. Rocky was looking thru his field glasses. We were all lying down and trying to make out what we thought were the pillboxes. Sgt. Rocky came over to me. I was down behind a tree trying to be invisible. I want-a tell ya, I was scared as much as I had ever been. This forest was thick and the underbrush was thicker. You could see where fields of fire had been cleared, so we all knew we were in view of a pillbox.

The Sgt. Asked, "Can you see the pillbox?"

"All I can see is a mound of dirt."

"That's it." He handed me his field glasses and told me where to look. I could make out a dark place at the center and bottom of the mound of dirt. "That's the aperture they're watching us thru. Al, you're the best shot in the platoon. I want you to fire at that aperture so they'll close up. Two of us will move up on both sides and throw a grenade into the box when they open it up again. The rest of the platoon will fire at the flanking pillboxes. Ok? I'll tell ya when to start shoot-n." This sounded good to me. "Al, are you sure you can see where to shoot?" he asked me again.

"Yeah," I told him, "I got it."

He took off on his belly, hands and knees. I did some dry firing at my target, then pushed off the safety. I was ready.

I watched Rocky. Soon, he was waving for me to shoot. I opened up and fired four rounds into the target. The other guys started firing, too. I saw Rocky and one of the other squad leaders jump up and run up to the mound; one on each side. Good old Rocky, he was showing the rest of us how it was to be done. All the firing stopped; then I saw the two throw grenades into the slit; it worked to perfection.

Rocky had told the others to fire on the flanking boxes. Then, he motioned for me to come to him. I got up and ran as fast as I could and flopped down by him. He told me to call to the men inside. I yelled as loud as I could, "Cambered, war schultze nicht." {We won't shoot} "Come-n z-out."

From inside, a man called back that they would surrender and come out. I didn't see what happened next. I guess the men inside came out the back door with their hands up in surrender

246

fashion. The pillbox in the rear shot all four of them dead. What a shame to kill men that way. Now we were all mad as hell.

That day, our platoon took four pillboxes and no one was even hurt. We captured two Germans. They were badly wounded. All the others were killed. Most of them were boys 14 to 16 years old. Some older men tried to give up, but the young ones shot them. How sad.

The engineers came in and blew the boxes to smithereens so they couldn't ever be used again. That was a day I'll never forget. Oh, how I wished Hank was with me. Oh God, how I missed him. I always cry about missing old Hank. I just hoped he was in a better place.

That night, I wrote a long letter home and one to Jennie. We had hot chow and plenty of hot coffee. It was strange as no one hardly talked at all. A day like this is hard to talk about. That night, I didn't sleep too well either. I cried again over my buddy Hank, I missed him. I knew what was in store for us tomorrow.

Before it got light, our platoon had been assigned an area to assault. The Captain told us we had done such a good job that he gave us an easy one to take this morning. He said a tank destroyer with its 75 would be ours for the day; oh joy for us!

It was deadly quiet in the forest. Not even a bird could be seen or heard, only the wind in the trees made a sound We moved in position under the cover of the breaking light. The sky gave us a cover of clouds. I thought it might rain anytime. Sgt. Rocky studied the situation a while. Then he told the commander of the tank destroyer where it should shoot. We could see a pillbox in our front. Another was high up on a hill just back of the one to our front. We couldn't see any on the flanks, but they were there.

CA-WAM! WOW, what a hole the 75 made in that bunker.

Three guys came running out and ran right on past us. I guess they were picked up in the rear as I never saw them again.

Two of our guys started to go have a look when the flanking pillboxes opened up on them. They didn't get hit at all, bad shots. Some of the German kids couldn't shoot very well, thank God.

Rocky had the 75 take the one on the right. CA-WAM! It blew a nice hole in the pillbox. No one returned fire from there. Next, the 75 took the one on the left. He must have hit some ammo as the whole darn pillbox blew sky high. No one could have lived through that. Next, we had to take the pillbox on the hill. The 75 couldn't get a good shot at it, so we had to take it on our own.

Sgt. Rocky called up a 60mm mortar squad from our heavy weapons platoon. Our boys laid down a perfect smoke screen. We moved up within fifty yards of the pillbox and waited for the smoke to clear. MY GOD, there was machine gun fire coming in every direction from that pillbox. We had a problem on our hands. We had to find the openings they were firing from and bring them under our fire. They had small slits to shoot thru. Once we found the slits, we poured a lot of BAR and rifle fire into them. That stopped their shooting at us.

When their shooting stopped, Sgt. Jimmy ran up to the pillbox and used his Tommy gun. He fired into the slits. Soon, all was quiet. I moved up and called as loud as I could for the men inside to come out. We heard nothing. A flame thrower came up and he let go thru a slit. There was a lot of screaming and yelling coming from the inside. That's one mean weapon. I sure wouldn't want to be hit by a flame thrower.

The men inside were begging to come out. I called for them to come on out. Sgt. Jimmy and I climbed on top of the pillbox. The men inside came out the back door with their hands in the air. The pillbox in the far rear started to fire on these men. With well-aimed shots, I hit the apertures where the firing was coming from, they closed up quickly. Our prisoners ducked and ran around to the front of the pillbox. These were three older men and two younger guys. They were all marched to the rear. Their time in war was over, I never saw them again.

Now, we had to go after the command pillbox that had been shooting at us. Again, the mortar boys laid a smoke round right in the German's lap. They put two more in front of the pillbox. That smoke blew right into the faces of the men inside. What luck to have the wind on our side. It started to sprinkle a little.

Little PFC J.P Niles came up with a bazooka and fired a round into one of the apertures. Boy, J.P. was getting good with that thing. The rocket must have gone right into the pillbox as we could hear a lot of yelling coming from inside. Ammo started going off inside. Poor guys.

Rocky told me, "Get in close and tell them Jerries to surrender." I did, to no avail. They didn't come out.

Rocky charged up to the roof and dropped a white phosphorus grenade down the ventilator. That started a lot more screaming and yelling. Again, I called for the men inside to come out. This time, they came out. One thing we were told not to do was ever go inside to bring prisoners out. I never saw a GI do that all the time I was fighting on the Siegfried Line. It was easy to follow orders when your life depended on it.

I kind-a figured our day was over as we had taken these pillboxes in good time. It wasn't. Sgt. Rocky was called to the CO's command post for orders. The platoon hunkered down and waited.

Rocky came back with orders for us to dig in. An observer aircraft had spotted German Infantry in force preparing to attack us. We heard that places on down the line where our guys had been pushed back with heavy German counterattacks. We sure didn't want to give up our hard fought ground. Once is enough to take a piece of real estate. So far, we hadn't lost a man to the enemy. One of our guys got shot by one of our own; bad luck. That's called friendly fire; some friend, huh?

The Jerries really gave us the works; they had artillery and mortars rain down on our position. I was glad I had dug my hole deep. They really had us zeroed in. It was as bad a barrage that I had ever been in. We had dug in around and between the pillboxes. We were told to stay out of the boxes. Now, it was raining hard. At first I though it felt good. Then I got real wet. Not so good.

The Jerries hit us with a strong Infantry attack just after dark. They tried to come around our flanks, but Rocky knew their tricks and they took a beating from our guys on the flanks. I guess they didn't count on anyone protecting our flanks. They really got the sh–t kicked out-a- them. Two of our guys with an M1919 machine gun killed 10 of them. We counted that many the next morning. Don't know how many got away or were wounded.

The ones who hit our front got a hell of a whipping. Our 60mm mortar crews lit the night with flares and turned the darkness into daylight. The enemy was sitting ducks. We had interlocking final protecting fire and it did its job to perfection. A rabbit couldn't have made it thru there. Our Platoon alone killed over 35 of the enemy.

Looking at the dead the next morning, I could see most of the dead were young kids. Some looked to be only 12 or 13. What a shame. I was sick as I had ever been seeing those young people laying there. Not a pretty sight. What a waste of the young men of Germany. We were told most of these young guys had been in the Hitler Youth and had been brainwashed to the point that they were more than willing to give their life for Hitler.

That night, our Company was pulled off the line and we

went into a quick rest camp. We got a shower and clean clothing. The best was we got a hot meal. The Company cooks outdid themselves. We got hot SOS and all the hot coffee we could drink. I wrote several letters, one to Mom and Dad, and one to each of my brothers. I hoped they would get to them somehow. Of course, I wrote a long letter to Jennie. I poured all the love I could into my words. God, I hoped it would find her. We had one day and one night out of the line.

The next day, we got another sector to take. I want-a tell ya, this wasn't getting to be fun.

Holy Cow, we got a new platoon leader. A shave tail fresh from OCS. I tell ya, he looked like a kid to the rest of us. He was a sharp dresser, I'll tell ya. He wore a well tailored uniform all starched and pressed. He looked like he had just stepped off the parade ground. He was still wearing his brass. The first thing the asshole did was to dress Sgt. Rocky down for not saluting when Rocky reported to him. Captain Cook must have heard him. The CO was talking to some of the men and hadn't introduced the jerk to us yet. That kid got hell from the CO. Man, I never heard so much cuss-n a man got that our new platoon leader got from the CO. If the Captain hadn't, the whole platoon would have had some target practice in the next engagement There's no better leader of men in all the Infantry than Sgt. Rocky. Every man in our platoon would have given his life for Rocky. You couldn't love a man more than that.

The CO told the jerk to get his ass behind Rocky and follow him around like a dog. "Every time Rocky says shit, you say where and how much!" He went on, "If you want to be a leader, you forget all the crap you learned in OCS. Rocky will teach you how to command men and be a leader." There were lots of smiles from the men in our platoon. In combat, you go on your instincts not by the book some nitwit wrote sitting at a desk in a nice warm office with a pretty secretary hanging on his shoulder telling him what a great man he was. When the bullets fly, you get the feeling you don't know a hell of a lot. There was no room for bull shit out here.

This new Lieutenant would learn darn quick or he wouldn't be around long. Later, we found the guy was from a wealthy family. You gotta give him credit as he had volunteered for this assignment. One of our guys was from his hometown. He told us the Lieutenant's father had been a bootlegger during the prohibition era. He said the old man was filthy rich and that he had all kinds of pull in Washington. "That kid can be anywhere he wants to be." Turned out, he wasn't too bad a guy. We took credit for that.

The next day, before daylight, we moved to our next mission. We were told this was the last group of boxes we would have to take. This was the end of the line for the Siegfried line.

Before we went in, Sgt. Rocky gave us a big talk. He said he was proud to serve with men like us. "You men are the best damn Rifle Infantry Platoon in the whole American Army, bar none." I really felt good having this man I so admired say that. He sounded mad when he said, "I want you men to be careful today. I ain't lost a man to enemy fire so far. I don't want it to happen today." I think he must have had a premonition about that day. Because he never gave anybody a pat on the back before, nobody.

We took the pillboxes easy. We were getting good at our job by then. We had taken ten prisoners. One was an older officer. The rest were young guys. The oldest must have been around seventeen or eighteen.

This was one of the saddest days in my life. Like when I lost old Hank.

Sgt. Rocky was searching the prisoners, when the older one was standing away from the group ten or so feet. As Rocky approached him, he pulled a pistol and shot Rocky point blank in the head. Rocky was dead before he hit the ground.

Me and several other guys, just by instinct, opened up on the bastard. I never emptied eight rounds so fast. Sgt. Jimmy jumped on top of the Jerry and fired his Tommy-gun until it was empty. That night, in my sack, I cried like a baby. I couldn't stop. I'll tell ya, I wasn't the only one. We all loved Rocky.

Sgt. Jimmy was made platoon Sgt., Corporal Fred Henderson was made our squad leader. Guess what? I was made Assistant Squad Leader and promoted to Corporal.

Captain Cook talked to the platoon and said Rocky was the finest soldier he had ever served with. The tears ran down his face as he spoke. As I looked around, there wasn't a dry eye in the whole damn platoon. Even the kid Lieutenant was sobbing.

That night, Sgt. Jimmy called the platoon together and told us about Rocky. Rocky had been born in the slums of Chicago, Illinois. His father deserted the family when Rocky was twelve. He helped his mother raise his brothers and a baby sister. From what Jimmy said, I surmised that Rocky would do anything to keep the family together. He had to fight all the time. Sometimes it might not have been legal what he had to do. He kept the family together until he joined the Army.

Rocky stood five foot nine or ten. Built like an outhouse and tough as nails. His ruddy face didn't give away his soft heart and pleasant disposition. He just looked tough.

Jimmy said Rocky never had a girlfriend. Never had the time for a woman. He had told Jimmy he would have liked to have found a good woman to settle down with on some Army post and raise a bunch of kids.

Rocky found a home in the Army. He had joined a jump or two ahead of the law. He really liked being in the Army. Jimmy had told him he might find a nice German girl after the war. Rocky was a Bohunk and liked the Germans he had met at home. He was looking forward to finding a girl he could love. He would have made one hell of a husband and father. WAR is HELL.

The Siegfried line cleared, the 90th moved to the West bank of the Rhine River. The weather had turned bad and we crossed the river on bridges.

My platoon spread out in a field. Our squad was the point squad. We were moving toward a village in the distance, when all hell broke loose. We were in an anti-personnel mine field. Four of my Squad were killed. The new squad leader was the first to go.

I started yelling for everyone to move back. No one had to be told. We all moved back in a hurry.

Captain Cook called in artillery and air strikes. There wasn't a foot of that field that didn't have a hole in it. That village in the distance took a hell of a pounding. Every weapon that was brought up laid on that village for an hour. I felt sorry if there were any people in the place.

When we entered the village, nothing could have lived thru that barrage. The village was nothing but rubble. I saw a few dead bodies, some were kids. WAR is HELL.

From then on, we met nothing but light resistance. The 90th was on the way to Czechoslovakia.

Chapter 6

War is Over

Can you believe it? I was made Squad Leader. Sgt. Al I was called. Me, eighteen and a Buck Sergeant. The Captain told me he had all the confidence in the world that I could do it. I told him, "I can do it, I had good teachers."

In the drive toward Czechoslovakia, we found the German national treasure in the Merkers salt mine. My squad got into the mine, we were the ones who found the treasure. What a deal, I'll never forget that day. I never dreamed there was that much gold in one place in the whole world. The whole division celebrated to hear what we had found.

Some of our units took the surrender of the entire 11th Panzer Division at the town of Hof. We captured over 13,000 men and all their equipment: tanks, halftracks, trucks and staff cars. Most of the Germans wanted to have the war over. We were glad to oblige them.

We had a bad thing happen. We found the Flossenburg concentration camp. What a horrible place. I will never get the sight of those people out-a my memory. How God let that happen I'll never know. The Captain called headquarters. They sent for the Red Cross and all the help they could muster.

We stayed almost a week helping the people interred there. What a mess, most of the people hadn't eaten in days. Most couldn't hold the food down. It was awful, I never want to see anything like that again, never in my life. If I live to be a hundred, never can I see a worse thing. The way people were treated in that camp…it's embedded in my mind forever. I was glad to get away from that place.

HOORAY! Germany surrendered, the war was over. On the Czech Border, we met some Russian units. They even had women in their ranks. I'll tell ya, some were darn good looking, some weren't. We had their company for almost a week. They danced, drank Vodka and had the best time. The Russians really liked to celebrate, and they knew how. The women made a big fuss over our boys. The CO pulled us back so's not to start another war with the Russians. Yeah, I think the Russian ladies were hot to trot. He saved another war. Some of our guys made out with-em anyway. Our kid Lieutenant was found with a Russian Girl in his sack. You never know about some guys.

I sent a long letter to mother asking her to try and find Jen or her folks. I gave her all the info I had on the family. I sent a letter to Jennie at her last address, hoping it would find her.

Captain Cook called me to the Company headquarters. I reported with a salute and said, "Reporting for duty, Sir."

"Al, you're not here to report for duty. I have news of your brother Tom." I want to tell ya, I had the most sick feeling come inside I had ever had. The Captain smiled and said, "Your brother is safe and on the way back to the States. I understand he has a broken leg and arm. From what I can gather, he had been spending some time in a Nun's Convent in Spain. I guess some French Partisans rescued him from a group of Germans taking him prisoner." I told the CO that was the best news I had ever had. He patted me on the back. "That's great news. I'm glad he's okay." I thanked him and returned to the platoon.

That night, I gave thanks to the Lord for Tom's safety.

The next day, the 90th was ordered back to the States. We were told about the suffering the division had gone thru. Over 21,000 men were killed or wounded and missing in action. A lot of our guys had non-battle injuries...over 9,000. Most of them were frostbite cases. All in all, the 90th had over 32,000 casualties. That's a lot of men.

Since I could speak German, I had a command conference with a Major from our Europe headquarters. He asked me to stay awhile and be an interpreter for the occupation forces. I'd get promoted a rank and live in style. "Sounds good to me," I told him. Now, maybe I could find Jen He cut orders for me to go take classes in German at a school in Berlin. I was promoted to a Tec/Sgt.

It was a sad day when I parted ways with my company. Captain Cook gave me a real nice send off. He called a company party. What a blow-out. I'll never forget all my buddies. Rocky and Hank would be with me always. A lot of other guys, too. If I live to be a hundred, Rocky and Hank will always be young guys to me.

Before I left the company, I got mail from home. I got letters from Mom, Dad and my grandmother. Her letters were hard to read but God bless her she tries. Dad wrote that brother Frank and his Marines had taken an island called Iwo Jima. He said proudly that Frank had been promoted to an officer, a field commission. That-a way-ta-go Frank! I was damn proud of him. I told all the guys my brother was an officer in the Marines.

A real sad thing happened. The 90th was recommended for a Presidential Unit Citation by General George Patton. His recommendation was returned as he could only give ten percent of his units this award. The 90th was the only Infantry Division Patton recommended this award for. That will tell you something about the fighting men of the TO 90th. What a proud day that was.

It took me a week to get to Berlin. What a mess that trip was. That could be another story. I had to go thru the Russian sector to get there. We Americans were not at all received with open arms by their soldiers.

In Berlin, the place looked like nothing I had ever seen before. It was all rubble, with people already starting to clean the place up. These Germans were industrious people. Looked to me like all the women in Germany were working to clean this mess up. You should have seen them. Those gals were cleaning bricks and shoveling like mad. I really admired these people. They had been bombed and torn apart for the last four years. Now, here they were, working their butts off to start a new life and rebuild their city. You just gotta admire them.

After asking a lot of people for directions, I finally found the building I was to go to school in. There were forty students and we had a really good looking teacher. A lady 25 or so years old, a real beauty. She had been in America as a teenager before the war, came back to Germany on a visit and got stuck here. At least that's what she told us. She said most of her family had been killed in the bombing and as soon as she could she wanted to get back to America. A lot of these GI's were ready to take her.

Before I settled in, a Stars and Stripes reporter was talking to some of the men. When I heard him say something about the Marines, I questioned him. He said the Marines had landed on an island called Okinawa and were taking heavy casualties. Now I had to pray for Frank's safekeeping. I prayed as hard as I could to keep Frank safe. That night, a Chaplain came to give all the students a service. I told him about Frank and the landing at Okinawa. He gave a prayer service for Frank and all the Marines. He was a great guy. All the people there prayed for Frank by name. That made me feel a little better.

We had nice quarters and all the good food one would want. I thoroughly enjoyed the class work and was learning all I could about the German language. This gal was a good teacher.

For some unknown reason, this lady took a liking to me. Not just because I'm a nice, polite, good-looking guy. She must have thought she was safe with me, me being so young. She was. The guys starting kidding me and saying I was gonna put the make on her. I might have, but I had Jen in my mind all the time, no room for anyone else.

Our teacher would take a few of us at a time out on the streets to talk with the Berliners. It was to help sharpen our German language. I enjoyed talking with the young kids. We always drew a crowd on the streets. Of course, we GI's had candy to give, that helped to bring 'em to us.

On one of these outings, we were talking with a group of teenage girls. The girls were chatting away like girls do. I wasn't paying too much attention to anything. About a half a block away, a hotel had opened for American service people to come and stay while making a visit to Berlin. I could see a bus being loaded with military personal. I wasn't paying much attention and when I looked back, I could see three white uniformed nurses waiting to get aboard. I was half listening to the girls chatting away. I looked back and saw the last nurse step up into the bus. My mind all of a sudden said to me, "That's Jen!" I stood there a moment frozen to the ground. I took off in a run after the bus. Of course, I couldn't stop it even though I ran a block or two trying.

I was so damn mad at myself I could bust. I sat down on the curb and did everything but cry. I was sick inside. Here she was staying a short block from me and dumb me never thought to go look.

My attractive teacher had followed me. She came and wanted to know what was the matter. I told her the whole story. She was so sympathetic, she asked me to stand, took me in her arms and kissed my lips. "What you need is a little female companionship tonight."

"No, no, I can't be with another woman."

It was getting late. She invited me to have supper with her. I did and later we went to a club and danced awhile. It was good to have a female in my arms again. Her smell and her cheek against mine felt so good. This lady was a temptress in every aspect.

Around midnight, I walked her home. At her door, she invited me in. I flatly refused. She said, "You American men are funny. Most would knock my door down to get in. You refuse my advances. You will make some woman a wonderful husband."

I pulled her close and proceeded to kiss her lips hard. I spun on my heels and got the H away from there. How much can a guy take?

Back in my room, I took a cold shower and went to bed. That time, I did not sleep. How could I be so unlucky to not have found Jen? I'll be mad at myself a long, long time. Part of it, too, was because I turned my back on the beautiful teacher.

At the end of the week, we were finished with school and I was assigned as an interpreter to a Major Joe Brown in a city in the American zone in central south Germany. My cut orders said I was to get there ASAP. I could get transportation at the motor pool in the American sector. I packed my bags and said my goodbyes to the teacher and the friends I had made at the language school. When I said so long to her, I thought I saw a tear in her eyes. What a devil I am. She was really a very nice woman.

At the motor pool, I introduced myself to the crusty old Master Sgt in charge and showed him my orders. He said, "We ain't got no vehicle for ya."

Now that made me mad. "My orders say you get me a vehicle or else."

"Or else what? See my stripes? I'm a Master Sgt. You ain't

but a Tec.- Sgt, so bug off."

I showed him my right fist. "This says I get a vehicle or else it's going to find a place in your face."

He could see I was mad, and I was. He pointed to the combat badge on my chest, "I wish I had won one of them."

"Yeah," I said, "A lot of guys, now that the war is over, wish they had one."

"Well, since you're a combat vet, can you ride a motorcycle?"

"You bet your sweet ass I can, had one at home."

"Well," he says, "I got one hid out. Was gonna save it for myself. I hope to find me a good looking Fraulein and take her for rides. Since you're a nice sweet guy, I'll let you have her."

"Get the SOB out here. I gotta get going."

"You gotta motorcycle license? Nowadays, you gotta have a license to drive or ride anything. That's orders from headquarters."

"Na, I ain't got one for anything."

"Well, come on in and I'll issue you one to drive anything, You can drive, can't ya?"

"Yeah, I can."

We went in his guard shack and he wrote one up. Then he went behind some trucks and came out pushing a motorcycle with a sidecar. He was petting the bike like it was a woman. "Ain't she a beauty?" he asked. She was a BMW German Army job with a side car.

I wasn't for any small talk. "Let's get her gas. I need to be on the way." I was ready to boogie. While I was gas-n, he got a phone call. When he returned, he said, "Well, what ya know, you got yourself a passenger. I'm told to hold you here until they get here. They're on the way."

"Ain't that the shits. Who is it?" I asked.

"Don't know. You gotta wait. They said your man is going

to the same town as you."

We waited for what seemed like an hour. Then, up pulled this staff car and out from the back door come a Lt. Colonel in his pinks and greens, behind him out came this gorgeous , I mean gorgeous, Wac blonde First Lieutenant. Every eye in the motor pool was on this woman. I said to myself, "I hope she's my passenger." Hot dog, she was!

I heard the old Sgt tell the Lt. Col that the motorcycle was the transportation. Man did the Lt. Col blow a fuse. I gotta admire the old Sgt. He stood his ground. He didn't back up an inch. "That's it, Colonel, and that's all there's gonna be."

The Colonel calmed down and told the Wac Lieutenant, "It'll be ok, honey." This guy was maybe forty and she was twenty or twenty-one. I didn't think he was her guardian.

They came over to me and, of course, I saluted and said, "Welcome, ma'am." The Lt. Col. asked me if I could ride this motorcycle. "Yes, sir, been ride-n a bike for years." Of course I lied. Who wouldn't if your passenger was this comely Wac?

All the time, this lady was giving me the once over. I said to her, "You'll need to change into something else. I don't think you'll be able to make it in that tight skirt."

In her musical voice she said, "I have coveralls in my bag." She proceeded to dig some out.

The driver of the staff car had set her luggage by the sidecar.

She asked the old Sgt., "Where can I change?"

He pointed to the guard shack and said, "It's all yours, ma'am."

She went over, went in and closed the door. All the eyes in that motor pool were on the door hoping it would pop open at the right time. It didn't.

When she came back, Lord, this was one good looking woman. The coveralls couldn't hide that figure. While she changed, the old Sgt., the driver and I tied all our baggage on the bike and side car. It looked like Okie's heading for California.

She jumped right in the side car, "Let's go driver." I handed her her make-up bag and told her she would have to carry it on her lap. She smiled, "Fine, let's go."

I kicked the starter and the BMW roared into life. I shoved her into low gear and off we went. When I looked back, the Lt. Colonel was dancing around on one foot. He must have leaned over to smooch my passenger and the side car wheel ran over his foot. I laughed to myself and I saw her looking back, too. She looked up at me and laughed a big hardy laugh. I could see we were going to get along fine.

Berlin was one big mess. Burned out building everywhere. Finding your way around was a major job. I stopped at an intersection and asked my passenger if she knew her way around this city. She looked at me with disgust. Some real bad language came out of that beautiful mouth. "If you don't know where we're at, how the hell should I know? You're the man here." I couldn't help myself, I started laughing. She really puffed up. Then she started laughing, too. How cute she was. "Let's put our heads together and find our way, okay?"

"Okay by me," I said.

"Let's ask that man," she pointed to someone on the sidewalk. I did and he told us we would have to go to the town of Hannover to get the road we needed to go south. He told us how to find the way to Hannover. She crossed her arms and said, "See, I'm no dumb blonde." I told her she was damn smart to ask for directions.

We arrived in Hannover well before dark and decided to go south. Hannover had been a real war zone. Many bombed out buildings. I told her we could look for a place to spend the night just as it got dark. In the next hour, it turned pitch black, no moon. In the next hour, we entered a small village. "Let's get something to eat and find a place to stay the night." I had to yell over the motorcycle loud motor. Sure enough, there was a bar and hotel in the village. I went into the place and asked if they would serve a meal and if we could get rooms. All affirmative. The owner showed me a place to park the bike where it would be safe.

We had a nice German meal and great beer. When it came time for the room, he told us he only had one room left. She said, "Take it. I'm tired." So we did.

The owner showed us the room. The bathroom was at the end of the hall. The room had a big double bed. She said, "I get the bed, you can have the armchair. I outrank you."

"No, lady," I said, "We'll flip a coin for the bed."

"Okay, I'll do the flip." She took out a coin, tossed it into the air and said, "Call it."

"Heads," and it was. My turn first.

I took my ditty bag and went to the bathroom. I had a nice warm shower. Returning to the room, the lady was in the bed all curled up and asleep. I raised the covers. She had on a SHORT NIGHTIE. WOW! Was she looking good! I shook her awake, "My turn for the bed."

She only said, "Go-a-Way." So I went around the bed, pulled the covers back, turned off the light and slipped in.

The next thing I knew it was morning. There she was sitting in the armchair putting on lipstick. Damn, I was hoping to beat her up and get my kicks watching her dress. Now, she would watch me. Oh well, I jumped up, grabbed my pants and pulled them on. All the time, she kept saying, "You're not bad looking, good body, too." She had a big smile on her face.

I said, "You some kind-a mind reader or just a nut?"

"I love good looking men, but you're too young for me."

I said, "Ain't that just great." I see this desirable woman

and she says I'm too young.

She said, "I'll bet I'm at least 5 years older than you."

I let it drop and asked, "By the way, what is your name?"

"Mildred Clinghoffer."

"Clinghoffer?" I asked.

"Don't laugh, that's my name."

"Okay by me. I'll call ya LT, okay?"

"Fine by me," she said.

After getting dressed, we had breakfast downstairs. The owner, who looked to be in his sixties, visited with us during the meal, a real nice old gent. He told us he was glad the war was over and that Hitler was no longer in charge, and he had a brother in the States. He hoped to visit him when everything settled down.

He helped me get the bike out and on the road. LT jumped in the sidecar. We waved good-bye and took off.

Back on the road, we would stop in small villages and ask questions about the road ahead. We always drew a crowd of young kids. I guess the war hadn't been over long enough for them to see many Americans. I had a bag of candy bars and packets of cigarettes. We tried to be good ambassadors. The children were great. I think we did a good job for Americans.

We stayed the next night in the city of Frankfurt. It once must have been a beautiful city. It had been bombed heavily. The people were working like honey-bees putting the buildings back in shape.

We had separate rooms in a hotel in the center of the city. The hotel was partly finished. The kitchen was up and running. What great meals we had there. Everyone was friendly and ready to answer any questions we had. LT had plenty. I tried to shut her up when she asked about the war. No luck, she kept asking. There were some amazing answers to her questions. Like how little the people had known what was going on in their country. They had had no idea how bad the War was going for them. They just knew their lives were bad and they were hungry. All of them said they were glad the war was over. We left early the next morning. It would be a long day to get to our posted town, Augsburg, Germany.

Chapter 7

Augsburg, Germany – Jen – Homeward Bound

We stopped for lunch at another small village. We had our meal at a bombed repaired café. During this time, we had a lot of people stop and say how glad they were to have Americans in southern Germany. The kids were great, we passed out all the candy bars we both had. What smiles we received from them. Lots of "danke-schons!" They made us feel right at home in all the villages we stopped in.

On down the road, I pulled off to the side as I wanted to have a talk with LT. I wanted to know why she was going to the same town as I. She told me she was to be an assistant to a Major Jones. "Major Jones has to go back to the states as there is something wrong at the Major's home. I will be the officer in charge while the Major is gone," she said proudly.

"Holy Cow, you'll be my boss," I said with a smile.

She just laughed. How cute she was. "You'll be my interpreter. We will be close all the time."

That made me laugh. I told her, "That will be great."

She told me she had a Ph.D. in social science and that the Major had been a Transportation Officer. "The army is throwing officers into jobs they know nothing about. I'm to help the Major help Germany to be a democracy."

We finally arrived in Augsburg in the evening hours. It was well after dark. I drove to the town hall. It was closed. A beautiful old hotel was across the town square. The hotel had some bomb damage but was being repaired. We drove the bike up to the front entrance and walked into the lobby. In the hotel, we met a Master Sergeant Dale Hanson a man about thirty-five years old, slightly balding. He had a friendly smile and a warm welcome. He told us he was Major Brown's Administrative Assistant and all the Army personal lived in this hotel. He had dinner with us and helped to check us into the hotel.

He said there was a detail of twenty GI's serving as occupation troops in this town. He told us he wasn't too happy with them. All of them had just come from basic training in the last several months. "Major Jones don't ride herd very well and the Sergeant in charge is a transportation trained non-com, not much of a leader." With that conversation, LT and I went to our rooms and to bed. I got a front room on the second floor overlooking the town square. LT got a room next door.

The next morning, LT and I took breakfast in the hotel café. The detail of GI's was there. No one said a word to us. We really got the once over. It didn't bother me, but LT said they were rude not to make us feel at home. I told her, "So what! We might interfere with their play house and they know it."

After breakfast, we reported to Major Jones. To our surprise, the Major was a Wac, Major Jo Jones, a lady in her early thirties. A redhead, not bad looking, showing a nice figure in her uniform. I could see she was uneasy in the job she was doing. She was pleasant and went overboard in her welcome to us. She said, "I want us to be friends. Be good to everybody. I don't want any trouble in this town." She told us she needed us. She said she didn't speak any German at all. She also said she was a lawyer and didn't know why she was given this job.

LT spoke up and said, "We'll help you all we can." That made her tear up and gave us a big smile. I thought for a second she was going to hug and kiss us both.

We sat and visited with her for several hours. She did tell

me to take off my blue infantry braid and infantry brass. "You're now in the Signal Corp. I don't want the town people to be reminded of the war."

I told her in no uncertain terms, "I want them to remember why we were here and that we were here to help them get their lives back together. I'll be damned if I'll quit wearing my Infantry Combat Badge." End of conversation.

She backed off pronto. I could see LT and I had a big job ahead of us.

Major Jo, that's what she wanted us to call her, told us she had to go home as her father was ill and she had orders cut to go. We would have to take over while she was gone. I could see LT would like to be in charge.

Major Jo was on her way home the next day. LT wanted to know where to start. Sgt. Hanson had her set a meeting to inform the boys that there would be no more screwing off and not paying attention to orders. LT really sounded tough. HA, HA! She was a real push over, so we found out. Things got bad, the boys got clear out-a hand. The Sgt. and I got LT to put in a transfer for the whole bunch, using disorderly conduct. Some people don't know how good they had it.

About a week later, this Lieutenant Colonel shows up. He said the 82nd Airborne Division was taking over the occupation duties in Southern Germany American zone and he was in command. He made it plain he was a no nonsense kind-a officer. Ok by me. He asked right away where LT wanted to be transferred. She said without hesitation, "Berlin."

I knew she wanted access to husband-finding territory. The Lt. Colonel said he would cut her orders pronto. He then asked M/Sgt. Hanson what he would like.

Hanson said, "I'm a lifer, any motor pool will do."

"Okay, Sergeant, you'll stay with us." He turned to me next, "What do you do, son?"

"I'm an interpreter."

"We have two in our ranks. Anything else you want?"

I told him "I just want-a go home."

"I'll have your orders cut. You'll be on your way in a few weeks."

LT left the next day for Berlin. She had a staff car to take her. Before she got in the car, I took her in my arms and planted a passionate kiss on her beautiful lips.

"Maybe I should stay? No," she said, "Al, you're too young for me, besides I want a man with money." She got in the car and I watched it drive away.

Hanson was there with me and I said to him, "I'm sure gonna miss that girl."

Hanson made a suggestion, "You have no duties, why don't you take a jeep and go look for the hospitals in the American zone. Maybe you can find your girlfriend before you ship for home."

Good idea. I asked headquarters for a list of hospitals, packed an overnight bag, hooked a jeep full of gas and headed out. The first two hospitals I visited, in one I found a nurse who knew Jen but didn't know where she was. The next was up by Stuttgart. I drove up a long road leading to the hospital. Outside, on a big front lawn, there were patients in wheelchairs and white uniformed nurses enjoying a sunny day. There were several dozen people.

I surveyed the situation closely, going from nurse to nurse. I saw one nurse kneeling down talking with a wheel-chaired patient. I looked past her to the next then for some unknown reason I looked back when she stood up. JEN! No doubt about it, it was her. I'd know that shape in a thousand.

I leaped out of the jeep, almost fell down and ran to within ten feet of her and said in a low voice, "Jen." She turned to see me standing there. She ran at me almost knocking me down.

She threw her arms around me and said loud and clear, "Al, where have you been? I've been looking for you all the time and everywhere."

"So have I, Jen. I was afraid I would never find you."

I'll tell you, a whole lot-a kissing and hugging went on for some time. The Nurses and patients must have thought it was a strange world that an officer and GI would make such a fuss over each other.

"Jen, I have orders to go home. Can you go with me now?"

"Yes, I have enough time, I can go anytime."

We went to her headquarters, got her orders cut immediately for her to go. She got her gear together. We drove back to Augsburg. The Lieutenant Colonel turned out to be an understanding fellow. He got air transportation from an airfield near Stuttgart to Fort Dix, New Jersey. I packed my duff and Jen and I got on a converted B-24 cargo plane. In twenty-four hours, we were back in the good old US of A. We hunted up a marriage license and an Army Chaplain. We got married in a small Chapel on the post. To our surprise, the Chapel filled to capacity with well wishers. We both were separated from the Army the next day.

Holy Cow, we spent our wedding night in the BOQ and what a night it was. My love was some lover.

We took a train to my home on the ranch. It was a reunion I will never forget. My folks, brothers and their families all fell in love with Jen. Who wouldn't? I went back and got my High School diploma. Jen worked part time in a local hospital. My folks offered me manager of the ranch, how lucky could a guy be?

My time with the 90th was unforgettable. I think of my buddies and friends all the time. Old Hank, Sgt. Billy Joe, Sgt. Rocky, Sgt. Jimmy Good and, of course, LT will be etched into my brain the rest of my life. They're all young viable guys to me. God Bless all the men and women who served in that horrible time, surely we will all meet again.

About the Author

F.M.Worden lives in Tucson, Arizona with his wife Beverly of 57 years. They have 1 daughter, 5 sons, 12 grandchildren and 3 great-grandchildren. An avid student of American history, his motto is "If you don't know where you've *been*, you sure don't know where you're *going*." He spent 13 and a half years in the Arizona National Guard, 4years in the Army Reserve. He's a graduate of Tank gunnery school, as well as NCO leadership school and Infantry Officer Training at Fort Benning, Georgia. A successful owner of three small businesses, he also enjoys racing quarter horses with one champion. F.M. Worden has also authored the novel *The Two Sams: Men of the West*.